Readers love *Dog Days*
by TA MOORE

"I really enjoyed *Dog Days* and I am really hoping there is more to come."
—Joyfully Jay

"…an amazingly captivating shifter story that is by far one of the most unique I have read in a quite a while. And I want more."
—The Novel Approach

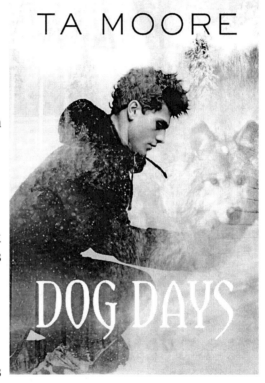

"I loved this story for the beautiful way that it was executed…"
—MM Good Book Reviews

"Trust me when I say you won't regret reading this… not if you love twists, turns, and horror."
—Rainbow Book Reviews

"…I highly recommend this to all the shifter lovers out there."
—Diverse Reader

By TA Moore

Dog Days
Liar, Liar

Published by Dreamspinner Press
www.dreamspinnerpress.com

LIAR, LIAR

TA MOORE

DREAMSPINNER PRESS

Published by

DREAMSPINNER PRESS

5032 Capital Circle SW, Suite 2, PMB# 279, Tallahassee, FL 32305-7886 USA
www.dreamspinnerpress.com

Liar, Liar
© 2017 TA Moore.

Cover Art
© 2017 Anne Cain.
annecain.art@gmail.com
Cover content is for illustrative purposes only and any person depicted on the cover is a model.

ISBN: 978-1-63533-570-5
Digital ISBN: 978-1-63533-571-2
Library of Congress Control Number: 2016960585
Published May 2017
v. 1.0

Printed in the United States of America
∞
This paper meets the requirements of
ANSI/NISO Z39.48-1992 (Permanence of Paper).

To my mum and grandparents, who always thought I could do it—
whatever it was—
and to the Five who have always told me to keep writing.

CHAPTER ONE

IT WAS past midnight when the small fleet of black vans bumped over the tire shredders and pulled up to the security booth. The bored security guard glanced up, back down at his graphic novel, and waved them through.

Syntech was Dyno-clean's biggest company, so they scheduled them in for a double-shift booking at the end of the night. Twice a month they doubled up the crew to make sure everything was spit polished and shipshape. It was as tightly organized as a military campaign.

Down in the parking garage, Jacob hopped out of the back of the van. He yawned until his jaw cracked, blinked back tears, and stretched his arms to work the kinks out of his spine. They'd been working eight hours already—four office buildings and the renovated dorm at the university—and the smell of disinfectant felt like it had soaked into his pores.

It had worn on the rest of the cleaning crew as well, especially with Jacob doing his bit to stir up existing tensions. So far there had been one accusation of sexism, a fight bad enough that the two cleaners couldn't be assigned the same floor, and everyone was quietly resentful toward the student who'd been caught reading his textbook instead of working. It had been two jobs since anyone had said a casual word or cracked a joke.

"Jacob!" the crew supervisor snapped, crooking a finger at him. He sauntered over, and she shoved a work order against his chest with stiff fingers. "You're doing the floors on the executive levels. Do a good job this time. You're still on a warning after what happened at the university last month, and if your next performance review doesn't improve...."

"I remember. I'm out of a job," he said. "Don't worry. I'll be on the top of my game tonight."

She squinted at him dourly, but he gave her his best trustworthy look. After a second she hmphed and stepped backward.

"I'm keeping my eye on you," she said. "Now get back to work."

He hummed contentedly to himself as he did what he was told. Everything was going according to plan.

THE HUMMING had turned into a tuneless whistle as Jacob stepped off the lift, dragging the buffer with him. He unwound the cord, snapped it to make it snake over the floor, and plugged it in next to one of the sullenly growing potted plants. The buffer juddered to life and skidded over the floor. He grabbed it by one hand and dragged it down the hall behind him, letting it swing carelessly back and forth over the floor. As he walked he bit the coating of glue and paint from his hand. The peeled-off strips of it went into his pocket.

The top floors were usually Naya's realm. She was presentable and polite, in case anyone was working late and she ran into them. And she spent all her time daydreaming about her wedding, so she didn't mind the boring jobs. The last few weeks, though, Jacob had noticed her creaming her hands every time she got into the van. Not with the cheap, greasy stuff the rest of them used either. Something from a department store.

She wanted nice hands for the big day. Not the raw, peeling mess of contact dermatitis she saw every time Jacob peeled his gloves off.

Jacob dropped the buffer off outside Nora Clayton's office and kept walking. He unzipped the top of his boiler suit, squirmed out of it, and let the sleeves dangle. It had been a while since he'd had to actually work on-site, but luckily it looked like he hadn't become any less of an asshole.

His brain ticked through how long his manipulation of the cleaning crew's various resentments and tensions would buy him before someone came to check on how he was doing up here. Gun would be slacking, trying to steal five minutes to read his textbook, Anna would be crying in the toilet, and Jim would be trying to run interference with Ella. Add twenty minutes to the hour it usually took Ella to get up there and subtract ten because she didn't trust Jacob to do a good job.

He pulled his T-shirt up and untaped the stripped-down electronics from his stomach. Plenty of time for what he needed to do.

Something jabbed at the back of his brain—a nasty little squirm of doubt that he couldn't quite pin down. He hastily flipped through the plan in his head to see if he'd missed anything. It seemed solid, but that bastard qualm kept squirming. With nothing to pin it on, he squelched the thought and loped down the tiled floor to the president's office.

The door wasn't locked, which was sweet. It was cold inside and the heat that built over the day had leeched out through the span of glass that took up the external wall.

Jacob let himself in, nudged the door shut behind him, and headed to the desk. It was slick, polished glass, and the keyboard flickered to life in squares of light on the surface as he touched it. Folding one leg under him as he sat down, his heel pressing against the back of his knee, he strung the code breaker together with confident fingers.

He couldn't make one himself—social programming was his specialty—but he understood how they worked. Once it was hooked up, the touchpad flickered dimly to life. He reached under the desk and plugged it into the hard drive.

While it worked he sat back in the chair. The leather settled under him as he chewed absently at the skin around his thumb. He'd had to get himself an honest job because security at Syntech was good enough to have plugged his usual sources of information—the careless e-mails, the social network logins, the chatty tech in the coffee queue.

If the computer security was that watertight....

He took a deep breath that tasted of ozone and Amouage and swiveled the chair around to face the glass. There were marks that shouldn't be on that sort of conspicuous display of prestige—linen-weft smudges and a few smears of hair gel stickiness where Porter had forgotten it wasn't the sort of wall you leaned against.

If gut instinct had been enough, Jacob would have been out of work a month before. Porter was cutthroat, but he didn't play games, and industrial espionage was all about games. Besides, Porter was arrogant. He listened to maybe two people in the company. Not the sort who'd admit they needed to steal someone else's idea.

Jacob stretched his legs out in front of him and watched the reflection of his sneakers move in the glass. Or he was wrong and Porter was a thief. Either way Jacob got paid.

It was Christmas out there in the dark. Jacob could see the red and green glitter of lights strung in the street and bright in the windows of office buildings. The feeling in the back of his brain poked at him again, but he shoved it down firmly and bit through the tag of skin he'd been worrying. The copper tang of blood was sharp against his tongue, and he pulled a face.

Bad old habit. He thought he'd broken it years ago.

The stop clock in his head ticked down the minutes as he waited. He wasn't at the panic point, but he was just about to start fidgeting when the code breaker hiccupped behind him. He dug his heel into the carpet and swung around, and his mouth quirked with satisfaction as the narrow monitor flickered to life.

"There you go," he said approvingly. He laced his fingers together and bent them back to pop his knuckles—another bad habit, but not one he'd ever bothered to try to break. He tapped quickly on the glass, and his knuckles broke the beams of light as he typed in commands. "Now let's see what we've got."

On the floors below, thirty-two machines obediently allowed Porter's computer to access their hard drives and the thirty-two trojans that Jacob had spent the last two months installing handed over the data they'd mined. The packets streamed onto Porter's computer and immediately bounced to Jacob's private server as the percentage bars flickered over the screen.

Jacob watched the flickering data intently and occasionally moved his gaze up to the door as he heard a noise in the hall. His foot juddered nervously, heel twitching, as the waiting started to work at his nerves with all the things that could go wrong.

The final byte disappeared off Porter's monitor. Jacob hissed out a sigh of relief between his teeth and stripped his equipment out of the computer system. The trojans went first, politely self-destructing with a minimum of damage, and then he wiped the current session from the computer menu.

He yanked the code breaker out of the computer as it shut down, broke it apart, and shoved it into the pockets on his boiler suit. No point in wasting time taping it back to his stomach. They'd never been searched on their way out.

The computer shut itself down, the soft glow on the monitor cut off, and Jacob tugged a ragged, bright-orange cloth out of his pocket. He scuffed his fingerprints off the glass. Not that they'd help anyone find him. His prints weren't on any database out there, as far as he knew. He'd just prefer to keep it that way.

A shrill rattle made him flinch and taste his heart in the back of his throat. He pushed back from the desk and his hip hit the chair. Then he realized it was his phone.

"Shit," he muttered.

Jacob took a deep breath, exhaled the panic, and grabbed the phone out of his pocket. He slid the chair back into place as he answered it.

"Hey."

"Hey, babe," Simon's familiar, rough voice drawled in his ear. He was gorgeous in person—all dark, controlled male beauty and long, muscled lines—but his voice hinted at how dangerous he was. "You free tomorrow?"

Liquid heat spread through Jacob's muscles, a cramp of want squeezed his balls like a hand, and that bastard itch popped back into his brain. There it was—what he'd forgotten about, or what he should have forgotten about by then.

"I thought you were busy?" he stalled.

Simon laughed—a short, cat-rough rub of sound. "Playing hard to get?"

"Doesn't sound like me," Jacob said. He should have started a fight and hammered in the crack that he could blame the breakup on. Not that he'd ever actually broken up with anyone—the last relationship he had that lasted longer than a week was his short experiment in being straight with his third-grade girlfriend—but he understood the principle. Except what came out of his mouth was "I've got a few things to clear up in the morning, but I'm all yours from eleven. I thought you were going to look at buying another rusty ornament for your drive?"

He shoved the door open and stepped out into the hall as he tucked the phone against his shoulder and gave the handle a quick polish. Better to break up in person. Easier to salt the ground so Simon would never want to think about him again. It was a smooth excuse—good enough that he felt a pinch of regret at Simon's hate—but he'd never been any good at lying to himself.

Professional liars never were. That itch was a smug little shit when you got right down to it. Jacob tried to ignore it as he headed back toward the abandoned buffer.

"Nora said they had a '69 Firebird," Simon said. "I asked them to send me pictures, though, and it wasn't. So I canceled, and I'm going to have to take Nora to the Cars-and-Coffee cruise in Austin so she knows what a Firebird looks like."

The elevator dinged. Jacob cursed to himself. They weren't meant to have phones, and recently fired employees *did* get searched.

"Simon, I gotta—"

"What the fuck?" Simon's mutter interrupted him. At the same moment, Jacob saw the buffer jerk backward as someone got hold of the lead and tugged on it. His stomach knotted with a sick premonition.

"I'm sorry." It was probably the most honest thing he'd said in a year.

"Sorry?" Simon said. He sounded distracted already. "What for? Look if you can't make it—"

The lead dropped, and Simon stalked around the corner, jacket tucked back behind the holster of his gun. He looked good, even under the lights that sapped the color from his tan, and then he saw Jacob, and he just looked... confused.

"This," Jacob said.

He turned on his heel and ran. The rubber soles of his sneakers squeaked on the tiles, and panic scattered his thoughts as he tried to plan on the run. He could hear Simon sprint after him, his boots heavy on the tiles and getting closer.

"Jacob!"

The first time they met, Jacob had seen Simon beat three men bloody. It had been hot at the time—and it wasn't like the gay-bashing assholes hadn't deserved it—but not so much right now. Legs burning, Jacob pushed himself to keep moving—hard enough that he nearly overshot the door to the janitor's closet. He swung himself to a stop and grabbed at the door to get it open. It was metal and heavy enough that Jacob could feel the weight of it in his shoulder. Out of the corner of his eye, he could see Simon grab for him.

Shoving the door open, Jacob fell through—just dodging Simon's grab—and kicked it shut. He put his shoulder to it and braced his feet on the ground. Simon hit it hard enough to make Jacob slide on the floor and shoved the door open an inch. His sharp, handsome face was bleak with rage. Jacob managed to get it shut again.

"You think you can hide?" Simon snarled and bashed his fist against the door. "Who do you work for?"

Jacob fumbled a screwdriver out of his pocket and wedged it under the door as a block.

"That's confidential," he panted. "Simon, fuck, this wasn't meant to happen."

"No. I'm sure you meant to rob us and go, not get caught." There was something thin as a razor in Simon's voice. It made Jacob flinch.

He felt an odd ache in his stomach that wasn't exactly fear or exertion. Whatever it was, it wasn't useful.

"Well, yeah," he said. "But I meant, you… and me."

The door jolted against Jacob's shoulder and made him flinch.

"You lying little fucker." There was the thump of a fist hitting the door. "There's nowhere to go. Come out, stay in. It's not going to change anything."

Jacob wedged the screwdriver that bit farther in and scrambled to his feet. He still couldn't breathe, and there was a stitch cutting into his ribs. Fuck, he really needed to start working out.

"Good to know."

He could hear Simon on the phone outside, snarling orders and demanding answers. While he was busy doing that, Jacob stripped out of his boiler suit. Simon was probably right. After all if anyone knew the security weakness of the building, or lack thereof, it would be the security consultant.

Shit.

As he dropped into a squat and worn denim stretched over his knees, Jacob shoved his hands into his hair and tried to think. There was a freight elevator shaft behind the wall of the closet. If he had a crowbar, he could pull the bricks out of the wall, crawl through, and… fall to his death, probably. He wasn't Tom Cruise.

"Damn it, damn it, damn it." Jacob clenched his fist in his hair as though he could pull an idea out of his head through his scalp. Why did everything *always* go wrong for him?

Outside he heard Simon yell at someone to "get a goddamn Masterkey to breach the door if you need it." Jacob lifted his head and bit his lower lip. It wasn't necessarily a *good* idea, but it was the only one he had, and there wasn't time to wait for inspiration.

He gave himself a second and squeezed his eyes shut as he waited for some—for any—other idea.

His phone was still lying where he'd dropped it as he fell through the door. He picked it up, wiped the dust on his sleeve, and tapped the screen with his thumb. It rang twice, and then the operator picked up.

"Hello, could you please state the nature of your emergency," a light, faintly accented voice—Wisconsin, Jacob guessed—said.

"I… look… this is embarrassing," Jacob muttered. He shifted away from the door to mute his voice. "I've had an argument with my boyfriend, and he's *really* angry. I've locked myself in an office and…."

He didn't deliberately put the accent on. He just picked up the inflections as she dropped them. Instinct or habit.

"We're at work." He answered the operator's questions quickly. At the same time, he'd pulled the code breaker out of his pocket, tore it apart, and ground the pieces underfoot. The waste made him twitch. "In Syntech. It's just off Beagle Road? He found out I lied to him about something, and I've never seen him like this."

Outside the door Simon hammered against the metal and cursed flatly. The operator murmured reassuringly and promised they'd be there soon. Jacob hung up on her, called his lawyer, and sat down on the floor with his back against the boast wall that butted onto the elevator shaft.

Leaning his head back against the dusty plaster, he listened to the ringtone and the bang of Simon's fist on the door. It had been *one* stupid decision in the middle of a well-planned job, and look where it got him. The minute it started to get tangled, he should have ditched.

Too cocky for that, or too greedy, and look what it got him.

Someone lifted the phone and mumbled something down the line.

"Hey, Allison," Jacob said. "I might need you to get me out of jail. In about half an hour."

CHAPTER TWO

TWO POLICE officers walked Jacob off Syntech property to a waiting taxi. Apparently, without evidence of wrongdoing, that was the most they could do. Simon stood in the window of his office, jaw clenched until his skull ached, and watched through the smoked glass as they crossed the carpark.

At the fence the blonde policewoman handed over Jacob's shabby, searched backpack and said something to him. Then she and her partner turned and headed back toward the building. Left on the property line, Jacob hitched his bag over his shoulder and looked up at the window. Simon had never brought him there, but apparently Jacob did better background checks than he did.

After a second, Jacob shrugged one shoulder and got into the taxi.

Simon pulled his phone out of his pocket, flicked it on, and speed dialed the security team.

"Murtagh? Keep a detail on him," he said. "I want to know where he goes, who he speaks to, and for how long. I don't want him without eyes on him from now until I tell you different."

He got a grunt in answer, and then Murtagh hung up. The taxi pulled away from the curb, and five minutes later, a Toyota pulled out of a nearby street and fell in behind them.

Simon dropped the phone back in his pocket.

His stomach was in a knot of closely collared rage, and the familiar itch of frustrated self-loathing crawled down his back. He should have known better. The minute he risked trusting someone—something—outside of the few family and friends he still had, it was just a matter of time until they let him down, or he let them down.

The anger slipped his leash, and he turned around, kicked the chair, and sent it spinning over the office. It hit the wall, bounced, and landed on its side. Still fuming he sent the bin flying after it. The thin metal canister buckled against the wall and spilled out crumpled paper and a Red Bull can.

It didn't really help. He wanted the solid pain of broken bones and split knuckles, the satisfaction of turning his feelings into blood and bruises. Not Jacob. The fucker might deserve it, but Simon couldn't bring himself to imagine it. Just a nonspecific face and nonspecific fists—the sort he never had trouble finding.

"I didn't know you were seeing anyone," Devon said from the door. He'd been polite enough to wait for the tantrum to be over, even though, as CEO of Syntech and Simon's brother-in-law—or whatever you called someone after their wife, your sister, died—he had grounds to interrupt.

Simon gave Dev an impatient look. "That's your takeaway? We've either had a thief with free rein of your office, or your security consultant locked a cleaner in the janitor's closet. And you want to ask about my dating life?"

Dev shrugged, straightened a chair, and spun it around so he could straddle it backward. His heavy shoulders bulked under his shabby band shirt as he crossed his arms over the back of the chair. The watch on his wrist was classy. The scars on his knuckles weren't.

"One is related to the next, isn't it?" he said. "According to Dyno-clean, Jacob Archer has been working with them the last seven months. Five months ago one of their cleaners quit, and they moved him onto our rotation. He passed their background checks, never raised a flag until tonight. Maybe he just didn't want to tell you he scrubbed our toilets for a living?"

"You think that's something I'd care about?"

"Not the right question. Do you think he cared about it?"

Simon made himself slouch and tried to fool his wire-twitching nerves into thinking he was relaxed. Despite his best efforts, his fingers drummed nervously against the desk.

"I don't think Jacob would know shame if someone express shipped him a packet of it," he said. An odd pop of inappropriate fondness made its way into his voice. He swallowed it and shook his head. "Under the circumstances I know it's a lot to ask. But trust me, we need to find out what he's done."

Devon waved his hand. "Don't be an idiot," he said. "Of course I trust you. I've already got people stripping my computer, and I assume you've got a team on Jacob?"

A bit of the raw tension in Simon's spine eased. After he came back from Afghanistan the last time, he was a mess. He wouldn't have taken a risk on himself if he'd been Devon, and with Becca a year dead, Devon didn't owe him anything. The last thing he wanted to do was let the man down.

It was a weird thought, considering how much they'd hated each other back in their hometown.

"Did he ever ask you anything that seemed suspicious?" Dev asked. "Even if only in hindsight."

Simon snorted and pushed himself up out of the chair. Energy itched under his skin. His body was convinced that being *this* angry meant a fight.

"I know how not to talk about my work," he said. "And he never asked me anything about here, not even if I'd be leaving for the night. He was in my house, though. I'll need to sterilize, see if there was anything he could have accessed."

Dev scratched his jaw and rasped his nails through dirty-blond stubble. "Okay," he said. "There's nothing we can do until we find out what he actually did. Go home, check the house, let me know if you find *anything*. And get some sleep."

The suggestion riled Simon's temper and dragged a snarl out of him. "I'm fine."

"Well, I'm your employer," Dev said as he stood up. He wasn't short—although the seventeen-year-old prick Simon had been insisted on snarking that he was short*er*—but the muscle made him look it. "And when there's something we can do, I want you in a state to do it."

It went against the grain to admit it, but that made some sense. Simon pinched his nose between his thumb and forefinger. He could feel the tug of the whiskey in the drawer. It promised a dreamless sleep if he just took a swig. Or two. Or more, since he'd never been a quitter.

"Fine," he said flatly. "I do need to strip the house down, anyhow. Make sure he didn't plant anything. What about you?"

Dev gave a tight grin that crinkled the corners of his eyes. "Like I tell Callie, do as I say not as I do. And you're not my kid, so you don't even get to argue with me for three hours and call me a hypocrite."

"She could be worse," Simon defended his niece out of habit. He was the uncle she'd seen at Christmas every other year before her mother died. So he curried favor by always being on Callie's side. "My sister would have just climbed out a window and gone to do whatever it was anyhow."

"Callie wouldn't let me off that easy. She wants me to admit I'm wrong," Dev said. The digression was a welcome distraction, but it couldn't last long. The smile faded from Dev's face, and he glanced down at himself. There was a smear of something tomato based on his T-shirt, and he picked at it with his thumbnail. "Speaking of Callie, could you sort out an Uber to go and pick up one of my shirts from her? I'm going to need to call the board."

Dev never sounded enthusiastic about talking to the board, and he sounded less enthusiastic than usual. Guilt hooked its claws into Simon's gut and shredded what should have been numb scar tissue by then if the world were just. He jerked his chin down in a short, hard acknowledgment of the request and pulled the door open.

"I am sorry." He ground the word out past a clenched jaw as Dev crossed the threshold. "If you want to me to resign...."

Dev thumped him in the arm with a loosely closed fist. "Shut up, Saint Simon," he said. The decades-old nickname—it predated Dev dating Becca, back when they'd been allowed to hate each other—made Simon scowl, despite his best efforts to look repentant. "Look, I'm not the security expert, and if they tell me different, I'll be happy to string you up like a piñata, but from what I can tell, the *only* thing that Archer could have gotten from you was dick and your schedule. Neither of those seems vital to his infiltration. So no throwing yourself on your sword. Okay? Not until I tell you to."

It was sort of a "get out of jail free" card, but it sat uneasily on Simon. He shifted his shoulders and leaned into it like forgiveness had a physical weight he could stop in its tracks. "I still fucked up. I should have known better."

Dev shoved his hand through his hair. "Yeah, you did. Maybe you should. So?"

"So?" Simon repeated, more exasperated than he meant to sound.

"So."

Dev walked away, and Simon slouched back against the doorjamb and shook his head. Fuck up in the military, and a dressing-down was the least you could expect, the *best* you could expect. More likely you'd get yourself, or someone else, killed.

A fuckup had ended his career in the military—dropped him back in his hometown with a messed-up shoulder and nightmares—and it hadn't even been *his* fuckup.

This mess deserved a more savage payback than a "so." Simon peeled his long body off the door. Not sleeping—despite Dev's veiled order—would do.

THE APARTMENT was huge and stylishly empty—all dull golden wood and heavy black furniture. Simon had bought it furnished and lived there for two years, and it was becoming clear that the only significant change he'd made in that time was Jacob. He had a boyfriend when he was discharged, but that crashed and burned because Dean was career military and Simon was actively fucked up. That was long before Simon moved in here.

There'd been a couple of one-night stands, a couple relationships that were just three one-night stands strung together by texts, and the month he'd spent dating Julie—because pretending to be straight and dating your AA sponsor was totally a good idea.

None of them had changed anything. Jacob's handwriting was all over the whiteboard, scrawled in red pen and decorated with exclamation points. His spare phone charger was plugged in next to the bed, and three bottles of that disgusting sugar syrup he had in his coffee sat in the cupboard, since Simon would rather keep him in bed than lose him to a Starbucks run.

Simon stood on tables and unscrewed light fittings, dismantled picture frames, and scanned the rooms for bugs hidden under plaster. There wasn't even a spider. He took his computer apart and broke the plastic down to circuits and wire, but there were no extraneous components.

He stared down at the dismantled Toshiba and chewed on the inside of his lip until he tasted salt. With nothing to aim it at, his temper was just a restless weight in his gut. It was like sourdough—wet, heavy, and feeding on itself to get bigger.

If he'd found some evidence of Jacob spying on him, of collecting information, at least it would make sense.

In a burst of frustration, he swiped his arm over the table and sent the components and plastic casing flying onto the floor. The single jolt of anger got him moving, and he supposed he might as well use the momentum. He stalked across the room, grabbed the few souvenirs of Jacob, and shoved the syrups, dog-eared magazines, and odds and ends into a bag. Glass rattled as he tied it shut, the plastic stretched under his fingers, and he tossed it in the garbage. Then he soaked a handful of paper towels under the tap and scrubbed the whiteboard. Jacob's crooked scrawl disappeared in a smear of red.

It took under an hour to wipe away any trace that Jacob had been in the apartment. All that was left was the realization that the only person who could stand to spend time with him had been lying about it.

Simon paced the apartment restlessly and texted orders to the security teams until the sun came up and fatigue finally hit. From experience he knew he could keep going, but there was no point in pushing the limits until he had to. The bed in the other room tempted him, but he resisted the thought of its comfort. Instead he folded himself down on the couch, closed his eyes, and willed himself to unconsciousness.

He slept hard, and if he dreamed, it wasn't anyone's business. By five thirty the next morning, he was back at Syntech, sitting on the opposite side of Dev's desk with Nora Reyes, his brother-in-law's slick, professional second-in-command and computer expert. She'd been Becca's best friend too. It wasn't nepotism. Exceptional people just liked Simon's sister. Always had.

One thing Nora wasn't, though, was lenient. Simon wondered bleakly if he should have packed up his office before he came.

"Here's my report," Nora said as she tossed a folder onto the polished desk. She sat down, took her glasses off, and pressed her fingertips against her tear ducts. "It's all in there, but I can tell you the short version. He cleaned us out. Last night a huge packet of data was uploaded to a secure location. The details of the transaction were wiped, so we don't know what data he was after. However, the cyber forensic team was able to pinpoint the targeted computers, and they're going to autopsy their hard drives."

Simon forced his jaw to unclench long enough to ask, "Do you want to fire me, Dev? Or would you prefer my resignation?"

"Stop trying to quit." Dev leaned back in his chair. Carrie had gotten the Uber driver and a clean shirt to him the night before, and Dev had already managed to make the stiff designer linen look crumpled and sweaty. He hooked a finger into his collar and absently tugged at it. "I'm not dealing with this without my chief of security."

Nora cleared her throat. "Your chief of security got you into this," she said. She shot Simon a quick apologetic look with a twist of glossy lips and a shrug. They were friends too—enough that she'd pass on a tip about a car she thought he'd like, not enough that he talked to her about his love life—but that just made her judge him to a higher standard. "The board will not be happy that he's still on the payroll."

"The board will be happy with what I tell them," Dev said, and that old sullen scowl settled on his brow. He'd always been that guy, the one who would cut his nose off just to spite whoever had told him not to. Nora frowned and went to say something, but Dev stopped her. "Enough, Nora. The board isn't your problem anymore, remember? I'll deal with them, you find out what data was stolen, and Simon will find our Mr. Jacob Archer."

Of its own volition, Simon's hand clenched against his thigh. His knuckles showed bony and white through the callused skin. "And then?" he asked, his voice rough with frustration. At himself. "What will happen to him?"

"Do you care?"

"Yes," Simon said. "I want to see him punished."

That was true. But it maybe wasn't the whole truth, not yet, and Dev looked like he knew that. It didn't matter. By the time Simon caught up with Jacob, it *would* be the truth. He changed the subject.

"The team I had on him lost his trail on Riverside last night," he said. "I have them staking out his flat, but I don't think there's anything there he cares enough to go back for. The worry is that his client was from out of the city or the state, because as far as I can tell, he's got no family or long-term ties here. I have teams watching any mass transit, but it is a big place, and you're rich, but not *that* rich."

Dev leaned back in his chair and tapped his pen against his knee. It was the beat to some country song, but Simon couldn't place it.

"What if he just drives out?"

Simon shrugged. "He can't drive."

It took a second, but Nora finally voiced the question that Simon asked himself every time he thought about Jacob.

"Are you sure he wasn't lying?"

"I considered it," Simon told her. "Unless it was a very long inconvenient con, though, I think this one thing is true."

He didn't say *why* he was sure. Pretty sure, at least. The night at the Raceway had been reframed in his memory as turgidly sentimental now that he knew he'd been a mark, but that didn't mean he was going to vomit it up for anyone else to look at.

But there were bits that still felt authentic. It had been hot, packed, and noisy. Simon spent most of the day leaning against walls, envying people their cold beers. Jacob spent it talking to mechanics and betting on cars. But when Simon offered to hire a car so he could have a go, Jacob had gone gray.

"I couldn't leave you sitting here," he'd objected. It was warm, and Jacob had already been sweating, but he was sweating more. "Besides, I wanted you to have fun."

Consideration and modesty were not traits that Jacob pretended to have. Probably because they weren't qualities he prized. So yeah, Simon trusted that one thing.

Simon pushed himself back from the desk and stood up. He shot his cuffs and tugged his jacket straight over his shoulders. Dev wore his suits with the resentment of a kid on the first day of school, but Simon found their strict lines reassuring. It was almost like a uniform. To keep the proper lines required the same posture.

"I'll find him," he said.

Dev rocked back in his chair, and the hinge creaked under him. "I know," he said. "And just as important? Find out *who* hired him."

Nora put her glasses back on. "My money's on Bres Industries," she said. "With the court's ruling in our favor on the lawsuit, they're going to have to pull out of their Arctic projects. That will be a big loss, especially if our experiments bear fruit."

"They're going to appeal," Dev pointed out slowly, but Simon could tell he liked the idea. It wasn't like Dev was stupid or easily led. He was one of the leading voices in a scientific community that Simon, despite having it explained with small words by a twelve-year-old, didn't completely understand. But it was personality, not intellect. He liked his problems straightforward—something to fix, whether it was a carburetor or the ozone layer, and someone to hit.

Simon didn't think it was going to be that simple. Syntech was on the cutting edge of geo-engineering. *Everyone* had problems with them— from hippies who thought they were interfering with Mother Nature to competitors who thought they might have a head start on interfering with Mother Nature.

He said, "I'll check them out first." If he'd owed Dev before, he owed him even more after the other night. So if he wanted an easy answer, Simon would do his best to get it for him.

CHAPTER THREE

THE CHAIR wasn't *right*. Jacob shifted, squirmed his shoulders against the leather, and frowned at the computer. Code streamed across the screen in flickering bars, sorting itself according to algorithms he'd had tailored for the job. The program was 75 percent finished, his playlist was finally streaming seamlessly to the speakers, and he had answers for his employer. He should have been happy, not dissatisfied and fidgety.

Maybe it wasn't the chair. Maybe the monitor was in the wrong place.

It had been a month since Jacob cleared out Syntech and his loft in the same night. Not the first time he'd had to do a flit, but for some reason, he just couldn't settle into his new place. The windows were too big, it turned out he didn't like wooden floors, and no matter how he tweaked it, he couldn't get his workstation set up just right.

Jacob sighed, sprawled back in the chair, and stretched his long legs out under the desk. His bare feet stuck out into a beam of sunlight, and the wood was warm under his heels. One of these days, he was going to fall down his own rabbit hole and buy his own lies, but not today.

There were three cardinal rules in his line of work. Okay, he'd made them up himself—it wasn't as though there was a trade school for corporate spies—but that didn't make them any less true. The first was "Don't get involved with the mark. You're a professional, not a British undercover cop pretending to be an ecoterrorist." He'd still done it, though, hadn't he? Hadn't been able to resist dark gray eyes and a sculpted mouth that rarely relaxed into a smile… or the shoulders. Although, to be fair, who the hell could resist those shoulders?

For a second, Jacob's mind drifted to somewhere sweaty and pleasantly dirty—elegant, callused hands pinning Jacob's wrists over his head, the heavy muscle and bone breadth of those shoulders, and Simon's teeth biting heat into Jacob's lips. The insistent press of Simon's cock against Jacob's stomach making his balls twitch in anticipation.

The chime of the program as it reached 100 percent interrupted his reverie and dragged him back to his grouchy reality, now with aching balls. He pushed himself up in the chair, wincing as his jeans pulled tight over his half-hard cock, and scrubbed a hand over his face.

Fine. He missed Simon. That was the truth. "Now suck it up," he told himself. His voice sounded loud over the pixie pop that his playlist had thrown up. "That ship's been sunk."

And if Jacob couldn't think of a way to manipulate someone into doing what he wanted? It probably couldn't be done. There was a reason he was so good at his job. So, since a box of Godiva wasn't going to mend his fences with Simon, he might as well get back to something that was going to pay off.

He hooked his foot onto the chair to give his cock a bit more room under his fly and typed in the commands to generate the appropriate reports and encapsulate the remaining data behind a password-protected partition on the remote server. Most of his clients saw the benefit in keeping things transactional, but there was always someone who got the idea they were starring in an episode of *24*. This way they were both protected—Jacob from someone deciding to stiff him, and the clients from a contractor who might turn on them.

All he had to do was meet up with his current client and he could take his payday and head to Bali to sweat the mope out on the beach—with a brief stop in Pennsylvania. Maybe hope just sprang eternal, but Jacob was sure he could find a surfer with irresistible shoulders in at least one of those places. Admittedly, that was probably more likely in Bali, but he wouldn't count Pennsylvania out yet.

He fired an e-mail off to the dead drop and pushed himself to his feet. His T-shirt stuck to his back. Once he was upright, his hips felt stiff and there was the whiff of a pulled all-nighter around him. He stripped off as he went and dropped his clothes on the floor as he headed into the bathroom for a shower.

Standing under the hammer pulse of the scalding, he had the best intentions in the world, but when his hand wrapped around his cock, it wasn't some interchangeable surfer boy he conjured up. He braced one hand against the tiled wall, and tension balled in his shoulders as he pumped his fist in slow, steady strokes.

It was Simon he imagined, with his hands on Jacob's hips and his mouth hot and eager on Jacob's balls as he twisted his hand along his cock in wringing, practiced strokes—Simon's dark hair slicked to his skull, the curl drenched out of it, and the long, clean muscle in the tanned slope of his back.

Jacob licked soapy water off his lips and swiped his thumb over the head of his cock. Precome was slippery against his skin. Reaction pinched through his nerves, twitched from his groin down to his knees, and pleasure pulled into a heavy, eager knot in the cradle of his hips.

He came with a jolt. The come was sticky between his fingers and on his stomach before it washed away. His hand slid on the tiles until his forearm pressed against the wet ceramic. The shower thudded water between his shoulders, and his hair hung in dripping knots around his face as he caught his breath.

"Okay." He twisted the taps off. "I'll admit rule number one is just fucked."

Jacob grabbed a towel from the rack and scrubbed his hair dry as he dripped his way back to the computer. The icon was flashing notification that he'd gotten a reply. He dried his hands on the towel, slung it around his neck, and flipped the e-mail open. He snorted to himself.

It was the first time anyone had ever asked to meet in a Starbucks, but whatever. Jacob could get a coffee, and with what Jacob had for him, the client might even pick up the tab.

Because, somewhat to Jacob's surprise, it looked like the client's suspicions were right. Devon Porter *had* stolen from him first.

SOMEONE SOMEWHERE had once done Harry Clayton the sartorial disservice of telling him to ditch the nerd wear. He was the sort of short, chubby guy who could pull off a meme T-shirt and a pair of dork glasses and make it look good. Instead he wore tailored suits with an air of resentment. Not sexy. Although Jacob was sure that the platinum card he had in his wallet made up for a lot of his flaws.

Although the fact he was too cheap to buy a contractor a coffee wasn't in his favor. Jacob sat down in the narrow, hard-backed chair and sucked cold coffee and cinnamon cream through a straw. The sugar hit the back of his tongue and gave his brain a buzzing jolt.

"Mr. Clayton."

Rather than responding, Harry folded his paper in half and pretended he was so absorbed in taking sparing sips of his black coffee that he didn't notice the lanky blond who sat opposite him. Simon took his coffee black too, but at least *he* drank the stuff like he enjoyed it.

Jacob caught the tail end of the thought and smothered it. Irritation pricked at him. He didn't usually spend so much time thinking about people he *was* fucking, never mind ones he used to. Certainly not when he was working. It was hardly professional.

"Well?" Harry asked as he glanced up from the weather report and gave Jacob a quick, sidelong look. "You said you found something."

Something made Jacob hesitate—the unhappy nagging feeling that twitched at the back of his brain like a kid tugging at his sleeve. He still couldn't put his finger on *what* it was. It *did* occur to him that it might be guilt, but he hoped not. So he tugged the square of cardboard out of his pocket and slid it over the table.

Harry covered it with his hand and slid it off the table. He glanced discreetly down and squinted as his contacts caught on the waterline of his lower eyelids.

"Doris Gallagher?" he said. "Who the hell?"

"There's a QR code on the back." Jacob sat back, hooked one leg up, and balanced his ankle on his knee. Since it was a business meeting, he'd made some effort with black trousers and a fitted black shirt. He drew the line at a tie. His clients liked to think he was a *bit* dangerous. "Scan it, and you'll get access to all the data I secured investigating your issue with Porter."

Harry immediately reached for his phone and leaned away from the table as he dug his fingers into his pocket.

"Obviously." Jacob drew the word out as he rattled the straw around his cup to mix in the cream. "That would be after you've paid the remainder of my fee, Mr. Clayton. Just a precaution."

Suspicion made Harry scowl. "How can I trust you to deliver once you have the money?"

"Because I'm not a con artist," Jacob said.

"You're a thief."

"I prefer Confidential Information Acquisitions," Jacob said mildly, and he glanced around to see if anyone was listening. He nodded pleasantly at a woman sitting opposite who looked up from feeding crumbs to her baby to eye him suspiciously. "It sounds nicer, I can talk about it at parties, and it has a badass acronym. Mr. Clayton, I'm a contractor. If I didn't deliver at the end of the project, I wouldn't get hired again."

Harry looked flustered for a second and then sighed. He set the paper down on the table and rubbed his hands over his face.

"I don't *do* this," he said. "I've always done everything aboveboard, got all the permits, made sure my workers were receiving a living wage, paid the taxes to the penny my accountant tallied up for me. I leave pennies at tills. I'm not doing this to profit or to steal anything from Porter. *He's* the one that stole from me. All I want is proof that Devon Porter isn't the genius everyone thinks he is."

Jacob stretched an arm over the table and tapped the card with his finger. "That's on here. And once you pay me, it'll be yours. As far as I can tell, the code you gave me has been used on a variety of Porter's projects over the last five years. Predominantly on something called Icarus."

Harry took a deep breath, and his lips puffed as he let it out. "I didn't want to believe it, but I should have known. That son of a bitch."

He swiped his thumb over his phone screen and tapped information into the keypad. "See, Porter always thought he could just take what he wanted, because whatever he was doing was so important. Because I just run a social-media platform. He took my code, and he made me look like a fool—"

Harry's low, angry mutter broke off, and he looked up. His forehead furrowed as he stared over Jacob's shoulder. Instinct made Jacob turn to scan the half-empty coffee shop. The only thing out of place was a man at the counter, sucking sugar out of packets as he waited for his coffee.

"I know that car." Harry grabbed his arm. His fingers dug into Jacob's muscle, hard enough to bruise. "What happened? You turned me in to Porter to save your own ass? Did he offer you a better deal to sell me out? Well, fuck you. You think I can't break your stupid encryption? That's what I *do*."

Harry bolted to his feet, grabbed his jacket from the back of the chair, and stuffed the business card into his pocket. As he shoved his way between the tables, he knocked Jacob's coffee over, and the half cup of coffee splashed out over the table and Jacob's knee. He cursed, grabbed a handful of napkins, blotted his wet knees, and made an abortive attempt to sop up the spill from the table.

It was pointless. Jacob dropped the sodden ball of tissue onto the table and grabbed his peacoat from the back of his chair as he chased after Harry. He caught the door as it swung to, and shouldered it open.

He shrugged his jacket on as he looked around for Harry and caught a glimpse of a broad back and a flying coat as it disappeared around a corner. Jacob followed and wove between the Christmas-present laden shoppers who filled the street. It slowed him down enough that, once he turned the corner, there was no sign of Harry.

"Shit," he muttered as he broke into a jog. He needed that payday to go and find his sexy surfer—

The arm caught him across the chest as he rounded the corner and hit him hard enough that he went down like a bowling pin. He saw the sky spin over him, and then he hit the pavement with a grunt. When he looked up and blinked away swimming dots of impact, he saw a man in a worryingly nice suit shove a limply unresponsive Harry into the back of a low-slung, smoke-windowed black car.

"Bring him," a man said. "We don't want anyone asking questions."

A swarthy man built like a small wall grabbed Jacob, hauled him to his feet, and jabbed something hard into the small of his back when he struggled. *That was not a cock.* Jacob sucked in a strangled breath through a bruised chest. Under the circumstances, a cock wouldn't be *ideal*—but better than the alternative. Fear ran down Jacob's back and clotted unpleasantly in his stomach.

"We need your mouth, not your legs," the man holding him growled in his ear. His breath was sour with cheap coffee. "So behave, and you might get out of this alive."

CHAPTER FOUR

THE MEETING with the board was heated enough that some words filtered through the wood-and-glass doors. Simon leaned against the wall, arms crossed, and listened.

"Gross misconduct."

"Serious cause for concern."

"We trust that this will be resolved without further incident."

"—revisit the decision to accept DOD funding."

Dev stalked out of the board meeting in a black mood and yanked the tie loose at his throat as though the thing were trying to strangle him. Most of the employees waiting to buttonhole him about some pressing bit of paperwork took one look at his face and realized there was something else they needed to deal with first. Simon and Nora were the only two who stuck around and followed along a pace behind him.

"What?" Dev pulled his tie off and shoved it into his pocket. The end of it dangled against his coat. He nodded down at Nora's feet in shiny designer shoes. "And how the hell do you move that fast in those shoes?"

"Practice," Nora said, answering his second question first. "And pain."

"You never used to wear them."

"People expect Syntech's chief operations officer to wear heels," she said. "You made me COO. I learned to wear heels. And to deal with the board."

"I deal with the board." Dev stalked down the hall to his office, pushed the door open, and absently held it for her.

"No," Simon said dryly. "You don't. You yell at the board."

"It's my company." He stripped his jacket off and tossed it over the back of a chair, feeling a bit less constrained once he was free of it. "Something they need to remember. They've been getting away with too much."

It was a low blow. Nora grimaced through it, and Dev didn't notice as he slouched into his chair and scowled at his computer. Simon winced for him and gave Nora a twist of his lips that tried to be both sympathetic and apologetic.

He hadn't been here when his sister died. It hadn't been his choice. He'd been in the desert killing people while the doctors tried to poison his sister just enough to save her life. Maybe he could have gotten a leave of absence, if he'd asked. He hadn't. So it had been Nora—Becca's best friend since the day they'd turned up at college and found out they were sharing a room—who took Becca to hospital appointments, let Callie cry on her shoulder, and took over running Dev's company for him while he was chasing a cure that nobody but him believed in.

It was the sort of thing you knew you should appreciate, but also couldn't help but resent. Especially when you were Dev Porter, a man who thought asking for help was the same thing as showing belly.

"If they want me to resign...," Simon started to offer again.

Dev scowled, and his heavy brows beetled over his sharp gray eyes. "You bring that up again, I'll fucking fire you myself," he said. "This wasn't your fault."

Nora sat down, crossed her legs, and laced her hands around her knee. "He could take some time off, save face *and* placate the board?"

"It won't save face. The minute he takes an extra-long lunch break, they'll be muttering about me backstabbing my loyalists." Dev impatiently swiped his hand through the air. "He can take a holiday when he finds my missing data. Buy me a geographically themed T-shirt."

There was rarely any point in arguing with Dev when he started to glower. Simon sighed his acceptance. "In that case," he said, "I want to put Icarus in quarantine—suspend work and contain all the files related to the project on an isolated server."

Nora unlaced her fingers and leaned forward. "Is that really necessary?" she protested. "Without Icarus our whole research team is hobbled. My autopsy of the systems didn't show any signs of the thief approaching the sectors housing Icarus."

Icarus was a bioengineering program that would use nanotechnology, climatology, and oceanography in a synergistic environmental improvement program. Or as Callie had explained it to Simon, her dad was going to save the world by using tiny machines to replace clouds and fix the ozone layer. Eventually. For now it was a money sink that had sired a bunch of unexpectedly profitable corporate projects.

"Without Icarus, whatever they stole won't replicate the effects they want," Simon said. "And if... our thief... wasn't their only operative, we want it safe."

Dev grimaced and rubbed his hand over his eyes, and the old calluses on his fingers scraped the bridge of his nose. "If we're not ready for the trial in the summer, we'll have to scrabble to make our case for the environmental gains. *Again*."

"Well, if you've lost control of the project to a competitor, that won't be a problem."

That got him a dirty look and, after a second, a resigned nod. "Do it," he said. "But only until the end of the month. That will give me a chance to finish the current projection before I have to commission new environmental studies for our off-site research stations."

Simon nodded. "Well, if I'm not resigning, I should get back to work."

"And we," Nora said, catching Dev's eye, "have some business to talk about."

"If it's about working for the DOD, I'm not interested. I don't care what the board wants," he said. "Syntech is supposed to be making the world better, not about finding better ways to kill people. I won't sell Icarus to people who want to use it as a weapon."

"Want isn't the same as will," Nora said. "It would be years before Icarus could be weaponized and deployed, and in that time, we'd have all the resources of the DoD at our disposal to develop the world-saving aspects of it. I don't know if Icarus would even be a viable weapon."

"Then you suffer a failure of imagination," Dev said. "The Icarus nanotech works like a virus, colonizing other molecules. It could be used to steal a country's oil. Or water. We're experimenting with using it as an alternative to chemotherapy, but it could also be used as chemical warfare by essentially wiping out an enemy's immune system so a cold sore could kill them. Or—"

Nora shook her head and held up her hand to signal an early surrender. It wasn't the first time they had argued. "I get it," she said. She sat back, crossed her legs, and rubbed the back of her neck. Her mouth quirked. "The DoD isn't a good fit for Syntech. Besides, that wasn't what I wanted to talk about. That ship has sailed. Laramie will have already allocated the money elsewhere. What we need to discuss is expanding our portfolio of corporate projects…."

Leaving them to it, Simon headed out of the office. He closed the door behind him and got on the elevator. Half the board left when he did. Last time he'd been stuck in a confined space with them, they'd thanked him for his service and played armchair general over how they'd run the wars better. He'd been their trophy veteran, and not just any veteran—a Marine.

They stood in stiff silence and pretended he wasn't there. He stood easily, defiantly not at attention, and watched the floors drop away on the glass display. It probably didn't matter, but he wondered if they were more annoyed that he'd been fucking a thief or that he'd be been fucking a male thief.

Jacob would probably have asked them. Not that he was an example to follow. Simon just got off at his floor and left them to talk about him the rest of the way down.

IT HAD been nearly a week since the last time Simon made it home from the office, and it wasn't the first week either. The apartment was starting to smell disused—not dirty, just empty. Simon stripped his jacket off, hung it up, and unbuttoned his shirtsleeves. His fingers grazed the ugly mess of old, blotched, and stitched scar tissue on his left forearm as he shoved the fabric back.

Coffee. A couple of hours sleep. A shower. More coffee. Then back to the hunt.

He poured fresh water into the reservoir and hunted through the fridge for a bag of coffee. The dregs of three different bags ended up in the filter. He flicked it on and leaned back against the counter with his arms braced behind him as he listened to it perk.

So far the hunt for Jacob had been fruitless. The syrups that Simon had tossed had been the only footprint he left behind. Archer wasn't his real name, he'd been renting his shithole loft with cash, and his fingerprints weren't on any database that Simon had access to—officially or unofficially.

Simon twisted his lips back from his teeth in a humorless smile. He supposed that if he were going to be taken for a mug, it was some comfort to be taken by someone who was good at it.

The harsh buzz of a call jolted him out of his coffee haze. He shoved himself off the counter and crossed the room in long strides to grab his jacket and fumble through the pockets until he found the phone.

He glanced quickly at the screen. Not a number he recognized, and only people he recognized should have his contact. He swiped to answer.

"Hello," he said, his voice flat and unencouraging.

On the other end, someone swallowed audibly. "Hey, Si."

For just a second, all Simon felt was pleasure at hearing Jacob's voice. Then the anger crawled back up from where he'd shoved it and scraped at his throat.

"You lying, thieving bastard," he snarled. "When I find you, and I will—"

"Yeah, 'bout that," Jacob said. He sounded ragged, and his voice shook as though he were cold—or afraid. "I need your help."

"Are you *fucking* kidding me?"

Jacob laughed—a short blurt of noise. "I suppose I deserve that, but—fuck me—Si, it's gotten out of hand. I don't know what to do."

Part of Simon wanted to tell Jacob to fuck off, but he still had a job to do. Swallowing the anger, he found a cool, steady tone for his voice. "Do you still have the information you stole?"

"Sorta. For now."

"I need to know who hired you."

He heard Jacob swallow, and his mouth sounded dry. When he spoke again, his voice was steady as he started to bargain. "I can tell you that. Once I'm out of here. Much good it'll do you."

Simon hunched his shoulder up to hold his phone, shrugged into his jacket, and grabbed his keys. "Where are you?"

Jacob gave a frustrated-sounding snort. "Fuck if I know. I'm in the parking lot of some La Fiesta."

"Use the GPS on your phone."

"No offense, Si, but if I *had* my phone, I wouldn't be calling you," Jacob said. "I'd be on with Uber. Hold on."

There was the click of the phone being set down, and Simon let himself out of the hall and headed to the elevator. He hesitated with his finger on the call button and wondered bleakly if Jacob was playing him for a fool again.

"Si? You still there?"

"Where are you?"

"Castroville. Thanks, Si."

The smart thing to do was play along, tap into their old connection—however unreal and shabby it had been. Simon hung up and stabbed the button to take him down to the parking garage. The expensively nondescript company car sat in his space, looking bland and gray.

He'd always known Jacob was trouble. Finding out he was a thief had just upped the ante.

The Castroville La Fiesta was locked up when Simon got there, the shutters dragged down over the doors. There was no sign of Jacob. Simon pulled up on the other side of the street and idled the engine as he scanned the parking lot through the smoked glass window.

There was a phone booth mounted on the wall next to the padlocked Reddy Ice freezer, and the handset dangled on the wire cord. The wind set it swinging back and forth.

He pulled his phone out and checked the messages. Jacob had said he didn't have his phone, but Jacob said a lot of things, and he *was* a thief. Not this time, though. The only notification he had was from one of his security team. No sign of Jacob at his favorite club.

Yeah, well, tell me something I don't know.

Simon swiped the phone shut and took a last glance up and down the street. He clocked the homeless guy at the end of the street, squatting in the doorway of a shop under a Mylar blanket, and a light in the window of a run-down house with a boarded-up window and a For Sale sign in the dead square outside. There was an overflowing bin on the pavement, stuffed with plastic bags and balls of grease-stained paper.

Habitual paranoia twitched at the back of his brain and dripped sour adrenaline down his spine. That wasn't unusual. Eventually he got used to it and it was just gibbering background suspicion. Then Simon got out of the car, gave his jacket a hitch over his holster, and strode across the road and the cracked concrete to the dangling phone.

He picked it up and put the handset back on the hook. The plastic was wet. Simon pulled his hand back, took a quick glance at the dark stains, and then grimaced and wiped his hand on his leg.

Maybe this time Jacob had lied to the wrong person.

Simon really didn't want to care. He crouched down, pulled a slim, finger-long flashlight out of a pocket, and flicked it on to examine the ground. It was hard to tell, and concrete wasn't the most forgiving surface for tracking, but he could see scuff marks.

"Damn it," he growled as he stood up.

Maybe he was going to kill Jacob, but he wasn't okay with someone else doing it. He glanced around and assessed the approaches *he'd* have used. There was no way that Jacob wouldn't have seen them coming—and he wasn't a fighter. He'd have run.

The nearest corner was to the left. Simon went that way, and with difficulty, controlled the urge to run. He looked out of place enough without drawing any more attention to himself, so he walked briskly and with purpose, as though he knew where he was going.

He saw the car first. An idling SUV parked on the other side of the road with tinted windows and no plates. Simon knew security-modded cars well enough to recognize one when he saw it. He slowed down, and the hit of real adrenaline, not just PTSD habit, punched his heart rate up.

Two men in jeans and unremarkable brown leather bomber jackets hustled out of the back of the supermarket. They were so wide they looked short, but they were easily hauling the long body of a blond man across the car park.

Jacob. He wasn't unconscious—or dead. Simon had seen enough people he cared about dragged out of firefights to know *exactly* how that looked. He was hurt, though. His sneakers dragged, and his ankles turned awkwardly every time he tried to cooperate with the walking. One of the two men—hair a ginger blush cut close to his scalp—twisted Jacob's arm viciously when he stumbled.

Anger hit Simon in the gut—acid hot. Maybe he couldn't feel just one thing about Jacob, but those two he could get a nice, clean hate on for.

"Hey. Hey, is he okay?" he yelled and stretched his legs into a ground-eating stride. He pulled his phone with his off hand and waved it. "I got a call there'd been some trouble."

The two men traded looks over the top of Jacob's head. The ginger man shrugged Jacob's weight off onto his partner and walked toward Simon with his hands out and a smile on his face.

"Our friend just had a few," he said. The fake grin that stretched his mouth didn't reach his dead predator's eyes. "We'll get him home safe. No worries."

Ginger moved like he knew how to fight. Put that with the quick professional communication with his teammate, and it pointed to someone spending a lot of money at some point to train this guy.

"Well, this is private property," Simon said, his voice crabbed and just a bit whiny. "You can't just come here—"

Without breaking stride he jabbed his phone-weighted fist forward into Ginger's face. His nose spattered across one cheek with a brittle cellophane sound, and blood and snot splashed out to stain his T-shirt. Simon grabbed the slimed jacket collar, wrenched him forward, and kicked his knee out of joint as he went down.

Unfortunately for him Uncle Sam had spent a helluva lot more money teaching Simon to kill.

"Fucker," the writhing ginger man got out. "Kill the fucker."

His partner let Jacob drop to the ground and reached for something under his jacket. That made it easier. He wasn't going for his phone, so whatever Simon did was justified. Not that he had been planning to hold back, but it would just make it easier if the police got involved.

Two long strides closed the distance between them, until Simon could smell the oily coconut hair gel on him. Unlike his ginger friend, the man was almost aggressively nondescript—from his no-color hair to his no-color eyes. Simon closed one hand around the man's wrist, gouged his fingers down into the nerves, and twisted hard. Pain knotted the man's face, thin lips peeled back from his teeth, and he aimed a short, nasty heel jab at Simon's jaw.

Turning from the hips, Simon avoided a broken jaw and caught a callused palm against his cheekbone instead. He felt the crack of bone meeting bone—hopefully not bone snapping bone—and a flash of red bolted through his vision. He ignored the pain, jabbed his fingers into the man's throat, and felt cartilage bend and the burp of trapped air.

Out of the corner of his eye, he could see Jacob struggling up off the pavement. He was only using one arm and held the other hunched close to his chest.

"Si—behind you," Jacob yelled as he lunged forward and grabbed at Mr. Nondescript's leg. He wrapped his arms around his knees and yanked, making the man stumble and rattle out a "fuck." Simon spun on the ball of his foot. Ginger had managed to get up, weight on his good leg, and he squinted as he raised a gun.

"What the fuck have you gotten yourself into, Jacob," Simon snarled and dove at Ginger. He ducked under the gun, hitting the man in the stomach with his shoulder, and drove him back down onto the ground.

Ginger screamed as he landed on that broken knee—the ripping sound suggested nothing good was happening in there. Simon grabbed him by the front of the face. His fingers slid in the slimy mixture of gore and hooked under his cheekbones. He used his grip to punch Ginger's head into the pavement. It only took one smack, and the distinct feeling of resistance turning to pulp traveled up Simon's arm.

Simon took the gun out of Ginger's lax fingers and rolled to his feet. His arm followed the direction of his eyes, and he swung the gun up on autopilot to aim at Mr. Nondescript. The man was wheezing, a bruise spread up over his throat, and he had a gun pressed to Jacob's head. The barrel dug into the thin skin over Jacob's temple.

"Drop it," Simon said flatly.

Twisting his hand in Jacob's scruffy curls, Mr. Nondescript yanked his head back. He ground the gun in harder and pressed it until it had to bruise.

"I'll blow his brains out," he threatened.

A smile twitched at Simon's mouth. "Then I'll shoot you. Right now I'm pissed off at him, so I'd put money on you being fonder of your life than I am of him. But it is up to you."

Mr. Nondescript curled his tongue over his top lip, wetting the stubble, and narrowed his eyes at Simon. Whatever he saw in the steady regard convinced him Simon meant what he said. He let go of Jacob, stepped back, and held up his hands with the gun dangling loosely.

"We don't need to… escalate… things," he said. His voice was broken and scraped past the damage to his throat. "I'm sure this is just a misunderstanding. My name is Shaw, and I work for some very influential people. People you don't want to cross."

Jacob scrambled toward Simon and got painfully to his feet as he went. Keeping the gun steady in one hand, Simon reached out to grab Jacob's arm on the way past. He yanked his ex to a shoulder-wrenching halt and dug his fingers into the firm muscle of his forearm.

"Drop the gun," Simon repeated, gesturing his own weapon toward the one still held by Mr. Nondescript. "Or I drop you."

A smug smirk twisted Shaw's mouth. "You're going to shoot me? In the middle of San Antonio? I don't think so. You don't need the attention."

"I'm a decorated Marine," Simon said, gun steady and mind icy clear and confident. "You're a thug with a gun I caught gay-bashing my ex. And I am sure your influential employer isn't going to go on record to contradict that. So drop it, or I'll take my chances with the press."

The calculation ticked in Shaw's eyes like clockwork. Then he mugged his best helpless expression and bent down to put the gun on the pavement with ostentatious care.

"Look. I don't think you quite understand what is going on," he said as he straightened up. "Mr. Archer here has just taken something that my employer wants. If he would just hand it over—"

Simon took two quick steps forward, sideswiped the gun into the road with his foot, and sent it skipping over the tarmac. Shaw's eyes followed the movement and then returned to Simon.

"This is a bad fight to pick," he warned.

"Go," Simon told him.

There was an equation to that sort of thing—reward divided by risk decides action or inaction. In this case the risk outweighed the reward. Instead of fighting, Shaw retreated, and once he was in the car, the invisible driver behind the black glass threw it into gear. It disappeared around the corner, and Simon lowered the gun. He breathed out and took a second to ride out the empty feeling, disappointed and almost resentful at missing a fight.

Dev thought he was an alcoholic. Drink wasn't what Simon was addicted to. It didn't help, but it wasn't the problem. More of a facilitator.

He used the corner of his jacket to wipe the prints off the gun and tossed it into the supermarket parking lot. Then he turned around, grabbed Jacob's elbow, and hustled Jacob into a brisk walk. The ragged huff and rasp of Jacob's breathing was too loud in Simon's ear and masked the noises of the street.

"Who were they?" Simon asked.

"Don't know," Jacob said. He ducked his chin to wipe sweat and blood off his face onto his shoulder. When Simon made a frustrated sound, Jacob shook his head. "I mean it. I've no fucking idea, Simon. This was a clean job."

"Clean," Simon said flatly. They reached the end of the road, and he paused to check the established landscape for any changes. The homeless man shuffled across the road, Mylar dangling around him like a cloak—too far away to pose an immediate threat if he wasn't what he looked like. "Not what I'd call it."

Jacob hesitated and leaned his weight back on his heels. "Simon. Look, I told you that I never meant—"

"And I don't care," Simon lied flatly and shoved Jacob into the road ahead of him. "If I didn't need answers, I'd leave you to get your own ass out of whatever mess you've got yourself into."

Arm tucked protectively over his ribs, Jacob hobbled toward the car. "I *just* said this wasn't me."

Simon thumbed the car fob, making the lights flutter, and reached past Jacob to get the door open.

"Get in."

As Jacob gingerly lowered himself into the car, Simon got a better look at him. He had a cut on his forehead and a puffy lip that roughed up the otherwise almost-pretty lines of his lean face. The hand pressed over his at-least-cracked ribs was scraped and raw, the skin split and bruised where someone had stamped on it. It could have been worse. Simon had *seen* worse, but he still had to wrestle the urge to go back after Ginger and Nondescript.

He slammed the door shut and loped around the car. Jacob was still getting the seat belt on as Simon got in, and struggled with working it one-handed.

"Can we get out of here?" Jacob asked as he shifted in the seat and looked out the window. His tongue swiped over the tender bruise of his lower lip, and he grimaced. "I need a doctor and a drink. Not necessarily in that order."

"You need a lawyer."

"I've got one."

Simon snorted as he pulled away from the curb. "Call her, then."

"No phone."

"My point."

The black car screeched around the corner, rear end fishtailing on the tarmac as it raced toward them. It clipped the homeless man and sent him flying. The Mylar blanket slipped off his shoulders and soared away on the wind.

"Son of a bitch," Simon snapped. He grabbed the back of Jacob's head, shoved him down against his yelp of protest, and tucked himself over him. The car jolted as bullets hit it, and glass sprayed over Simon as they shot out the windows.

As soon as the gunfire stopped, Simon unfolded himself. The engine was still running, and he gunned it and peeled off down the road. Jacob got his elbow on the passenger-side window and pulled himself up. He hissed a groan between his teeth as he uncreased his abused ribs. Then he brushed glass out of his hair with a shaking hand and stared out through the hole where the window used to be.

"Wait," he said suddenly. "The old guy—they hit him. We have to call the cops or an ambulance or something."

Simon swallowed, tasted adrenaline, and tossed Jacob his phone. He hadn't even thought about the old man. His brain was still locked into violence and mission parameters.

"Hit 911. We were just passing—"

Jacob fumbled with the phone and snorted. "I think we can both agree, I know how to lie," he said. The operator opened the line, and the pain left Jacob's voice as he said, "Hello? I think something might have happened...."

CHAPTER FIVE

A BLOODY facecloth dropped onto the floor. Mint-green mouthwash and blood hit the scraped porcelain of the sink and swirled down the drain as Jacob flipped the tap on. He wiped his hand over his lips, looked up at his reflection in the mirror, and grimaced at the more-or-less okay face that stared back at him. A zombie-green bruise was spreading down from his temple, and his lower lip was scabbed and puffy, but he'd seen his sister with worse after her "kickboxing for kuties" classes.

It wasn't a face that was going to earn him a free pass. Although he suspected he could look like Keifer Sutherland on hour twenty-three and it wouldn't get him a sympathetic hearing.

He took another swig of mouthwash. The inside of his mouth stung as the alcohol hit it, but he swilled it around his teeth and spit it down the drain. Time to face the music—or fake a medical emergency. He half-seriously weighed that up in his head as he grabbed a towel, wiped his face, and left the bathroom.

It was a Comfort Inn. It looked like every other Comfort Inn he'd ever stayed in, from the shiny bedspread to the butt-scarred computer desk. Simon's long, lean, expensively dressed body looked out of place slouched against the wall, arms crossed, and attention on the darkness outside.

Hot, but out of place. It seemed like a camera should flash at any minute and capture the lithe lean of his body and clean-cut, reserved beauty of his face for the pages of a high-end magazine. Untouchable.

Jacob swallowed the ridiculous urge to wrap himself around all that muscle and bone, to prove he could touch him. Even if he hadn't burned that bridge—and, let's be honest, he had blown that bridge up, set fire to the bits, and pissed on the ashes—it wasn't the sort of thing Jacob did. He didn't *need* people. His sister said he was like a cat—fun to pet, made all the right noises, but fended for himself just to make the point he didn't need you.

Cats probably didn't have to deal with being kidnapped from outside a Starbucks, though.

He sat down on the end of the bed, felt the base shift under his weight, and tried to think of the right thing to say. It was usually easy, but the thugs who'd grabbed him seemed to have rattled the smooth right out of him.

"I think my hand's broken," he said.

"It's not," Simon said flatly without looking around.

Jacob wriggled his fingers and flinched at the hot ache of pain that started in his knuckles and ground up into the bones of his wrist.

"It hurts."

"Good. It still isn't broken." Simon finally dropped the curtains closed, sealing off the view, and turned around to look at Jacob. His eyes were flat and cold, and the slant of his mouth was somewhere between contemptuous and impassive. The anger made Jacob feel weirdly closer to him. He could see the flaws, the bony callus of an old break making a bump on Simon's Greek-straight nose, the divot of a small scar that nicked the corner of that irritated mouth. It probably said something about Jacob that he preferred the flaws to the perfection. "What I want to know is why Harry Clayton hired you? He runs a social-media platform. There's no overlap with an eco-engineering firm."

Apparently he was more interested in what Jacob had told him on the way there than in Jacob's battered fingers—which was probably fair enough.

Jacob supposed he was violating some sort of implied confidentiality. Except it wasn't like he'd added a chapter on professional ethics to his imaginary rule book, and who would he have been trying to kid if he had?

"He thought that Porter had stolen the code for an operating system he wrote," Jacob said. He shrugged one shoulder and regretted it as his skin grated over his aching ribs. "He might have been right."

Simon narrowed his dark eyes. "He wasn't. Dev's not a thief."

"Not what his juvie record says."

"That's sealed."

"Kind of my job," Jacob pointed out. "Look, it didn't matter to me—I got paid either way—but I found the code in the information I—"

He hesitated, and Simon finished the sentence for him. "Stole. The information you stole, Jacob."

The contempt in his voice was dry as dust. It would have stung, if Jacob had *any* shame in his body.

"Clients usually prefer information acquisition," he said. "But yeah, stole works. Like I told you, Simon, it was a clean job. All Clayton wanted was information related to his code—no industrial secrets, market information, or dirty pictures. I handed it over—"

"I thought you still had it."

Jacob flexed his hand again, like it might have stopped hurting in the last few minutes. It hadn't. "I do," he said. "Getting kidnapped interrupted the process."

He stopped and cleared a throat that had suddenly filled with sand. In the back of his nose, he could still smell the sweat and gun-oil reek in the car, and when he swallowed, he could feel the hard muzzle of the gun shoved into the small of his back. It hadn't been cold—just hard. The red-haired gunman had been so close that Jacob could feel the stale heat of his breath on his ear as the guy threatened him with a disturbing lack of passion. Jacob had been scared, but not *really*. That came later, when the gun went off.

"Gonna puke," he announced abruptly and jolted to his feet. He lurched into the bathroom and hunched over the too-low toilet. Bleach fumes stung the inside of his nostrils as he coughed up the dregs of coffee and the stale sandwich he'd been tossed to shut him up earlier. Somewhere outside his sweaty misery, he heard the door open and shut.

It would have been a good time to make a run for it, but Jacob's stomach responded to that thought by trying to turn itself inside out again. Every retch made his ribs burn and cramp, and the pain made him dizzy and hot. He leaned his forehead on the cold rim of the toilet, not caring about the multitude of asses that had farted there previously, and tried to think about nothing.

The sound of the door interrupted him again, and he lifted his head just as Simon stepped into the bathroom.

"Here." He crouched down and held out an open can of Pepsi. "Drink it."

"Did they not have Sprite?"

The stern line of Simon's mouth twitched with… maybe humor, probably irritation. "Drink. It."

Jacob took a sip, grimaced at the hit of sugar and flat caramel taste, and rubbed the can over his forehead. The frosted metal spiked a headache through his skull bones and cooled his bruises.

"Thanks," he said and reached out to slap Simon's knee with his hand.

It was a casual gesture, unthinking contact. Not even intimate—not to anyone healthy. It *felt* intimate, though, and the tension suddenly thickened like resin between them. Simon pulled away first, rocked back on his heels, and stood up with easy grace.

"We aren't done yet," he said flatly as he turned his back and walked out the room. "And I need you talking, not puking."

Jacob swallowed, his mouth sticky with puke and soda, and reached up to put the can next to the sink. If everything had gone according to plan, he'd have been on a plane home for a longer-than-usual visit with his family. So it could be worse.

Last time he'd gone to visit, his sister had left him with the kids, taken off to Mexico, and gotten stopped coming back over the border with contraband. It had been the rugrats' first visit to court—all in one long weekend.

Compared to that an awkward conversation with an ex was nothing. But he supposed that was true of most things. His family had made him. That was proof enough they sucked.

He dragged himself to his feet, flushed the toilet, and headed back into the bedroom. Simon had stripped his jacket off and rolled his sleeves up, exposing lean forearms and old scars as he braced his elbows on his knees. The black canvas straps of his holster were snug around his body, stark against the tight-fitting white linen of his shirt. It was probably meant to be intimidating, but it was kinda hot.

Simon looked up, his dark eyes narrow over knife-edge cheekbones.

"Who grabbed you?"

"Don't know."

"Why?"

"Don't know."

"For someone whose job is information, you don't seem to know much."

Professional pride a bit ruffled at that, Jacob scowled at him. He regretted the expression as his battered face twinged around the hinges. "I didn't exactly have my usual prep time," he said. "They were thugs in cheap clothes and a nice car. They were not particularly nice. That's all I got. They weren't interested in talking to me."

Simon played with his watch and adjusted the strap around his wrist so the fob lay flat on his arm. "What about Clayton? Maybe he just didn't think you were worth your payslip."

"No, I don't think so," Jacob said. He felt vomit balling up under his diaphragm again and tried to think about something else. Anything else. He rubbed his hand nervously and pressed down on the bruises. "He was... he wasn't the type. Clayton was out of his depth with *me*, never mind these guys."

Simon clenched his jaw.

"I'm very tired of being lied to, Jacob," he said after a couple of seconds that felt like they dragged on for hours. "So I'm going to give you one chance. What are you hiding?"

Jacob folded his arms and snorted indignantly. "I didn't lie any more than normal people do. Withheld the truth, a bit, but—"

The last of that sentence caught in his throat as Simon stood up, grabbed his arm, and marched him toward the door.

"Hey, what are you doing?" Jacob leaned back against Simon's grip.

"Showing you out," Simon said as he yanked the door open and shoved Jacob through it. "I know Clayton was the one who hired you, and apparently you don't know anything else. So what good are you to me?"

He waited for an answer. Jacob hunched his shoulders and glanced around. All the peepholes lined up down the hall felt like tiny black eyes on him. At the end of the beige carpet, a woman in pajama bottoms and a white shirt leaned on the ice-machine button and weathered the rattle as she filled a plastic Walmart bag with cubes.

"Look, you know who wanted to steal the data, and I'll give the packet back to you," he said. "No harm, no foul."

Jacob tried to get back into the room and got stiff-armed into the hall.

"Ow." He hugged his ribs and tried to look pathetic.

Simon crossed his arms. His face was stonily ummoved, but his dark gray eyes were tight with anger. "Either tell me what you're hiding, or get out and fend for yourself. I'm sure you can spin a good enough lie to talk your way into someone's bed."

"Fuck you."

"You did, and then you fucked me over," Simon said. The corners of his mouth twisted. "Now fuck off."

He slammed the door in Jacob's face. At the end of the hall, the woman in business nightwear had finished filling her bag of ice and watched Jacob with bleary-eyed, unabashed interest.

Shit.

Jacob slapped the flat of his good hand against the door. "Simon, please. You can't just throw me out."

Except he could, and Jacob couldn't even really blame him. He leaned his head against the doorframe, and the molded wood dug into his forehead as he tried to think. Given a clean phone and access to high-speed Internet, Jacob could be up and running—*away*—in a couple of hours.

The problem was finding a clean phone in the middle of the night with no cash, no credit, no ID, and no coat. All he had were bruises, the taste of puke in his mouth, and a new ability to feel guilty about things that weren't his fault. That wouldn't even help him get a drinking problem.

And he was scared. He didn't want to be on his own.

"Okay," he said. "I'll tell you."

Nothing. He kicked the door in a burst of frustration and then glanced around to pull an apologetic face at the woman letting herself back into her room.

"Simon," he said. "Open the fucking door and stop being a cock. Okay? You want to know, let me in and I'll tell you."

The door opened, and Simon dragged him back inside with a hand cupped at the back of Jacob's neck in—again—that familiar way that suddenly felt strange.

"Talk," he said as he kicked the door shut. "What happened with Clayton?"

Jacob stalked past him into the room. He wished Comfort Inns stretched to a minibar instead of a tepid fridge. He wanted a drink with more of a kick than just caffeine and chemicals.

"I know Clayton isn't behind this," he said. The words dried up on his tongue, and he hesitated. He wasn't even sure this was a good idea, but it wasn't like he had a lot of choice. "Because those guys—I think they killed him."

That was a lie too. Sometimes Jacob just couldn't stop himself. They had definitely killed Clayton.

CHAPTER SIX

PRIVACY WAS hard to find in a hotel room with paper-thin walls. Simon took the elevator down to reception and kept his mind in neutral as he wondered what had left the Brazil-shaped stain on the carpet and *not* what Jacob had gotten himself into. The elevator dinged, and the doors slid open to reveal a lobby decked out in gold-and-green tinsel and a sweaty, bickering family in shorts with matching luggage.

He stepped out and held the door for them as they struggled into the space, and he hid his irritation behind tight lips.

"Thank you," the mother said as she reached between the suitcases to slap a finger out of the smallest child's nose.

"You're welcome," Simon said and let go of the door. It slid shut, and he dropped the social smile from his face. He stalked across the lobby, detoured around the clot of guests draining tepid coffee from a thermos, and headed out into the parking lot. A tired-looking woman with bags under her eyes and foundation drying around her hairline was smoking a cigarette in a businesslike way by the door. Simon caught her eye. "Don't suppose I could snag one of those? I quit, but it's been that sort of day."

She pleated her mouth in a smile, offered him the pack, and flicked the lighter for him once he'd picked his poison.

It had been six months since Simon had last smoked. He sucked down a lungful of hot, acrid smoke and couldn't remember why he'd stopped.

"Thanks," he said and exhaled slowly. She gave him the addict's smile and finished her butt while Simon stepped aside and pulled the phone out of his pocket. Dev was still third on his speed dial, since he'd never gotten around to taking Jacob's number off. It didn't mean anything. He hit the number and prowled out into the parking lot as it rang.

"Uhh?" Dev answered, audibly yawning until his jaw cracked.

"I found Jacob."

"Fuck. Really?" Dev mumbled. "Hold on."

Simon stalked across the dry tarmac to his car and winced at the sight of the damage, even though he was responsible for 40 percent of it. Bullet holes caused comments. Crushed car doors invited judgment. Even though it was only borrowed from the Syntech carpool, he ran a consoling hand over the hood.

"Okay," Dev said, his voice unfuzzed by sleep. "What happened?"

"He turned himself in." Simon shifted to keep an eye on the hotel. It seemed like making a break for it had been the last thing on Jacob's mind, but then a month ago, Simon would have said stealing information was the last thing Jacob had planned for the day. "Apparently things got out of hand. Clayton was the buyer."

"Clayton? *Harry* Clayton."

"Yeah."

"No way. I went to college with Clayton. He's a computer guy, right?"

"Social media. He's the founder of PeaPod."

"Yeah, that's him," Dev said. "Nothing to do with me or my research. Why the hell would *Harry* send a corporate thief into my company? He's cheap, and we're friends. Were friends. What did he even want from Syntech? Our areas of interest don't exactly form a Venn diagram."

Simon leaned a hip against the hood of the car. He took a pull on the cigarette, and the tip glowed ember-bright as he exhaled smoke into the darkness. "He didn't want anything. He thought you'd stolen code from *his* company. Or something. Jacob has the data, but we've not managed to access it yet. Like I said, things got a bit more complicated."

He heard a door creak as Dev padded out of his room and down the hall. "Look, Simon, I'll talk to Harry or get the lawyers to talk to his lawyers. The last thing the board wants is the publicity of a criminal trial. If you can get my data back from Jacob...."

"Another party has gotten involved. And Harry's dead. Maybe."

Silence for long enough that Simon felt a tweak of worry he'd been disconnected. Then Dev huffed out a shocked "fuck" and Simon heard the clink of glass on glass and something being poured. Bourbon probably. Dev liked his bourbon.

Simon rubbed the heel of his hand over his eye. He could do with a drink. "I said it had gotten complicated."

"Do I need to call you a lawyer?"

"No."

"What happened?"

"Not clear yet," Simon said. "Jacob claims that he met with Clayton to deliver the payload, they both got grabbed during the transfer, and he managed to get away at some point."

"Do you believe him?"

Simon made an unenthusiastic noise. "I do, but then I did before too. Look. I don't know what's going on yet, but if someone is grabbing geniuses with a connection to this data...."

"I can take care of myself—"

"In a brawl, sure. But these guys were professionals. And you don't just have yourself to think about, remember?" Simon finished the cigarette, tossed it onto the tarmac, and ground it out under his sole. "There's a guy I served with, he does close protection now. I'm going to give him a call, and you're going to hire him."

"You're overreacting." Dev's voice was a growl of offended pride.

Simon got up off the car, and the suspension creaked quietly as amusement quirked the corner of his mouth. "He's good. He's an asshole, but he's good."

"Great. Then he's not going to miss my business."

Stubborn bastard. Simon sighed and gave up, for the moment.

"I'll call you tomorrow," Simon said. "By then I should have a better idea what's going on."

"Maybe you should call the cops," Dev said. "If Harry's really *dead*, this is out of our league."

Not entirely true. Until he'd been invalided out, dead people had been Simon's stock in trade. Mostly he'd dealt with making them that way, of course, rather than the cleanup afterward. Addiction tickled at the back of his brain, and the nicotine of five seconds past was of absolutely no comfort to craving neurons.

"We don't even know if Jacob is telling the truth about Clayton yet," Simon said. "If he is, cops would be more of a hindrance than a help. They don't have the operating parameters for something like this, and even if they did.... Let's be real, Dev. If I didn't know we hadn't done this? I'd think we had."

"Flattering," Dev said. "Fine. I'll hold off for now."

Guilt caught in the back of Simon's throat. He owed Dev, and he wasn't sure if he was acting solely in Syntech's interests. There was also the lure of adrenaline's uncomplicated hit... and Jacob. Jacob would end up in jail if they went to the police—for the theft of intellectual property if nothing else. And even if the little shit deserved it, Simon couldn't *quite* stomach the idea.

"Thanks."

Simon hung up, fired off a message to his security team—he didn't need Dev's permission to put them on high alert about the CEO's safety—headed back into the hotel, and grabbed a coffee on the way past the front desk. It was only when the elevator let him back out on his floor that two things occurred to him. First, that neither he nor Dev had even suggested calling Clayton's family, and second, that he didn't have to disguise the taste of smoke on his breath.

Simon tossed the coffee into a nearby bin, strode back down to the room, and swiped his card to open the door. There was no sign of Jacob, and it gave him a second's pause as he wondered if the idiot had snuck out through the back—or let someone in.

"Jacob?" He kicked the door shut behind him and reached under his jacket for the gun. A bed creaked, and he heard someone sigh in the dark.

"Thinking about where it all went wrong," Jacob said.

"When you took up a life of crime, maybe?"

"Nah, I think it was Friday."

Simon bit his lower lip, folded it tight between his teeth, and looked up at the ceiling. He didn't want to laugh, but Jacob's deadpan refusal to be anyone else but himself was... Jacob. He let go of the gun, allowed the weight of it to settle back into the holster, and walked down the short hall into the bedroom. Jacob was slouched in the low bucket chair in the corner, a lumpy, dripping washcloth resting on his battered hand. His hair was unruly, and one of his eyes was going black. He wasn't a handsome man. He was almost pretty in a way that depended more on mobility and charm than on his unremarkably even, bony features. He wasn't handsome, but he looked particularly rough just then. It didn't matter. The lean sprawl of his body and the stubborn humor in his eyes clenched a familiar heat in Simon's stomach.

"Tomorrow, you're giving all the stolen data—and the analysis— back to Syntech," Simon said. The hard edge in his voice was more for him than Jacob, although not much more. "After that you're on your own."

Jacob started to say something and then visibly changed his mind and closed his mouth.

"What?" Simon asked shortly. He wasn't sure if he was more irritated by the thought of Jacob begging, or the thought that he might give in.

"I told you I was going to see my sister over Christmas," Jacob said. "So I'm not going to be on my own."

Simon stared at him for a second and then rubbed his fingers over his eyes. "Jacob, you really want to lead people you think might have killed a man home to your family?"

"You have *not* met my sister," Jacob said dryly. Then he added, still from his prone position, "And neither will they. I know how to disappear, Simon."

"I noticed," Simon said. "Short-term leases, no friends, nothing you actually care about—you don't leave much of a mark on the world, Jacob. If you hadn't gotten away from those two men last night, would anyone have ever noticed?"

Jacob asked, "My sister? My lawyer?"

"Two whole people," Simon said. "Congratulations."

He turned to grab the remote from the TV stand and thumbed the worn-down-to-pink power button to make the screen flicker to life with a rerun of *The Big Bang Theory*.

As Sheldon ran gawkily across the screen, Jacob added quietly, "You."

He glanced over with a frown pinched tightly between his eyebrows. "What?"

Jacob shoved a hand through his dishwater-blond hair. His fingers caught in knots of sweat and blood, and he looked uncomfortable. "You," he repeated. His mouth twisted into a crooked smile, and the scab on his lower lip cracked. "You'd have noticed."

Except he wouldn't have. Jacob could have been rotting in a shallow grave, and Simon would have gone on cursing him until there was nothing left of him but bones. It wasn't a good thought.

"Dead or running," Simon said, denying Jacob that third person. "How was I meant to tell the difference, and why would I care?"

If there was an answer that would make him feel better, apparently Jacob didn't know it either. He just sighed and waved a hand at the beds. "You care which bed I take?"

"You're going to sleep?"

Taking that as a no, Jacob gingerly stripped his shirt off. His ribs were dappled with bruises that ranged from pale blue to nearly black and blood blisters that looked raw where whoever had worked him over had worn rings.

"I'm tired," he said. "There's a bed. Unless you have something else in mind...."

Jacob pointedly yanked the covers back and sprawled out over the mattress. He draped his arm over his eyes, and his fingers curved around the point of his jaw. For someone Simon had seen nod off while lying on a stone wall, it took him a long time to actually get to sleep. He shifted and fidgeted, sighed and groaned as he tried to find some comfortable way to lie.

Despite his best intentions, Simon studied him. He knew the curve of muscle that led from Jacob's ribs up into his shoulders, the snorting snore than Jacob denied he'd ever made, and the way he kicked in his sleep.

And what, Simon wondered dryly as he sat down on the end of his bed, *had* he seen in Jacob again?

It was half an hour later and halfway into an episode of *Cops* when Jacob twitched awake and pretended he hadn't. Simon glanced away from a meth head swearing at a police dog and watched Jacob do his best impression of a sleeping person. It wasn't bad, if you were someone who'd never woken up to a heel in the shins from your lover.

"You okay?" Simon asked, after a minute.

It took a second, but finally Jacob ducked his chin in a quick nod. "Yeah, I'm fine," he said, his voice dry and scratchy. He didn't look it as he panted miserably into the crook of his arm and sweat soaked the sheets under him.

Simon tossed the remote aside, got up, and shifted beds. The mattress dipped under his weight, and Jacob lifted his arm enough to scowl. "I'm *fine*."

"Yeah. You look it." Simon put his hand on Jacob's shoulder and felt the heat of his sweat slick under his palm. "Have you ever seen anyone die before?"

After a sullen pause, Jacob shifted his arm back until it was tucked behind his head. "Die? Yeah," he said. "My grandmother had a heart attack at Thanksgiving, and my dad told God he was sorry he'd said there was nothing to be thankful for that year."

Simon eyed him dubiously. "Is that true?"

"Sadly enough, yeah." A wry smile curved Jacob's mouth and then faded. "My dad's an asshole. Surprise, right? When I'm such a prize?"

As distractions went, it was weak. Jacob *was* off his game if he thought that would work.

"You ever see anyone get *killed*?"

Jacob licked his lips, and his tongue followed the curve of his lower lip and skidded over the scab. "No," he said. He gave a short, dry laugh. "My line of work, it's more angry CEOs and sweating accountants. Ugly enough, I guess. They just... he was the one who tried to get away. I was scared. I just didn't want to piss them off. He ran, and they shot him. That's when I got the chance to run."

"You weren't scared. You were smart."

"No. I was scared," Jacob said.

Simon squeezed his shoulder. "So you were smart *and* scared. If you'd run first, you'd have been the one shot."

"So?" Jacob asked. "Like you said, there's two people that'll miss me. Make it 'mourn,' and I'm probably down to three quarters of a person."

If it had been an appeal for sympathy, Simon would have slapped it down. Jacob had made his own bed. But it wasn't. It was a mixture of self-pity and self-loathing. Still indulgent, but in a weird way, it felt honest—real, sharp, and unlovely.

So Simon kissed him. He tangled his hand in Jacob's hair so his knuckles pressed against the back of his skull and scraped his lips roughly over the bruise-swollen curve of Jacob's mouth. It had to have hurt. He tasted the metal tang of blood on his tongue, but Jacob still kissed him back with wet eagerness.

Of course he did. He needed Simon on his side, didn't he? Even more than he had when he used him to get to Syntech. That had just been money. This was his freedom, his life.

Simon's cock thickened, lust twisted his balls until they ached, and he didn't care if Jacob was using him. He would take it. He'd take whatever he could get. It was pathetic—he knew that—but it was private. As long as Jacob didn't know, as long as Simon didn't admit it, nothing would change.

He shifted position, braced his elbow on the mattress, and arched his back to leave space for Jacob's battered ribs. Bruised fingers fumbled at his buttons, and Jacob spit a frustrated "fuck" between their lips and then gave up and just yanked the tails of Simon's shirt out of his trousers. The linen rucked up around his forearms as Jacob ran rough palms up the hard curve of Simon's ribs until they caught against the tight straps of the holster.

"Damn it. You're so hot," Jacob groaned and planted wet, rough kisses along Simon's jaw. "I missed you."

"Liar."

"Not *always*."

It wasn't good enough, was it? Simon pulled Jacob's hands from under his shirt and pinned them to the mattress. His fingers wrapped easily around the wrists. Tendons pressed against his palms as Jacob strained against his grip and then relaxed back into the bed.

"Ow."

"That was a lie," Simon said.

He pressed his mouth against Jacob's throat, tasted salt, and felt the stutter of his pulse. Instinct wanted him to bite down, to leave a mark, but Jacob had enough bruises. He loosened his fingers around Jacob's wrists and dragged his palms along Jacob's lean forearms as he slid down the bed. The dark bruises were hot under his lips, and even the pressure of his breath made Jacob wince.

"Why'd they work you over?" Simon asked.

"I wouldn't give them the server," Jacob said. "Professional ethics, rule number three."

"Which is?"

"No play if you don't pay."

Simon sat back and splayed his hand over Jacob's stomach. His fingers brushed the thin, tender skin that stretched over Jacob's hip bones, just above the waistband of his jeans. "Does that apply to me?"

"This isn't business," Jacob said. He broke off, and his voice caught in a guttural curse as Simon worked the buttons of his fly free. His hips arched up off the bed, and the semihard curve of his cock was freed from the denim. "Fuck, Simon."

His own cock was so hard it ached where it pressed against his trousers with a dull, eager throb. Simon shifted his weight to take some of the pressure off it and peeled Jacob's jeans down his lean thighs. There were bruises there too—the imprint of a heel going purple against his hip and indistinct lines that barred his legs just above his knees.

Anger sliced hot through Simon. He should have taken the opportunity to do some serious damage to those thugs when he had the chance—more than a ruined knee and a couple of concussions.

"Still making friends everywhere you go," he said as he gripped Jacob's thighs and shifted them apart. Jacob's balls hung in a vulnerable dip, and Jacob gasped as Simon cupped them in his hand and rubbed a finger along the tight thread of skin that stretched back to his ass. Jacob's hands twisted in the washed-thin sheets, and his knuckles poked in sharp jabs under his skin. His cock hardened and curved up toward his stomach in taut reaction. Jacob threw his head back, with his eyes squeezed shut and his chin pointing at the ceiling, and groaned Simon's name.

Simon squeezed his handful of balls just hard enough to make Jacob blink open and focus light blue eyes as he squirmed on the bed in a way that suggested *this* little pain he didn't mind.

Simon met his gaze. "You know, this doesn't mean we're okay. You're still a liar and a thief."

"Yeah." A wry smile tucked the corners of Jacob's mouth. "But nobody's perfect."

It shouldn't make him want to laugh, but it did. Simon muffled the snort with a mouthful of cock and wrapped his lips around the firm shaft. He curled his tongue under the ridge of the slick head, tasted the penny-sour taste of precome, and dragged a rough sound out of Jacob that started as a curse and ended as a groan.

Simon let the cock slide out of his mouth and licked his way down. With his tongue he traced the ridge of veins under the velvet soft skin. Jacob caught his shoulders with his long hands and kneaded Simon's clenched muscles through his shirt as he mumbled encouragement.

"God, Si," he groaned. "That feels so fucking good. Don't stop."

"Maybe I should." Simon lifted his head. He shackled Jacob's cock with one hand and rubbed his thumb along the base of it as he looked up the sprawl of sinewy, bruised torso to his lover's lean face. It made his balls cramp with lust, and the ache of it settled in his thigh muscles. Before Jacob he'd never known he had a type—when you were as far in the closet as he had been in school, you fucked whoever stumbled in there with you—but he did. Or maybe it was just Jacob. "Teach you a lesson?"

"Oh, I never learn," Jacob said. He roughed his hand through Simon's dark hair and tugged until he made Simon shift. "Now come up here and fuck me."

He wanted to. The thought of Jacob under him, all tight muscle and tighter ass, made his stomach heavy with hot, angry need. The only problem was going black in knuckle-shaped patterns over Jacob's ribs.

"You're hurt."

"Yeah, well, if I don't need a hospital…." Jacob snarked. He rolled his eyes when Simon scowled at him. "I'm not *you*. If it hurts, we'll all know about it."

The mattress creaked as Simon rolled off him and stood up. Left sprawled and hard on the bed, Jacob cursed him irritably.

"I'm *fine*."

Simon unbuckled his holster, tugged the straps down his shoulders, folded it over, and set it on the bedside table. The absence of its weight at his ribs felt strange. A sweaty itch crawled over his skin.

"I actually don't have any reason to care, do I?" Simon took his shirt off. "Just remembered."

Somewhere in the pit of his brain, something twitched at exposing his left arm. Scars stippled it from shoulder to just above his elbow, half from the trauma and half from the surgeries to pin the joint and bones back together. It wasn't vanity… it wasn't *just* vanity. When Simon looked at it, he could see the weakness—the shoulder that dislocated easier every time, the staple lines where they'd replaced bone with metal, the damaged muscles and nerves to target in a fight—basically all the reasons that the Marines didn't want him anymore.

Jacob still did, though. He had hitched himself up on one arm, and his eyes trailed over Simon's chest and arms with lazy appreciation. One hand was curled around his cock, and he tugged at it with slow, lazy strokes.

Simon shed his trousers and joined Jacob on the bed. He cupped the back of Jacob's neck and scruffed him into a kiss. Stubble scraped his skin as he caught Jacob's lip between his teeth and tugged.

"I do care, though," Simon admitted reluctantly. "So shut up."

Simon sprawled on top of him, braced his weight on his arms, and slowly rolled his hips against Jacob's. Sweat and precome slicked their cocks as they pressed together, caught between the flat planes of their stomachs.

Jacob grabbed Simon's ass, flexed his fingers against the hard rise of muscle, and arched his hips up to grind his cock against Simon's abs as they thrust against each other.

"Fuck," Jacob groaned. He screwed his eyes shut as he gasped.

Electric pinches of reaction stabbed down Simon's cock and twisted his balls up tight between his thighs. The long muscles that strapped his back pulled tight and kicked off that old, familiar nag of bitch pain in his shoulder. The hit of endorphins blurred it and shoved it down for later. Simon kissed Jacob deeply, until they were breathless and gasping for air around tangled tongues.

Simon dragged his mouth away from Jacob's and bit kisses down his jaw to the taut line of his throat. He scraped his teeth over the pulse point in Jacob's throat, and it throbbed against his tongue as he thrust his hips roughly against Jacob's.

They still weren't okay—but this was close.

He buried his face against Jacob's neck, where the cropped blond hair was matted with sweat. Their cocks bumped and slid together, and each thrust twisted a knot of hot pleasure tighter at the base of Simon's spine and twitched through his muscles.

"Simon. Si," Jacob said. He clawed up Simon's back and dug into the slabbed muscles over his shoulder blades. His voice was cracked with lust and the lingering scars of fear. "I need you. I fucking need you."

His hips jolted against Simon's as he came and come smeared, wet and sticky, between their bodies. As Jacob went loose and boneless under him, it occurred to Simon that there was one lie Jacob had never told him—that he loved him. If he had....

Jacob twisted a hand in Simon's hair and dragged him around into a kiss—all panted breath and scraping teeth.

Simon pulled back long enough to grit out between clenched teeth, "You're still a fucking liar." And then he came into the mixture of sweat and come that glued them together.

He collapsed on top of Jacob and pinned him to the cheap hotel mattress. They sprawled in the mess they'd made and breathed wetly against each other's skin. Eventually Jacob winced and shoved at Simon's shoulder.

"Ribs," he grunted.

Simon rolled off him and debated rolling off the bed. In the end it didn't seem worth the bother of getting up. He fit himself around Jacob and stretched his long legs and bones over the bed. The TV was still on. People bickered over storage lockers in the corner of the room.

"It wasn't a lie," Jacob said suddenly, his voice rasping in his throat. "This. It was never about the job."

Simon dropped his head back against the too-thin pillow and licked salt from his lips. "That makes it worse, Jacob."

Jacob was silent for a second and then sighed. "Wish you'd fucking told me that before I spent a month scrubbing the skidmarks out of your boss's toilets."

It wasn't funny. Simon pressed his lips tightly against the smirk that wanted to escape.

"Go to sleep." He made his voice harsh. "You're going to have a busy day tomorrow if you want us to let you off the hook."

He waited for the smart remark, but apparently even Jacob ran out of those sometimes.

CHAPTER SEVEN

BRUISED RIBS and dried come were *not* a good combination. Jacob stood under the spluttering shower and picked last night off his stomach. It hurt to breathe, and his bruised hand was stiff and turning green and blue between the bones. It throbbed every time he moved his fingers.

He tilted his head back and closed his eyes as the stream of water hit his face. Last night might not have been the best idea. Good—his mouth ticked up at the corner as he remembered the heavy thrust of Simon's hips and the ragged need of his breath—but not the best idea.

The only thing sex ever fixed was being horny. Even *that* was temporary.

A fist hammered the bathroom door. "Jacob."

He tipped his head back out of the spray and spit soapy water from between his lips. "What?"

"Get out here."

Jacob sighed, turned the taps off, and batted the shower curtain out of the way as he climbed out of the tub. He'd forgotten to put the curtain inside the tub, and there was water on the tiles. Crap. He used his foot to drag a pile of towels through the puddles.

"Give me a minute."

One towel left. Jacob scrubbed most of the water off with it and tugged his wrinkled clothes from last night back on. A glance in the mirror made him wince. He pulled his mouth to the side to rearrange the bruises along his jaw. That was more memorable looking than he preferred.

No help for it, though, he supposed. He slicked his hair back and opened the door. Simon was leaning against the beige wall with his arms crossed over his lean-muscled chest. He'd already been showered and dressed when Jacob woke up. Somehow he managed to make last night's suit look freshly pressed. The sharp lines of his face were uncompromising, but Jacob could remember what the generous curve of his lower lip tasted like.

Simon glanced past Jacob's shoulder into the bathroom and screwed up his mouth at the mess. "You know, of all the things that could have been part of the lie, your allergy to tidiness had to be real?"

Jacob spread his hands. He gave Simon the best smile he could manage with his still-aching lip. "What you see is what you get."

Simon waved his hand impatiently toward the door. "Move it. We need to go."

"It's not even light out," Jacob grumbled. It was for show, mostly for show. He wasn't a fan of early starts, but sometimes they were necessary. He grabbed the door and pulled it open. "You know we don't have to check out until eleven, right?"

He hesitated in the doorway, and his chest hitched with a chilly weight. Stupid. If the men who killed Clayton were there, they wouldn't hang around in—

Simon planted a hand between his shoulder blades and shoved him out into the hall. There was no one there. Jacob took a deep breath and turned to give Simon an embarrassed look.

"I was just—"

"Trying to remember if you left anything behind?" Simon asked dryly. He closed the door behind him and nudged Jacob into motion. "Don't worry about it. Everyone gets the yips at some point."

It sounded good, but Jacob would put money on it that *Simon* never had. He slouched down the hall, scuffing his feet over the carpet, and tried to ignore the itch at the back of his neck. It was stupid. Until then, if anyone had ever asked, he'd have said he dealt well with stressful situations.

Turned out he *lied* well in stressful situations.

Dealing with them was apparently something different. They rode down in the elevator in silence, and Jacob nursed his hand in the crook of his elbow and kicked futilely at a wad of pink bubblegum dried into the carpet. It had never been difficult talking to Simon before. That had been part of the problem. Sex was a lot simpler when there was no conversation after. Now, though....

Lying had backfired, the truth hadn't worked, and small talk was just lying about nothing.

He finally came up with something as they were leaving the lobby. "Where exactly are we going?"

"Whatever hole you've been hiding in."

It was still early enough to be cool, and dew dripped off the butt-studded potted palms that framed the smokers' corner. Jacob balked on instinct—since the loft *did* hold all the evidence Simon would need to prove what he'd done at Syntech. And other places.

"All I need is a burner phone and an Internet connection," he protested. "I can get that in a Walmart with a McDonalds *and* enjoy the breakfast menu while we wait."

It would be an admittedly long wait—the data packet on its own was pretty sizable, never mind his various backups—but it *could* be done.

Simon stopped and turned to face him, and his eyes narrowed over the high line of his cheekbones. "Let me get this straight. You don't trust *me*?"

"That's not what I said."

"It's what you meant. Look, I told you. Get me the information you stole, and we're done. You're free to go and enjoy a shitty Christmas with your shitty sister."

Some childhood habits you never grew out of. Jacob glared at Simon. "Fuck you," he said. Temper set off hot little sparks behind his eyes. "Your shitty brother-in-law is a *thief.* Remember?"

Simon's jaw clenched, and he grabbed Jacob's shoulder and pulled him a step closer. Jacob's knuckles itched with the urge to throw the first punch. Playground experience told him that it would *probably* also be the last punch he got to throw, though.

"No, he isn't," Simon gritted out. "Whatever you *think* you found is wrong, so keep your mouth shut on it. Understand?"

"Yeah, well, keep your mouth shut about my sister. And her Christmas," Jacob muttered. The jolt of adrenaline was fading, and starting a fight over someone calling his sister "shitty" wasn't looking like such a good idea. She *was* shitty, after all. It was a family trait, and the way Simon was studying him made him feel uncomfortable. It was like he'd seen something Jacob hadn't put up to be seen. He tried to squirm out from under Simon's hand and scowled. "Can we go already?"

After a second, Simon gave in and lifted his hand. Whatever he'd been thinking was gone from his face, leaving the sharp lines chilly and composed. "Gladly," he said. "The sooner I know you're out of my life *and* my city, the better."

"Not your city," Jacob muttered and scuffed his feet across the gritty tarmac.

"What?"

"Nothing."

The sullen sound of the word on his tongue made Jacob cringe in embarrassment. Apparently he had actually regressed to preschool. He took a deep breath, tasted heat and the sour nicotine that had soaked into the plants, and tried to find his mental footing. Jobs had gone wrong before—not this spectacularly, but still wrong—and the key had always been to keep his head.

But around Simon the head that made bad decisions was in charge.

"I've been renting a place in Southtown," he said.

Simon snorted without looking at him, unlocked the battered car with a beep, and folded his lean frame into the driver's seat.

"What?" Jacob asked.

"You're secretly a hipster," Simon said as he started the engine. "Good to know. We can stop for some artisanal cheese for breakfast if you want."

Jacob slid into the passenger side, pulled the seat belt over his chest, and anchored it with a click. "I had to move in a hurry, if you remember," he said. "A friend had an open property there."

"You have friends," Simon said dryly. "Who knew."

Friend might be stretching it, Jacob supposed. Mani was more of an asset—a cheerfully amoral property manager with a portfolio of executive rental properties whose details she didn't mind selling on to a few trustworthy white-collar crooks. Lovely lady, though. She gave him a discount on the rent. Well, she *said* she gave him a discount, and it was the thought that counted.

It was half an hour to Southtown. After fifteen minutes of grim silence, Jacob flicked the radio on and bounced down the stations.

Adele. Awkward.

Metallica. Weirdly more awkward than Adele.

Opera. Yech.

The news…. Without taking his eyes off the road, Simon whacked Jacob's fingers away from the scan button.

"Leave it," he said.

Jacob leaned back into the soft leather seat and fidgeted as he tried to find a position that didn't cramp or stretch his sore side—political sex scandals, protests at the Alamo, and a dead body found in Riverside, near Nueva Street.

Shit. Jacob sat up as the name of the street where he lived caught his attention. He nervously ran the tip of his tongue over his upper lip. It could be a coincidence. Riverside was hardly a dangerous neighborhood, but it was popular, touristy, and sold booze, so things did happen.

Or....

Simon had heard it too. He flicked the volume up and filled the car with the smooth-edged voice of the presenter.

"A body was found in the San Antonio river this morning. According to reports, a man in his midthirties was discovered floating in the river this morning by a jogger. Bexar County Medical Examiner has yet to formally identify the dead man, but sources in the San Antonio Police Department have suggested that the body could be that of Harrison Clayton, founder of the PeaPod social network, who has been missing since Wednesday. Clayton was last seen in a coffee shop in the company of an unknown young man and may have made a tragic reappearance. In more cheerful news, the San Antonio Missions have signed a promising—"

The voice died midword as Simon flicked the volume to mute.

"Well, shit," Jacob muttered. He glanced over at Simon, and one of them had to say it. "It could be a coincidence?"

Simon changed lanes and slid in behind a battered old SUV. "If you were that lucky, I wouldn't have caught you at Syntech," he said. "Whoever took you... they're making a point that they know who you are."

A man ran by, arms pumping as his sneakers hammered the pavement. A sweat-soaked T-shirt was plastered to his chest, and his blond hair was dragged back in a ponytail. Pretty, but.... Jacob twisted his mouth in self-directed annoyance. Even before last night, these days everyone was "pretty, but." That'd teach him to stick to his rules in future. Because he wasn't seeing any way to fix it, and he had a feeling this one might actually hurt.

And he'd always preferred ripping the Band-Aid right off.

"No," he said. "They know who Jacob Archer is."

Simon snorted. "Of course. I don't even know your real name. I'd forgotten."

"You're not missing out on anything. It was a stupid name."

"It was you."

"It really wasn't," Jacob muttered. He dragged his attention back into the car and cracked a smile. "If it makes you feel any better, it did still start with a J."

"They're setting you up for Clayton's murder." Simon glanced over his shoulder as he changed lanes. "You really find that funny?"

The crack of Clayton's head hitting the concrete floor wasn't all that dramatic. It was a dull sort of thud. Stupid and clichéd, but it sounded like a melon hitting the dirt. The sound of Clayton's heels battering against the floor as he seized was louder.

Jacob swallowed the clot of dust in his throat. "Not really. But there's nothing I can do about it, is there? Except get out of town." He leaned forward, cursed shortly under his breath as the seat belt pinched his ribs, and pointed. "Turn left here. It's on Cevallos."

SIMON STEPPED fastidiously around the tangle of old jeans. "Tell me this is all a carefully plotted grid so you know if someone has been in your space?"

"It's laundry." Jacob considerately kicked a pile of towels under the couch. "Sit down."

A sneer curled Simon's mouth. "No."

"Suit yourself."

Jacob left Simon to disapprove of the mess and headed into the kitchen. There was a beer in the fridge, a strip of painkillers in the drawer, and a box of Christmas chocolates that he needed more than his sister did. He washed the pills down with a mouthful of cold froth and a coffee truffle and then leaned against the sink while he waited for the ibuprofen to kick in.

It didn't. He shoved another two truffles in his mouth and coated his teeth and tongue with chocolate. Then he nearly choked on them when he heard his sister's voice in the other room.

"Where the hell are you? I haven't heard from you in *days*, and you've turned Find My Friends off *again*. Why can't you—"

He nearly tripped over his own feet as he lurched back through the door with "shut up" on the tip of his tongue. His sister wasn't there, just her voice and Simon holding the old, unjailbroken phone that Jacob kept for his family.

"…whatever you're doing, you had better remember to get me and the kids presents. I've e-mailed you a list. There's a drum kit on there, but do NOT buy that for Jamie. Understand? And—"

Jacob stalked over, grabbed the phone from Simon, and glared at him as he swiped the speaker off. His sister's voice dropped from clarity to an irritated, singsong mumble.

"…if you buy me that—"

"Sis," Jacob interrupted and put the phone to his ear. "Not a good time."

"It's less than two weeks to Christmas. You haven't bought a single present, have you? Admit it. That's why you've been avoiding my calls."

"You're annoying. That's why people avoid your calls," Jacob snapped. He stopped and pinned the irritation behind his teeth. People were trying to kill him or send him to jail. Either way he probably shouldn't end what might be his last call with his sister on a bad note. "Sis, I love you, but this is a bad time. I have to go."

She ignored him. Jacob hung up anyhow. He shoved the phone into his back pocket, and the denim pulled tight over his hip bones. He glared at Simon. "That was private."

A dark eyebrow twitched up at a sardonic angle. "So was the information you stole from Syntech."

"That was business," Jacob said. It was also complicated. Simon might be brooding over the "never really knowing you" thing, but he already knew more than most people. Not that Jacob had *meant* that to happen, but it was still disconcerting, and giving him more info wasn't the way to deal with it. "This was my sister, and she's not involved in any of this."

"Okay," Simon said.

It was too easy. Jacob eyed him suspiciously, but it didn't seem as though Simon had anything else to say. After a second, Jacob shook his mood off and walked across the loft to his computer, which hummed along discontentedly. He really *should* remember to turn it off, he thought absently as he set his beer down on a stack of receipts.

"This is going to be quicker than Walmart," he said as he pulled the phone out of his pocket and shoved it under a folder. "It's still going to take a while, though."

Simon nodded agreeably. He flipped his jacket back and put his hands in his pockets, all broad shoulders and lean waist.

"Do you think those men from last night will leave your sister out of it?" he asked.

Jacob wiped his hands on his jeans and flopped down into the chair. The sudden weight sent him sliding backward. He refused to let Simon's question sink in deep enough to be a worry.

"They have no reason to go after her. They have no reason to know who she is." He dragged himself back to the desk by his heels. Then he hesitated as he reached for the keyboard and his fingers hovered over the keys. "You didn't say anything, about—"

"I didn't get the chance." Simon pushed a tangle of shirts off the couch and sat down. He leaned back and hung an arm along the back of the cushions. But there was nothing *relaxed* about him. "What does she think you do?"

"Market research," Jacob said. He impatiently hammered the space bar with his finger until the computer woke up and the screen flickered back to life. He caught Simon's snort, glanced over, and shrugged. "It's not a *lie*. It's just market research with a bit of theater. Most of the time."

"You pretended to be a cleaner for months. You created a fake sweepstakes and paid for a holiday to Europe, so you could get a place on the Syntech crew. It's a bit more complex than calling up and asking if we watch Fox News or ABC."

"That was your fault," Jacob said absently. A pulsing notification sat in the toolbar at the bottom of Jacob's screen. He clicked it and quickly scanned down the names, half his attention on that and half on his conversation with Simon. Two job offers, ten updates on his no-sleep series, and a bunch of bad jokes from people he didn't want to have to explain to Simon. He cleared the list, swiped the cursor back over to his server, and tapped the password in at the prompt. His bruised hand fumbled the keys until he gave in and hunt-and-pecked it in one-handed. "Security was too good to get *anything* remotely. I had to do it old-school."

That got him another snort. He pulled up the Syntech data packets out of the archive and keyed up the program to bundle and transfer them to the segmented subnet. As the percentages started to count down, he grabbed the beer. Simon raised his eyebrows at whatever message he read on his phone.

"It doesn't make any sense, you know," Jacob said.

"What?"

"This." Jacob waved his bruised hand at Simon. "Any of it. There's nothing in here that's worth killing someone over. The code was part of Clayton's PhD thesis. It's accessible through the college's library catalog, if someone really wanted it. The only value in this data is that it proves Syntech was using it without permission."

Simon frowned and tapped one finger against the back of the leather couch. Tap, tap, tap.

"It sounds like you're saying Dev's the only one with motive."

Jacob sat back and rested the beer bottle on his thigh. "It occurred to me," he admitted. "Seriously, though, it's not worth it even for him. Getting caught using code that's just been sitting in a thesis gathering dust? It's a settlement, a carefully worded nonapology, and a few years of tight smiles when it comes up in interviews. It's not worth killing someone over. I can make a guess at how much Clayton would have gotten, and it's a lot to me. But it's cutting a decade's worth of annual donations to the Alzheimer's Society for your boss."

Jacob remembered how Clayton's bitten-short nails scrabbled at the floor as he died, and the crack of a palm against his face as the thugs tried to bully him into not dying. It was weird how loud it was when someone stopped breathing. He hadn't known the man. It had been a shock watching him die, but that wasn't the same as caring. Still it felt like a waste.

"Clayton died for a principle and what's basically pennies at that level of rich." Jacob shook his head, pulled open a drawer, and grabbed a burner phone still in the plastic. He tried to rip the plastic apart, huffed irritably, and took his teeth to the corner when it resisted him. Around the mouthful of plastic, he grumbled, "I don't know if I should think it's tragic or stupid."

CHAPTER EIGHT

Brave hadn't even occurred to Jacob as an option.

Jacob had gone to get changed and left the computer to work. Simon's stomach started to make itself heard over the two missed meals. He stood in front of the fridge and tried to work out what to make of the sparse selection—a jar of pickled onions and peppers, a can of corned beef, and three cheese slices that were curling and dry at the corners.

And two bottles of beer, chilled and waiting on the shelf. He tried to ignore that, or how *good* his brain insisted the bottle would feel in his hand or the beer on his tongue.

A quick hunt through the cupboards turned up a slightly stale roll and a jar of preserves with smears of butter mixed in with it.

Not promising, but he could work with it. He found a frying pan in the cupboard, so dusty that it was obvious that Jacob wasn't the first person to live there who didn't cook. Simon wiped it out with a wad of paper towels and put it on to the stove, clicked the gas on, and left the metal to heat. Then he grabbed the corned beef and peeled the can open.

What had he seen in Jacob to start with? The man was a liar, a coward, and a slob—and he'd only hidden one of those things from Simon. His only virtues were a tight ass and a straight cock. As angry as Simon had been over being made to look the fool, maybe he'd been the one lying... to himself.

He dumped the corned beef into the pan and crumbled it. Then he added salt and a handful of silvery onions and wet red peppers to the simmering meat. While the grease melted, he sawed the roll in half and shoved it in the oven to toast the stale out of it. The smell of hot bread filled the kitchen.

"You cooking?" Jacob asked behind him.

And add that he was a mooch to his other sins. Simon flipped the corned beef with a spatula and glanced over his shoulder to catch Jacob tugging a worn T-shirt over his head. His ribs were a mess. The bruising had stained out into the surrounding skin, but the red had started to cool into muddy blues along the edges.

He was a train wreck *before* taking into account that he was a criminal, and Simon still wanted to kiss his bruises and breathe in the smell of his skin.

"I missed dinner saving your ass," he said.

"And I said thank you."

"Actually no. You didn't."

Jacob flashed him a quick grin. "Consider it said, then." He pointed with his chin at the pan. "Your hash is burning."

It was. The meat had blackened around the edges of the pan. "Fuck." He swung it over onto a cold burner and wrapped a dishcloth around his hand to pull the bread out from under the broiler. The roll lost its crisp shape as the juice sank into it. He piled the hash on both halves and added the dried-out cheese slices.

"I mean, I am," Jacob said. He boosted himself awkwardly onto the counter, still babying his injured hand by not putting weight on it, and leaned his shoulder against the wall. "Thankful for you saving my ass. You know."

He could feel the sting of the hot metal through the dishcloth as he shoved the pan back under the heat.

"Why did you call me?"

"Told you." Jacob shrugged. He poked dubiously at the last slice of cheese. "They had my phone. Yours was the only number I could remember off the top of my head."

"And what if Syntech had been behind the hit?"

Simon pulled the pan out, shoved it onto the stovetop, and folded the dishcloth over the edge of the oven door when he was done.

"Didn't have a choice," Jacob said. "Didn't matter if they were. I knew *you* weren't involved. You going to eat both of those?"

Someone else might have called that trust. Simon glanced down at the overpiled sandwiches.

"You have any plates?"

They were plastic and from Ikea. Simon slid the food onto the colored dishes and grabbed a fork from the drawer. His stomach growled as he dug into his sandwich and carved out gloopy, neatly squared chunks of meat, cheese, and bread.

Jacob made an orgasmically appreciative noise as he chewed on a mouthful, finally swallowed, and wiped his mouth on the back of his hand.

He tucked his foot up under him and then hissed and rearranged his legs. Balancing his plate in one hand, he rubbed his thigh with the other.

"So, do you still need me?"

Simon knew what he meant, but for a second, he let himself dwell on the notion of what it would mean if… if the lying, mooching, slobbish waste of space had meant something else. It felt too good to think about it, considering everything else between them.

"Maybe I should ask that question," Simon said. "You're the one who got kidnapped."

A shrug and another mouthful of sandwich. "I have a fake ID and a hideously suburban home to hide out in over Christmas. I'll be okay. The data transfer will be done in a couple of hours. Everything I got from Syntech is on there. After that…."

Simon's jaw felt stiff, as though that were some sort of terrible surprise. He ignored it and spat the words out precisely. It had felt the same when the doctors told him his shoulder was ruined—as though if he didn't *say* "I understand," it might not be real.

"Then I guess, after that, we're done. You can do what you want."

Jacob left half the sandwich on the plate and rubbed his greasy hands on his jeans. "I guess." He slid off the counter, caught his weight on his unbruised leg, and hesitated. "Look, I… had a good time, you know. If I hadn't gotten caught that night in Syntech, who knows."

One last bite of sandwich. Simon put the plate and the fork in the sink. "I do. If you hadn't gotten caught, you'd have kept lying to me. That's nothing real. There was nothing real."

Jacob scrubbed his hand through his hair, which made it stand on end. "It was as real as I get." He scuffed the floor with a bare foot and then smirked crookedly. "And hey, if you fancy hitting Bali in the new year, you know my number."

After an awkward second hovering, Jacob left the kitchen. Simon didn't have his number, actually, and he wasn't going to ask for it.

If he had it, he'd call it.

Instead he texted Dev with an update on what was going on.

INSTEAD OF Dev it was Nora who called Simon back an hour later with a terse, "And?"

Simon hesitated, and his fingers hovered over the touch screen. "Where's Dev?"

"Trying to explain what's going on to the board," she said. Her voice cracked in disbelief as she asked, "Maybe you could explain it to me. How did industrial espionage turn into murder?"

"I don't know yet," Simon admitted. "Clayton was the one who hired Jacob—"

"I know that," Nora said. "What I want to know is why Harry Clayton is dead, why I had to hear it from Dev, and somehow your little thief is still breathing. And, according to Dev, in possession of the stolen data."

Simon understood the suspicion. Unlike him, Nora had no reason to extend Jacob even a begrudging benefit of the doubt.

"He's not involved," he said. "Not with Clayton's death anyhow. Jacob's a thief, but he's not a killer."

Nora gave a shuddering little laugh. "Yes. I'm sure he'd never stoop so low."

"Are you all right?" Simon asked.

"No. This isn't what I—it's not what I signed up for," she said. "I know how to bully the board into allocating money for research projects that they don't really understand, and I'm a good computer engineer. But theft? Murder?"

"Dev wants to go to the police."

"I'm surprised the police aren't here already."

"They don't know why Clayton died," Simon pointed out. "For now, Jacob's the only thing that could draw the line straight from Clayton's corpse to Syntech. Which would be all it would take. We know we're not involved in this, but it doesn't look good."

There was a long moment's silence, and then Nora sucked in a slow breath and let it out on a sharp sigh. "You're right. I know you're right. Everything is still under control. We just need to keep our heads. I should go and save Dev from the board. What does he need to know from you?"

"If everything goes according to plan, I'll be back in an hour with all the data," he said. "Syntech will be made whole, and we can start an internal investigation into why this data was worth a third party killing for."

"Good," Nora said. She sounded relieved as she told Simon to keep them updated and then hung up on him, probably because she didn't know how few things had been going to plan lately.

Fucking Jacob last night hadn't been part of the plan, for a start. Or making him breakfast. Or imagining the lean, long-legged blond sprawled and probably naked on a beach in Bali.

Pushing that image out of his head—before he did something stupid—Simon turned to look at Jacob, who had leaned over the back of his chair and supported his weight on crossed arms as he eavesdropped on the call.

"Well?"

"Nearly done," Jacob said. He moved his attention back to the screen for a second. "I'm just handing back the raw data. If you want my analysis, I'll give you a competitive quote. Very reasonable."

"I think that Syntech would rather run their own analysis," Simon said dryly. "What with you being a thief and all."

"Work smarter, not harder," Jacob said. "Or if you can get away with it, be like me and don't work at all."

"Didn't you win Employee of the Month at the cleaning company?"

It was in the file. Jacob looked embarrassed, as though he'd been caught masturbating, not making a good impression. "Fine. Work sporadically. Enjoy the rewards. In this case, the down payment on the reward, but I'll get by."

The computer made a smug sounding *bing*, and Jacob unplugged the slim portable hard drive. He tossed it underhand across the room. Simon caught it one-handed and turned it thoughtfully in his fingers.

"That's everything I got off Syntech servers," Jacob said.

"The only copy?" Simon tucked the case into his pocket behind his phone.

Jacob jabbed a key on the desktop. "It is now. Simon…." He wrinkled his nose at whatever he was thinking.

Simon knew he should let it go, that whatever Jacob came out with *wasn't* going to be what Simon wanted to hear. Knowing didn't help, though. He still asked. "What?"

After a beat Jacob snorted softly. "I don't know," he admitted. "I don't really do good-byes, not usually."

Simon closed his eyes for a second and then gave in for the last time. "It goes like this. No hard feelings. Have a good flight."

"That it?"

"Yeah."

Jacob glanced down at his feet and then back up and blew out whatever regret he had on a sigh that ended in a smile.

"Damn, I picked that up quick," he said.

Simon snorted and headed for the door. He'd just reached for it when Jacob caught up with him, grabbed his head, and pulled him down into a kiss. The bite of pickled jalopenos lingered on his breath, and the spit and thrust of his tongue against Simon's clenched a reaction all the way down to his cock.

"Come to Bali," Jacob said against Simon's mouth. He slid his hands into Simon's hair and pulled on it. His body was hot and hard where it pressed against Simon's, and his voice cracked with nerves and uncertainty. "We can fuck in the sea, eat… whatever the fuck they eat in Bali. You can learn to surf."

The "yes" growled at the back of Simon's throat. He wanted to say it so much that it made it easier to swallow it down—nearly as easy as it had been to set the bottle down that last time, when Dev offered him something to do other than self-destruct.

"No." He pulled back from Jacob and wiped his mouth dry on the back of his hand. "I don't run away, Jacob, and I spent enough time lying to my family about what I do, who I am. And you're still you, still a liar. You're not going to change in Bali."

He saw the honesty in Jacob's face for a second—a mixture of hurt feelings and feline calculation on how to pull an "I meant to do that." Then he hid behind a smirk and a hand shoved boyishly through his hair.

"No," he said and stepped back. "I suppose I won't. Good thing we already said our good-byes, or this could be awkward."

For all his crimes—literal crimes—he made Simon want to laugh when he least expected it.

"Good-bye, Jacob," he said. "Take care of yourself."

For once he even got the last word as he closed the door behind him.

THERE WAS nothing out of place in his apartment. His clothes were either in the wardrobe or in the laundry basket, his fridge was stocked with basic provisions, and everything was laid at right angles. Usually

Simon found it soothing, a reminder that he didn't need the Corps to keep his life in order. Not today. Today it just looked like an echo chamber.

Simon stripped his jacket off and felt the weight of the hard drive tugging it down as he hung it over a chair in the kitchen. He pulled the fridge door open, grabbed a jug of orange juice, and sucked down the cold liquid until his chest cramped.

He needed a change of clothes, he had to book his car into the body shop, and he should probably already be at Syntech to drop off the hard drive with the cyber department.

It could wait. Simon took another swig of orange juice, tasted the bitterness that time, and twisted the top of the jug back on. At least it could all wait long enough for him to get into a clean suit. He shoved the jug back in the fridge, took off his holster, and set the gun on the counter.

He was almost into the bedroom with his shirt half-unbuttoned when his phone rattled against the shell of the hard drive. He shrugged the shirt back on and stalked over to grab it.

"Yeah?"

"Stay where you are," Dev ground out between clenched teeth, and his words rasped down the phone. He was on the move. Simon could hear doors slam and loud voices in the background. "Don't come in. Don't take any calls."

"What? Why?"

"Who have you talked to about our current situation?"

"You, Jacob. Why?"

"I'm being sued by Clayton's company. Apparently they've got evidence I stole that piss-poor code he wrote. How the hell did they get that, Simon?"

"It wasn't Jacob," Simon said. He hoped that was the truth. "What happened to Clayton scared the hell out of him. All he wants is to get out of town in one piece."

"Maybe Clayton told someone what he was doing, then," Dev snapped impatiently. "It doesn't even matter. Whoever it came from, they have *something*, and until I can prove it's bullshit, I've been suspended by the board. Fuckers."

Simon used his free hand to shove the tails of his shirt into his trousers. He grabbed for his gun and slung the strap over his shoulder. "I can come over now. If whoever was behind Clayton's death has anything to do with this, you could be in danger."

"I'm a big boy."

"Callie could be in danger."

Dev grunted, and Simon heard a car door beep. "Stop it. I'm putting up with your security team following me around like sad puppies. They can keep an eye on Callie at the house. We're fine. Right now what I need is for you to stay where you are. Understood?"

"Yeah," Simon said flatly. He leaned back against the counter, tucked the phone against his shoulder, and dug his knuckles into the knot of cold muscle in his shoulder. "Call me if you need anything."

"I need this last month to have not happened," Dev grunted sourly. The line went dead. Simon plucked the phone away from his ear, wrapped his hand around it, and squeezed until his knuckles ached. He wanted a fight, but failing that…. Everything in the apartment had its place, including the half-empty bottle of whiskey that he'd "forgotten about" in the back of the cupboard—an excuse that might have qualified as half-assed, if it weren't for the fact that Simon had been on the wagon since before he moved in.

He pulled the heavy bottle out from behind the balsamic and the sweet-chili sauce bottles and poured the honey-yellow liquid into a tumbler. The first swig was harsh, a shock of booze and iodine, but the second was mellower. Or his tongue had just remembered how not to taste it.

It was a bad idea, but fuck it.

He finished the glass and poured himself another. Then he took it and the bottle to the couch. Stretching his legs out in front of him, he took another drink and let it soak into his tongue while he stared at the blank walls.

He swallowed and let the whiskey blur through him. Maybe he'd get that fight after all.

The phone woke him up. It had gotten dark and there was an empty bottle on the table. Simon rolled off the couch, and his throbbing head and sour stomach reminded him exactly where the booze had gotten to as he staggered to grab the phone.

"What?" he growled.

It was Dev, his voice rough and impatient, as though it had been Simon who called *him* and was wasting his time with questions. "You got the news on?"

"No."

"Turn it on."

He hung up. Simon growled and threw the phone onto the counter, and the plastic skidded along the polished melamine until it bounced off a can. He grabbed the half-drunk jug of orange juice from the fridge, and took a drink to rinse the musty taste off his tongue. The remote was lying on the floor, so he picked it up, turned the TV on, and squinted painfully at the blare and glare of a cereal commercial. He turned it down to a mutter and flicked up through the channels until he hit the local news.

"—in the river this morning. The suspect was apprehended at his home this afternoon."

It meant nothing. Simon scrubbed the heel of his hand over his eye and tried to grind out the ache while he scowled at the TV. The shot cut to one of the journalists standing in Southtown, staring into the camera with a solemn expression on his face.

"We don't know, Lisa, what connection the suspect had with Harry Clayton. Details are sparse, and his neighbors say that he moved in just last week."

"Fuck," Simon spat out as he finally put the pieces together.

Jacob was *not* heading to Bali, and despite that crawling snake in Simon's brain, it wasn't a good thing.

CHAPTER NINE

IT WAS the *smell* in the cells that Jacob couldn't get over—a sour, years-old fug of sweat, spunk, sick, and shit, overlaid with the eye-watering ammonia reek of bleach. After a night spent trying to breathe through his mouth, it was a relief when a uniform came down, keys rattling, and escorted him back up to the interview room.

The man shoved him roughly into a chair with a hand heavy on his shoulder. Then he left Jacob alone with his thoughts and the mirror. He stared at his reflection in the wall of dark glass and wondered if there was already someone on the other side watching him.

If there was, he looked like shit. His bruises were at peak ripeness. His lip—resplit when they arrested him—was scabbed and puffy. They'd sent a doctor to check him over, but all that got him was a couple of painkillers and a cold gel slick of ointment between his knuckles.

But looking pathetic might be more useful here than it had been with Simon.

He sat back in the hard chair, and the back dug into his shoulders as he tapped his fingers on the table.

The last time he was in a cell, he was fourteen and his boyfriend was with him. They'd been caught fucking in the town cemetery, although the officer who caught them told his father they'd been drinking underage. Which they *had* been doing as well.

Fourteen-year-old Jacob had been terrified. Not that he admitted it to anyone back then, not even himself. He supposed the officer who lied to his dad had picked up on it, under the snark and the smart mouth.

At least this time....

No, this was still worse. Jacob had only *thought* his life was over at fourteen. Now it actually might be. He didn't want to go to jail. He wanted to go to Bali.

The door opened, and the wiry, fair-haired officer who'd arrested him walked in, trailed by a soft-looking woman with hard eyes.

"Mr. Archer," the man said as he sat down. "I'm Detective Barnes. This is Detective Morena."

"I asked for my lawyer," Jacob said.

"She's on her way. This isn't an interview. We're just making sure you understand your situation, Mr. Archer. It's not a good one."

So Barnes was going to be the good cop. That left Morena with bad cop or—Jacob mentally weighed up the options he'd have run with in this situation—flirty cop, maybe. The fact Jacob was queer didn't really matter there. It wasn't about sex. It was about making the mark feel powerful.

"My lawyer advised me not to say anything until she arrived."

"You don't need to, Mr. Archer. Just listen," Morena said flatly. "Or do you need your lawyer's permission to do that too?"

Bad cop, then. It wouldn't have been Jacob's choice, but it wasn't his con. He rested his elbows on the edge of the table and waited. After a second, Barnes picked up the folder he'd brought in with him and dealt a selection of photos onto the table.

Grainy black-and-white CCTV shots of the street outside the Starbucks where Jacob had met with Clayton. They showed both of them arriving and both of them leaving—cutting them in half toward the edge of the deck as they left the surveilled area—but none of them together.

"That," Barnes said as he poked a finger at Clayton's nervous face in one image, "is Harry Clayton, a very rich and—as of this morning—very dead man. And this other man?" His finger tapped the glossy image. "That's you, isn't it, Mr. Archer?"

It was in profile and fuzzy. Jacob supposed it could have been another blond man of his height, in his clothes, but he wouldn't want to try to convince a jury of it. He sighed. "I'd rather wait until my lawyer gets here."

Morena smirked at him. "Good," she said. "I like it when perps are stupid."

"You see, the thing is that it might not be in your best interests to hold your tongue," Barnes said. He pulled another sheet of paper out of the file. It was covered in small-type dense coding. Clayton's code. Or that's what Jacob assumed. It could have been a page from an Intro to Computer Science text, for all he could tell. It didn't matter. The page represented that they knew about Clayton and his code. Barnes smiled, and wrinkles creased around his eyes. "This here—this was what Harry Clayton died for. Wasn't it, Mr. Archer?"

He was overdoing the name repetition. It made the attempted manipulation obvious.

"Can't say anything until my lawyer gets here." Jacob shrugged helplessly.

"That's all right. We don't *need* your confirmation. We already know." Barnes put the sheet back into the folder and set it in the middle of the table in front of Jacob. "You were hired to prove that Devon Porter had stolen this piece of computer code from Harry Clayton. And you did. Impressive work. A real coup to add to your resume."

Jacob bit the inside of his cheek and sat back in the chair. He folded his arms across his chest. It wasn't so much the need to defend himself that he had to fight, it was the need to snark. Luckily Morena did it for him.

"Or it would have been," she said as she sat back and folded her arms in mirror imagery of Jacob. "Except you fucked up, didn't you? Got yourself caught and then...." She pursed her lips and shrugged.

"What did happen?" Barnes picked up the thread of the conversation. "Did Devon Porter buy you off? Pay you to tell Clayton that you'd found no evidence? That was what you were at the coffee shop to do, wasn't it? Except it went wrong."

"Do you think my lawyer will be here soon?"

"We don't know exactly what happened yet. Maybe Clayton didn't believe you. Maybe you tried to extort more money out of him. But what we do know is that Clayton ended up dead in the river near where you used to live, as it turns out, and you ended up in the company of Syntech's head of security. That's interesting."

Jacob smiled at him and shrugged. "Couldn't say."

"Think about that," Barnes said. "We have Porter. We have your computer. One of them is going to give you up sooner rather than later, so a smart man would get in first. If you tell us what happened, how Syntech is involved, maybe we can work out a deal. Your problem is Syntech's lawyers are already here, and the deal's on the table for them too. So... up to you."

"I'll ask my lawyer when she gets here," Jacob said. And really, *Law and Order* was on infinite syndication. Did anyone actually fall for the "only one deal on the table" gambit anymore?

"I told you," Morena said impatiently. "Ramsey is the one we should be talking to."

Barnes made a helpless, graceful gesture with his hands and pushed himself up from the table. "Let us know if you change your mind about holding your tongue, Mr. Archer," he said. "Just remember the clock's ticking."

They left the room and closed the door behind them with the sort of click that involved an automatic lock. On the scratched white table, the beige folder they'd left behind lay like a temptation. Jacob ignored it, sat back, and took a deep breath that stitched through his sides.

The computer wasn't a problem. All the incriminating stuff was stored on the server, and if the cop techs could backtrack to *that*, they would have gone into business for themselves already. All they'd get out of his hard drive would be some eye-watering porn and his Bali research.

Syntech's involvement was more concerning—*if* Syntech was involved and it wasn't just a shot in the dark by the cops.

Although that raised the question, how *had* the cops known where to find him?

His fingers itched to crack the folder open and see exactly what the cops had on him, even though there was no way Barnes had put anything useful in there. It was a trap, even if Jacob wasn't sure yet what they expected to get out of it.

So he did nothing, and nothing happened. Stuck in the small box of plaster and glass, boredom started to nag as time dragged. Jacob rocked onto the back legs of the chair and balanced on two and then on one. That got old after a while, and he got up to pace the room. Nervous energy made him move and fidget.

It had probably been twenty minutes, but it felt like more. Finally Jacob gave in and hammered on the closed door until he heard footsteps approach down the hall.

"What?" Morena snapped as she opened the door.

"I need to piss."

Her mouth twisted. "I'd have thought you needed your lawyer for that."

"She holds my hand, not my cock," Jacob said. "Can I use the restroom, or do I pick a corner?"

Morena studied him for a second with her lips pursed and then shrugged. "Wait, and I'll get someone." She closed the door again, and Jacob heard her footsteps retreat. It didn't sound like she was in a hurry. He went back to pacing the room, and the ache in his bladder grew in urgency.

The door finally opened again, and a uniform built like a fireplug gestured to him with a scowl. "Come with me."

The cop escorted Jacob through the bull pen and shoved him as a means of directing him through the maze of desks, kicked-out chairs, and scowling detectives. Morena and Barnes were both at their desks, heads lifted from their work to watch him go past.

Jacob glanced around as he walked and looked down corridors and through blind-slatted windows into small offices. There was no sign of Porter or Simon, although they could be in one of the other interview rooms. Behind the closed door of the captain's office, a man in a suit held forth at whoever was at the desk. He looked like a lawyer, but he had the matte look of a corporate shill. Criminal lawyers favored suits with a bit of shine to them.

Besides, if the CEO of Syntech had been dragged down for questioning, no shark worth their chum would leave his side during interrogation.

The toilet was opposite the elevators. It was grimy, with dirt worked into the grout and stains rusting around the drains. The uniform stood with folded arms and uninterested eyes while Jacob unzipped and pissed into the urinal.

Jacob shook, tucked, and zipped back up. A quick wash of his hands, the soap sickly sweet with lavender, and the cop shoved him back into the hall.

"Move," the cop ordered impatiently and gave him a shove when Jacob dragged his feet.

Halfway back to the interview room, Morena intercepted them.

"Bellick." She nodded to the uniform. "I'll take him from here. Thanks."

"Of course, Detective."

Morena took Jacob by the sleeve and walked him back the way he'd come.

"Detective," Jacob said. "I'm still waiting for my lawyer."

"Yeah, you'll be waiting for a while," she said. He looked at her curiously, but she didn't elaborate. "Don't worry. We're done with you for now. But don't leave town."

"Of course not," Jacob lied smoothly.

Morena let go of his arm as they reached the elevators. She jabbed the call button and then leaned back against the wall, crossed her arms, and bit the patchy lipstick off her lower lip.

"You're in over your head, Archer," she said abruptly.

"Lawyer," Jacob replied.

"I've released you from custody."

He side-eyed her. After a moment she tilted the corner of her mouth in acknowledgment, "You don't strike me as a killer. So if you did kill Clayton, it wasn't your own idea. Tell us who's involved and maybe we can help. Maybe not. You don't tell us, we'll never find out."

He nearly told her. It surprised him how much he wanted to spill his guts. Maybe she was better at running a con than he'd thought.

"I'll bear that in mind," he said.

The elevator doors slid open and let out two officers and a harried-looking geek with a laptop bag and a scowl. Morena stepped back to let them pass, and while she was distracted, Jacob dodged behind the geek into the car and insistently hit the button for the ground floor.

"We will solve Harry Clayton's murder," Morena told him through the closing gap of the door. "If you didn't do it, don't let Syntech bring you down with them. If—"

The doors bounced together, and Jacob leaned back against the wall. His head dropped back and bonked against the polished steel, and he stared up at the ceiling as the elevator lurched toward the ground.

Shit.

He made his living with words, the use and abuse of them, but right then he only had the one.

The whole situation was shit. He was *in* the shit. The job had gone to shit, and he had to work out what the fuck to do about it.

Okay. Two words.

The elevator jolted to a stop, and the doors opened and let Jacob out into the hall. He pushed himself off the wall with a huff of effort and let himself out. After the dim ecofriendly lights inside, the midmorning sun half blinded him. It didn't stop him from recognizing the man who leaned against the hood of the sleek blue Chevy parked by the curb. Simon wore his off-duty uniform of jeans and a white shirt, and Wayfarers covered his eyes.

Jacob envied them as he squinted one eye shut and lifted his hand to shade his face.

"I thought we'd done our good-byes?"

"That was when we thought we could wrap this up quietly." Simon pushed himself up off the hood. "Before *you* got arrested and Syntech ended up all over the news. Now we need to talk. Get in the car."

Jacob hesitated and twisted his mouth regretfully. "No offense, Simon, but the police turned up awfully quick after you left last night. I think I'd rather wait for my lawyer. I need to discuss her leaving me high and dry in jail, for a start."

A straight eyebrow quirked over the dark sunglasses. "Allison Moynihan, right? Same lawyer you called at Syntech that night."

Jacob didn't answer. Apparently he didn't need to.

"She's not coming," Simon said. "Her car was run off the road last night. She's in the hospital. Whoever is behind this, Jacob, they aren't going to let you jet off to Bali. So. Get in."

Once you let yourself feel guilt over one thing, it apparently took it as an open invitation. Jacob caught his breath against it and hunched his shoulder.

"Is she okay?"

Simon looked at him as though it were a strange question. Maybe Jacob couldn't blame him for that, but he'd known Allison for years. She was the closest thing to a friend he had in professional circles.

"Broken bones," Simon said. "It's not good, but it's nothing that won't heal. Jacob, you said you trusted me."

"That doesn't sound like me."

"No," Simon said wryly. "I suppose it doesn't, but we both know it's what you meant. I got Syntech's lawyers to get you out as part of the lawsuit they're threatening the police with right now. Why would I do that if I was the one who turned you in?"

Jacob thought about it for a second. Then he sighed and got in the car.

MIDDAY AT the Café Olé, right in the middle of Riverwalk. If whoever was behind Clayton's murder tried anything, there would be a hundred witnesses and a thousand Walden-filtered Instagram photos for evidence. Jacob sat under a striped umbrella and poked desultorily at a plate of salsa and unsalted chips. His phone lay on the table while PayPal was busy sending a fresh bouquet of flowers to Allison's hospital room. He was a bit surprised to realize he knew what flowers she liked.

"I appreciate you getting me out of the cells before they booked me," he said as he found a chunk of jalapeño. "But I already told you what I knew. I don't know what gave Clayton the idea Porter had stolen his code, I don't know why anyone would care enough to *kill* him over it, and pursuing me is a waste of money. I have no dog in this fight. If they had just let me leave town, I would have been done with it."

"Maybe they thought you had a moral center."

Jacob snorted and crunched the point off a chip. "Then they haven't been paying attention."

Simon braced his elbows on the table and pressed his knuckles against his mouth. He was still wearing his sunglasses, which left the only clues to his mood the tight line of his mouth behind his fingers and the pinched groove in the skin between his eyebrows.

"Why did you think that Dev had stolen Clayton's code?" he asked.

"I don't know. Because it was all over the servers?" Jacob tossed a chip over the rail to a loitering duck. He tried not to think about the fact that Clayton's corpse had been floating in the same murky water not twenty-four hours before. "Believe it or not, I was actually surprised. I read Porter as the type who'd cut his nose off to spite the board rather than admit someone could work something out that he couldn't."

"You weren't wrong," Simon said.

"I kinda was."

"Could the information have been planted?"

Jacob tried to think of any way that might be true. He thought about lying to give Simon the answer he wanted, but this might actually be one of the rare occasions where the truth was best.

"I'd have noticed," Jacob said. "My job is to get answers, not be fed them. The code wasn't just sitting, taking up space in a Dropbox folder. There were over a dozen projects where this code was installed during the testing simulations. It was actively in use."

Simon's mouth went sour, and he took a drink of the coffee he was nursing and pulled a face at the burnt-bean taste even as he took another swallow. The clean line of his throat worked as the coffee went down, and his Adam's apple bobbed under the freshly shaved skin. Jacob caught himself watching—staring—and pulled his attention back up to Simon's face.

"That just proves that *someone* took the code, not that Dev did."

"Maybe."

They both knew that was a lie. Porter had his fingerprints on every proposal that got through to the R&D stage. Simon sighed, leaned back, and rubbed at his temples.

"Fine. Ignore that," he said. Jacob squinted at him dubiously. It seemed a big thing to ignore. He opened his mouth to say so, but Simon impatiently waved a hand at him. "For now. How did PeaPod get hold of all this information now?"

Jacob sat back and brushed crumbs off his fingers. "Not from me. Not from Clayton."

"And if the code was in so many projects, Syntech's had it for a while, right? Why did Clayton suddenly get this bee in his bonnet about Dev stealing it?"

"I don't know." Jacob shrugged. "I did ask when I started the job, but Clayton was... on edge."

"When he was hiring you?"

"Yeah. He was just twitchy—about breaking the law, about trusting me, about how much I charge, about what people would think if they found out. Or maybe he just knew what a shit storm this was going to turn out to be."

"Can you find out?" Simon asked. He shrugged when Jacob looked askance at him. "You're supposed to be the information-acquisition specialist, aren't you? So go acquire some information. Impress me."

Jacob hesitated. "I don't know. This is not my—"

"It is," Simon corrected him. "And you owe me. Despite the fact you conned me, I saved your ass the other night. And if I hadn't stepped in, you'd still be in jail."

He had a point. Jacob picked up his soda and sucked the cold sugar-rich stuff down. It chilled his throat, but it didn't give the injection of energy he was after. It probably wouldn't have helped, even if he'd been sucking the syrup straight from the spout.

It wasn't the 90s anymore. He couldn't pack up his troubles in a dead infant's ID and disappear. Not *easily,* not *thoroughly.* If Jacob Archer got framed for a high-profile murder, it would impact. It wasn't as though he had a lot of marketable skills outside of telling what lies people wanted him to tell them.

Besides, like Simon had said, Jacob did owe him something.

"I'll try," he said. "I can't promise anything."

Simon raised an eyebrow at him and took a sip of his coffee. "I thought you were good."

"I am," Jacob said. He sounded more confident than he felt. Good? Yeah, he was. He was also under suspicion of murder, and that complicated things. A bit. "What are you going to be doing while I try to pull your boss's ass out of the fire?"

A raised finger called their waiter over with the bill and an offer to box up the tortillas. Jacob refused awkwardly. He'd have felt bad for hogging the table, but it wasn't as though there was a crowd waiting for a seat.

"Not ignoring things," Simon said, and he handed his card over.

CHAPTER TEN

THE BROWN-DYE hair mousse smelled like bleach and left dirty marks on everything it touched. Simon frowned at a teardrop stain on his wooden floor. A dye job that would run in the rain and borrowed clothes didn't strike him as a good disguise, but Jacob seemed to think it was good enough.

Worry poked at the back of Simon's brain with fretful nails and tried to push through his impatience with the staticky on-hold music that filled his ear. He growled and strode over to stare out the window.

The sound of someone hammering on his door interrupted his brooding.

"Simon." Nora sounded irritated. She rapped the door again impatiently. "Are you in there? Answer the door."

He pulled himself away from the window and let her in. She frowned up at him.

"Where have you been?" She pushed him out of the way and stalked through the door. Her bag slid off her shoulder, and she tossed it onto the kitchen table. "Do you even know what's happened at Syntech? Have you heard from Devon?"

The mixture of worry and exasperation in the rapid-fire series of questions she threw at him surprised Simon. If there was anyone he expected to be in on Dev's plans, it was Nora. That was why he called her. The fact Dev hadn't told her he'd benched Simon meant… something… or nothing. Maybe he hadn't had time or he didn't want to put Nora in an awkward position with the board. Or maybe he did have something to hide.

"I've been called to heel for this one." He pushed the door closed behind her. "I might have fucked up. Dev wants me off the case until it blows over."

She snorted and started to pace. The sharp heels of her shoes clicked angrily on the wooden floor and dug divots in the weft of the rug as she crossed it. "No. That's what I wanted, Simon. For your sake as much as anything," she said with one hand dismissively in the air and the metal band of her watch reflecting the light. "But until yesterday Dev seemed to think your personal involvement would just give you more motivation to find out who'd made a fool of you. Why change his mind now?"

Simon shoved his hands in his pockets and exhaled his temper through clenched teeth. He *had* been a fool. In fact there was every chance he was still being a fool—not that he was going to share that.

"I don't know, Nora." Despite his best efforts, he let his frustration seep into his voice. "Maybe he changed his mind when the board suspended him."

"It's Devon," Nora said, giving him an annoyed look over her shoulder. "He doesn't change his mind. He just digs his heels in and doubles down... and he can't afford to right now."

"He told me it was under control."

"That's what he thinks. I think he needs to hire a really good lawyer and sell out your weaselly little ex, before the board takes this opportunity to get him out."

"Can they do that?"

Her sigh hissed between her teeth, and she threw herself down on a well-padded chair. She rubbed her forehead in frustration, as though she were trying to sand out the nascent wrinkle between her eyebrows.

"If they're motivated to work together," she said. "And they have just cause to believe he's not working in the company's best interests. Both of those things they have right now."

"Crap. What do they have on him?" Simon caught himself and corrected. *"Think* they have on him."

"Evidence," Nora said flatly. "I haven't seen it all. The board is keeping *that* circle of trust small, but I know there's an audio recording of Clayton calling Dev to accuse him of stealing the code and there's a request filed with the University of Texas to see Clayton's PhD."

"That's sloppy," Simon said. "The board's aware that Devon's a genius, aren't they?"

"They're aware he's *arrogant*," she said. "They're aware that the evidence shows that Devon and Clayton hated each other, and for good reason, apparently. It's not looking good, Simon."

"You think he did it?"

Nora inhaled and held it. "No," she said, too slowly to be convincing. "Maybe. You know Devon as well I do, Simon. He can be ruthless."

"In business. He wouldn't *kill* someone."

"Of course not. I know that. You're right. Not on purpose. It might just have… gotten out of hand, though. If Clayton was threatening him, or if Devon was scared he'd lose everything. Maybe it was an accident and he never meant for it go that far?" She stopped, shrugged helplessly, and raised her hand in front of her face. "Or maybe you're right and I should have more faith. I'm sorry."

Simon wished he had more of that. He didn't think Devon was a killer, but… he'd told Dev where Jacob's safe house was, and then the police turned up, and there was a silver box full of information that Dev was doing his damnedest to keep away from the board. Simon didn't *think* Dev was involved, but two days earlier, he'd have *known* it. And ten years earlier, he wouldn't have questioned Dev's guilt. Before Dev cleaned up his act to date Becca, he'd had a violent streak. He'd broken Simon's ribs once, although to be fair, Simon had put one of the dents in Dev's nose.

He went over and perched on the end of the coach nearest Nora. He linked his hands together between his knees as he leaned forward.

"What happens next?" he asked. "At Syntech?"

"They've already quarantined all of Dev's computers, revoked his access to the network, and sent his computer to be analyzed for any proof of the theft or of Dev's involvement in Clayton's death," Nora said. She pushed her lips together, pressed her knuckles against the seam, and folded her fingers around her chin. "If they do—"

"They won't," Simon said. He hoped he was right. "Nora, is there any way you can get me the evidence that PeaPod has gotten their hands on? Whatever you've got, anyhow?"

She huffed. "I don't know, Simon. I hate to rub it in, but you're not looking good here either. You dated the thief. You're Dev's brother-in-law…. What even happened to the data you were going to hand back in to Syntech? If anyone finds that, it makes Dev look even worse…. Clayton didn't just have suspicions. He had solid proof."

Simon didn't look toward the gun safe. He kept his eyes on Nora.

"I'm an uncle," he said. The ploy left a bad taste in his mouth—guilt and the memory of the burned cupcakes his sister had made him eat when they were kids—but it was a good lie. Jacob was rubbing off on him. "If any of this is true, I need to know for Callie's sake. You were friends with my sister, Nora. For Becca. For her daughter."

It took a second, but eventually Nora gave a damp sigh. "I'll send you copies," she said. "The way things are going, they'll be public domain soon enough anyhow. Hell. I hate this."

"Me too, Nora," he said.

"Do you have a drink?" she asked as she leaned her head back and closed her eyes. "I need one."

He did. It was a strange question to ask someone with a drinking problem, though. She knew it too. He didn't keep it a secret. For a second Simon wondered how it'd look if he relapsed on top of everything else Nora had just listed. Bad for Dev, good for his second-in-command? It was a petty, paranoid thought, though, and he regretted it. Nora'd never wanted to be in charge of the company. The only reason she'd taken it on had been to help while Becca was sick. Dev was always joking about how glad she'd been when he came back and took it over again.

"Sorry," he said. "Cupboard's bare."

"Ah," she said. They sat quietly for a second until Nora leaned forward. She braced her hands on her knees, unconsciously mirroring his posture as she leveled a steady gaze at him. "If you find out anything, if Archer turns up again, you'll let me know, Simon? Dev's not talking to me. He says he doesn't want to drag me down if something happens."

He promised. Nora stared at him like she didn't believe him. Then she grabbed her bag and left.

"Take care of yourself, Simon."

She closed the door gently behind her, and a tug made the lock click into place. Simon went to the fridge for a beer. The scalloped edge of the edge dug into his thumb as he flicked the cap off. He took a swig and almost relished the reflexive jab of guilt that clenched between his ribs.

He did like Nora. He owed Nora for everything she'd done for Becca. In the end, though, it was down to Dev that he'd dragged himself out of the drunk tank and sobered up. So he wasn't going to tell Nora anything.

If any of it was true, well—Simon took another spiteful swig of beer—then it served Dev right that Simon had screwed over his sobriety. Dev should have told him. He was family. Simon would have backed him up, no matter what—even if he was being a fucking idiot. Jacob could have been talked around, could *still* be talked around. That was one benefit of having the Artful Dodger as your boyfriend. Ex-boyfriend.

Simon took another drink and then set the beer down on the counter. So he wasn't going to turn Dev in, even if he had stolen the code. He was going to kick his ass until Dev could taste his own balls when he swallowed, but he wasn't going to turn him in.

And if Dev had Clayton killed and framed Jacob for it? Simon picked up the beer to wash that thought away. He needed to know why Clayton had died. He needed answers before he made any big decisions. And whatever he felt about Jacob, he didn't trust him enough to leave it up to him to get them.

The gun safe was bolted to the wall in the closet by the front door. Simon didn't use it as religiously as he should—bad habits and the fact that he lived alone. He trusted himself with guns, and if someone broke in and took them off him, he deserved to die. The safe did come in handy sometimes, though. He pushed the code in and took out Jacob's silver hard drive.

It should have felt heavier. All those secrets should have had a weight.

Since they didn't, he tossed it idly in his hand as he headed for the couch and shoved a cushion out of the way to sit down. His laptop was under the coffee table, nearly as sleek, slim, and silver as the hard drive. That made sense, he supposed, since it was Jacob who had convinced him to upgrade from his battered old Toshiba.

He hooked the hard drive up and waited as it synced. At the prompt he tapped in Jacob's password from memory. He didn't even need to check the card. After a few years memorizing coordinates in the desert, he was good at recalling strings of numbers.

The drive opened automatically, and folders and files laid themselves out like decks of cards. Most of it might as well have been in Urdu, for all Simon understood it. He was hardly tech-illiterate—you couldn't rise in the ranks these days without the ability to use a computer—but converting ACQ files was a bit above his paygrade.

What he needed was barely above meat-space tech, just a list of all the projects that Clayton's code had been used in. It took a couple of minutes of clicking through files and organizing by type, but eventually he found them.

Fourteen projects had used the code, twelve where the project had been built on it. He grabbed a screenshot of the list to start with, threw it over to his phone, and then disconnected the drive. Leaving it to tick itself to sleep, he pulled up the link to the Syntech network server.

Another set of passwords and an automated virus scan of his hard drive, and he had remote access to the Syntech servers. He wondered—as he quickly archived his e-mails and set them to download to his laptop—if he could take the fact that Jacob had never tried to get access that way as proof that he had been, as much as he could manage, honest?

It was a nice thought, but it didn't hold up to scrutiny. Simon's access was second only to Dev's, but this server was basically just admin—bank accounts, personnel records, reports, and red tape. Nothing you'd want someone outside the company laying eyes on, but the meat and marrow of Syntech—the R&D, the global virtual simulations, the genetics of their science—was only accessible from inside the building. That was mostly for security, but partially because some of the files were so big and resource heavy that just looking at them would give a laptop an inferiority complex.

That was what Jacob had needed to prove his case—not the budgets and the HR complaints. Luckily enough, however, budgets and HR was exactly what Simon needed.

It took two hours of cross-referencing and another bottle of beer, but there'd been two researchers who worked on most of the code-corrupted projects—Ryan Lau and Mathilde Delacourte. According to the employee records, Mathilde was currently at a symposium in Berlin and Ryan had sent in his notice after being stationed in a research station in Alaska for three months.

Simon actually remembered that. It was weird. Ryan had spent three months living in a shack with only a radio and two loved-up British ornithologists from Xeon, the Chinese company that built the research facility. He'd been within a working week of a bonus and a free flight home when he e-mailed his resignation.

It was weird enough that Simon discreetly put a security detail on him for a month to make sure Xeon's happy hippy lesbians hadn't convinced him to break the no-competition clause in his contract.

Nothing raised a red flag... at the time.

Simon braced his elbows on his knees and pressed his knuckles against his lower lip. According to the reports for the board, there was no unifying theme between the fourteen projects that had used the code. Four had been looking into the nitrogen cycle, five at various botany models, one into solutions to reef bleaching, two into noise pollution, and the last two had been climate related. All of them used Icarus heavily.

It was research for the data model on one of those that had sent Ryan to Alaska.

Simon tapped his knuckles against his lip in an absent tattoo as he considered the evidence. It still didn't make any sense, but to so pointedly not make sense across a cluster of disciplines? That read deliberate to him.

He checked Ryan's personnel file. The last time security ran a trace on him, he'd been in Portland and teaching a few science classes at a local college. Again—weird, but hardly a red flag.

After signing out of the server—the virtual desktop wiped itself out of existence neatly—Simon closed the laptop with a slap. He leaned back and flinched as the scarred muscles in his shoulder cramped from being hunched over too long. He breathed out and rolled his head to first one side and then the other to work his way through each set of muscle groups until the pain settled down to the familiar, steady ache.

Could have been worse, he reminded himself. But it didn't help much.

The abrupt shrill of his phone interrupted him before he could wallow any deeper into self-pity. Simon wedged the pain down into the back of his mind and checked the screen. He didn't want to talk to Dev—not until he knew what they had to talk about.

It was Jacob.

Concern clenched in his stomach like a fist. Last time Jacob had called, he'd been about to be murdered and dumped in the river.

"You okay?" he asked roughly.

"Yeah, don't worry. No one is trying to kill me," Jacob said. He sounded out of breath, but his voice was steady. "I'm in the PeaPod offices. It's the sort of place that has standing desks and a yogurt bar at reception, so security isn't such an issue."

"Yogurt bars and good security aren't mutually exclusive."

Jacob snorted. "The sort of place that has a yogurt bar wants their employees to feel trusted, like they're a little family, and the investors to be impressed with their sense of community. They put it in their publicity packs. I do this for a living. Places like this are a utopia for people like me."

He paused and grunted. Something clattered in the background. Simon frowned. "What are you doing?"

"Making friends and influencing people," Jacob said. "Anyhow, we need to go to Clayton's house. He did most of his work from there. Only came into the office three or four times a month."

"Nice work if you can get it."

"I have it," Jacob pointed out. "Sometimes I only put on pants once or twice a week."

Simon's brain seized for a second on that and painted an image of a naked Jacob sprawled out on the couch with a frappucino and a tablet. He had to clear his throat and turn his back on his imagination.

"Point?" Simon said.

"Clayton was on edge, even before he hired me. He was obviously playing his cards close to his chest…."

"Not that close," Simon muttered.

"What?"

"Nothing. I'll tell you later. Go on."

"Anything useful? He's going to have kept it at his house, not in his office. Somewhere he'd feel it was safe and he could check on it for reassurance when he got cold feet about me."

It wasn't something that Simon would have known a month earlier, but because Clayton's name had turned up in the investigation and the news, Simon had had a crash course in the man's life.

"He lives out in Thunder Valley."

"And I don't drive."

"You need to learn."

"Don't want to. Pick up in an hour. Okay? I'll be done here by then."

"Wait," Simon barked. "Ryan Lau."

"Who?"

"Doesn't matter. You don't need to know."

"So what about him, then?"

"Just keep an eye out for his name. He's a climatologist, and if he's had any dealings with Clayton or PeaPod? I want to know. Even if he sent them a letter."

Jacob snorted down the phone at him. "I usually get paid for this, you know."

"I usually don't fuck liars," Simon said. "So we're all trying something new this year."

He hung up before Jacob could snark back at him. He needed to stop throwing Jacob's lies in his face. It was starting to blunt the edges of Simon's resentment and turn it into a shared joke instead of a grudge. He made one last call to give an old contact two names and no explanations. It was a Hail Mary pass, but what were old debts for if not risking a long shot?

"You'll owe me," his contact said.

"I thought you owed me?"

"Yeah, taking this call at all pays off that debt. Running these names, we're setting up a new tab."

"Do it."

The call ended without the social nicety of a farewell.

Two beers a couple of hours apart was hardly enough to get a buzz on, but he had started with an empty stomach and a hangover. He tucked the phone into his hip pocket and headed for the coffee machine in the kitchen. If he was going to be a getaway driver, he wanted to be awake.

Chapter Eleven

It stung to pay out cash on props when he wasn't going to recoup the money. Jacob straddled the secondhand bike and pulled the helmet on. He glanced down at his foot where the dog lay on its side, bored and yawning as though it had known him for years instead of just twenty minutes.

"Ready?"

The dog flicked a bat-tipped ear. It was some sort of terrier with a pointy noise and a heavy coat as dense as tree bark. According to the waitress he'd rented the dog from, his name was Fozzy and he liked bacon. Until then Jacob had always assumed he was more of a cat person—if he were going to be forced to have a pet—but Fozzy was even more low-impact than the cats he'd met.

"I'll assume that means yes," Jacob said. Then he sniffed his hands. He had spent the first hour and a half of his day going through the garbage, and while he'd scrubbed them in the cafe toilet, he wasn't sure the sickly lavender covered the stink of quinoa salad, old yogurt, and toner. He rubbed his hands on his thighs, shifted position, and braced his foot against the pedal.

In case anyone was watching, he pretended to fuss with his watch while he kept one eye on the reflection in the window opposite. PeaPod had bought up office space in the old San Antonio Light building the year before. The neon sign still hung outside, just over Jacob's head, and Abby Milgray, the office manager, had a designated spot for her bright blue Smart car in the attached car lot.

She also had a phone and bad habit of….

There. Reflected pink flashed in the window as she reversed out of her space. Jacob twitched the dog's lead to get Fozzy to grumble onto his feet. He kicked down on the pedal and pushed the bike into motion down the pavement. Fozzy huffed an aggrieved sigh and trundled into a trot, his heavy coat barely moving as he panted out a wet tongue and long ribbons of drool.

He'd timed it just right, and the front wheel bumped off the curb just as the office manager turned out into the street. And like she had on her errands or coffee runs that morning, she steered one-handed with her phone held at shoulder-level as she waited for her Bluetooth to kick in.

His plan would have worked even if she'd been paying attention, but it would have hurt more.

He yelled, put his feet down, and let the bike spin out from between his legs. It hit the side of the car with a clatter, and he threw himself down like he was playing for the Cowboys as the office manager hit the brakes.

Fuck. Pain scraped through his chest and spread out along his ribs. He'd forgotten about his ribs, but apparently they hadn't forgotten about him. He rolled onto his back and tried to find some way to hug himself that didn't hurt, but he swore through clenched teeth with every breath that made his ribs pulse. That was okay. He pressed his skull back against the road. It would make the lie better.

The leash had slipped out of his hands. Fozzy stood stolidly at the curb and looked at him. Then he turned and trotted off in a businesslike fashion with the leather lead trailing behind him. It was ideal, but Jacob still felt a bit betrayed.

"Oh my God!" Abby scrambled out of the car in a flurry of wedge sandals and dress shorts and dropped into a crouch next to him. Her hands were cupped over her mouth and nose and her words filtered through steepled fingers. "Are you okay? I am *so* sorry. I didn't see you."

Jacob sucked in a breath and carefully levered himself up into a sitting position. It didn't take any acting skill to wince and favor his side. "It's fine. I'm… ahh… bit sore. My bike?"

Abby's face was caught between concern for him and the looming horror of an insurance claim. She scrambled up and hurried over to the bike and propped it up. One of the wheels had a kink in it where it had skidded under her tire. She binged the bell hopefully.

"It's okay," she said. "Bit banged up, but nothing that can't be fixed."

"I was going for coffee," Jacob said vaguely. He blotted at his lip with the back of his arm. The bruise was a few days old, but hopefully she wouldn't put that together. "I needed to get out of the office…. My dog! Have you seen my dog?"

"No. I mean, I did, but I don't know where he went. Oh my God. Oh my God." Abby doubled over and pulled her hair back from her face as she tried to peer under the car. "He's not…. I don't think he got…."

Jacob grabbed the bumper of the Smart car and kept one arm pressed against his ribs as he pulled himself up. He hoped that going down like that hadn't pushed *cracked* into broken.

"Fozzy," he yelled and then tried to whistle between his teeth. "Fozzy, boy."

It was lunchtime. There were people about, and they started to look.

A man walking by on the other side of the street stopped, pulled his headphones out, and looked over curiously. "Everything okay?"

Abby grimaced a smile. "It's fine. Sorry. It's all under control. Just a bit of a spill."

The man looked dubious and cocked his head to the side as Jacob patted his hand against his thigh and whistled again.

"You sure?"

"Yeah," Abby said. "I'm just going to get him inside. Get him a coffee and a chance to sit down."

She caught Jacob's elbow, pulled him up off her car, and tucked herself gingerly under his arm while she tried to avoid touching his grubby clothes.

"I can't." Jacob stalled halfheartedly. "I have to… ah… find my dog."

"I'll send a couple of our interns out to look for him," she said and tugged him toward the office door. "They'll find him. Don't worry."

"His name's Fozzy," he said. "Tell them he looks like a beige Westie."

"Oh, a Cairn?" Abby said. "My friend has one. Lovely dogs. Very independent. He'll be fine. Just take this step here." She shoved the door open with her arm as she shooed him inside.

Cold air hit Jacob as he limped into PeaPod, which was a relief after lurking around in the heat outside. He swayed a bit, leaned on a convenient desk, and braced himself with the heel of his hand. The young receptionist pulled back from the desk, and his face curled with dismay as Jacob stumbled in, looking like a hobo.

"What on earth—"

Abby batted her hands at the air. "Rob, we had a bit of a spill outside. Mr…. umm… I'm sorry, I didn't get your name?"

"Jim. Jim Bell," Jacob lied. He leaned a little heavier and gave Abby a wonky, pained grin. "I hit your boss's car with my bike."

Rob pulled an "oh shit" face, hopped up from his chair, and loped around to grab Jacob's arm and prop him up. "Are you hurt?" He looked over Jacob's shoulder at Abby. "Should I call an ambulance?"

"No," Abby snapped at him, but then softened her voice. "Not yet. Let's just give Jim a chance to sit down and pull himself together."

She and Rob helped Jacob limp to a low indigo couch next to the yogurt bar and lowered him down onto the cushions. "I'll get you something to drink," she said. "Do you want water? It's got vitamins in it."

Jacob gingerly peeled his gloves off and winced as the tight pleather peeled off his bad hand. The swelling had gone down since the first night, but it was still bruised and sore-looking—enough to make Abby hiss in dismay.

"Tea?" he said plaintively. "And do you have any ice?"

"I'll get you some," Abby promised. "Just sit here. Catch your breath. Okay? I'll find Fozzy."

She dragged Rob away and hissed to him in a tight, angry voice that carried more than she probably thought it would. "Ambulance? Right now, we do *not* need any more publicity. Okay?"

"It's hardly our fault, what happened to Harry."

"I *know* that," she snapped. "It's still hardly the corporate image we want, and now I've run down some man with his dog? Let's just see if we can keep this quiet and off my insurance."

She rubbed her hand over her forehead and glanced at Jacob. He tried to look like he wasn't listening as he tilted his head back and poked with careful fingers at his ribs.

"Right. I'll go get some ice from the store," she said. "You keep an eye on Jim there and send a few of the interns out to find a terrier that answers to Fozzy. His *dog*, you...."

She crimped her lips and took a deep breath through her nose. "Look. Just look for his dog, get him some tea, and make sure he doesn't die. Okay?"

Rob nodded. "I'll round up a few interns to hunt around. Don't worry."

Abby took a deep breath, rubbed her hands through her hair, and huffed out an exhausted sigh. "First poor Harry, and now this. Did I break a mirror?"

She hurried out, and Rob retraced his steps to check on Jacob. "Is there any tea you'd like? We have green tea, honey and lavender, ginger...."

"Ginger. Sounds good," Jacob said. He took a deep breath and pulled a tightly pained face as his ribs protested the movement. "Can I use the bathroom?"

Put on the spot, Rob spluttered for a second and then gave in. "Yes. Hold on. I'll show you where it is. Can you…?" He made an "up" gesture with both hands.

Jacob made a slightly laborious exit from the couch—he needed to look injured, not on the point of death—and nodded.

"Lead on."

Rob looked relieved he wasn't going to have to help carry "Jim" to the toilet. He gestured for Jacob to follow him down the hall.

"We were going to redesign all this," he said conversationally as he waved his hand at the bare walls. "It was going to be all open plan. Don't know what we'll do now, though. I mean, did you see the news about our boss?"

"I don't know." Jacob said uncertainly and lagged a few steps behind so he could check the offices as they passed. He stuck his hand in his pocket and tapped the IM idling on the screen. "Are you moving out of the city? I didn't watch the news this morning."

Rob twisted around and walked backward. "God, no, he was killed. It was… pretty bad."

"Damn. I'm sorry."

"Remember the guy in the river?" Rob asked. He nodded when Jacob made himself look startled. "That was him. Harry Clayton. It's a real shame. He was a bit distant but a nice guy. He—" The phone rang, and he hesitated as habit shifted his weight back to head for his desk.

"Do you need to get that?" Jacob asked. "I can wait…?"

Rob dithered for a second and then pointed. "Just to the bottom of the hall and turn right. It's through the doors at the end. Just head back to the desk when you're done? I'll get someone looking for your dog."

"Thanks," Jacob said. "Poor guy will be freaked out."

Rob waved a hand in busy acknowledgment, ran back to his desk, and grabbed the phone with a breathless "Hello. PeaPod connects."

Jacob got to the end of the hall and glanced back to make sure Rob was distracted by the call. He was. The phone was tucked into his shoulder as he scribbled in a notebook. Good. Jacob had paid one of his old colleagues enough to call in and pretend to be the press. Besides, there wasn't much time. Jacob turned away from the door and loped down to

Abby's office—he'd identified it earlier from an interview she gave when the company moved into the building.

The door wasn't locked—that sense of community and all. He bumped it open with his hip and stepped inside. It was a mess. Folders and sheets of paper were piled up on the desk and stacked on the floor behind it. Pens chewed down to shrapnel were stuffed into an old cracked mug with a *Buffy* logo on it.

Jacob sighed. If he had more *time*, this would be a goldmine. Since he had minutes, he'd have preferred a neat freak. But he'd see what he could get. He pulled a battered memory stick out of his pocket. Without a good computer and an excellent VPN, he couldn't access most of his usual toys. However, the stick had been part of his industrial-espionage starter kit, thanks to a computer forensics professor who liked to demonstrate a bit too much. It would do.

He plugged it in to the computer and tapped the space bar with his knuckle. The screen woke up—a tasteful beach scene nearly obscured by a maze of files, jpgs, and icons. It was enough to make his eyes hurt. Jacob shook his head, pulled his sleeves down over his hands, and set the program to cloning the computer. It wasn't as sophisticated as some of his other toys, but it would get something. Besides, sometimes the most useful information was still hard copy. He grabbed the notepad sitting next to the phone. Usually he'd stick to scanning the relevant pages, but he didn't have the time, and it didn't really matter if PeaPod knew they'd been cleaned out—as long as they didn't know it was him.

He stuffed the notebook down the back of his jeans and tugged his shirt over it. Let Abby think she'd mislaid it. By the time she realized it was gone, he would be too.

A quick flick through the papers on the desk turned up nothing obviously interesting. Jacob quickly pulled out the drawers and found half a bar of dark chili chocolate, sachets of Swiss Miss hot cocoa, and an envelope with "Receipts" scrawled on it. The envelope went into his pocket, pressed awkwardly against his hip bone. He snapped off a square of chocolate and stuck it under his tongue.

The stopwatch he'd set in his head was ticking down. He dropped to his knee, hunted through the bin, and dug out scraps of paper from under the banana peel and leaking pens. His fingers ended up smudged with ink and sticky from the dregs of fruit smoothies. The bits of paper went into his pockets or down the side of his shoes, spread out so they wouldn't call attention.

From over his head, the computer binged an acknowledgment that the cloning program was finished.

Jacob sat back on his heels and glanced over the stack of folders behind the desk. His fingers itched to have a good look through them, but he had to prioritize. After the last few weeks, he thought he'd used up all the luck he could push. If he hadn't gotten anything useful, they'd just have to make do.

He hooked an elbow over the edge of the desk and hauled himself to his feet. The light on the side of the memory stick flickered green. He unplugged it with a tug and tucked it into his pocket as he headed for the door. The plastic was uncomfortably warm against his fingers. It might be time to put that particular device out to pasture.

The hall was still empty when he stepped out of the office. He wiped his sticky hands on his shirt and headed for the toilets, where he was meant to be. The doors opened into a white unisex room with scrubbed white tiles and a pervasive smell of bleach. There were Gameboys in a tray by the door. To use instead of magazines, Jacob supposed, although he didn't fancy grabbing one.

He washed his hands with scalding hot water and a bar of heavy creamy soap and splashed his face with a palmful of honey-scented water. He was about to run his fingers through his hair when he glanced into the mirror and the vaguely unfamiliar reflection pulled him up short. The lank brown hair changed his appearance enough that he didn't think anyone who'd seen the security footage would immediately recognize him, but he doubted the mousse was waterproof. Dye running down his neck would probably make someone suspicious.

It was sloppy. He shook his hands, shedding lather and drops of water over the pristine white bowls, and frowned at his reflection. The dark-haired bruised man in the mirror frowned back. It didn't look quite how he expected—less stern and more sullen. The mess had gotten him into bad habits.

Fuck.

"Mr. Bell?"

The voice out in the hall sounded suspicious and a little worried. Jacob flicked water on himself, leaned over the sink, and filled his palms with water. After a second the door was stiff-armed open, and Rob craned his neck around the frame. The tight expression on his face softened as Jacob mugged a surprised expression at him.

"Hey, sorry," Rob said. He straightened up and gave his sleeves an absent tug to settle the expensively pastel-striped shirt over his shoulders. "I wasn't sure if you were still in here. You've been a while."

"Yes, sorry." Jacob wiped his wet mouth on his sleeve. He gave a quick wipe to a convenient dark stain on the hip of his trousers. "I don't think Fozzy was the first dog to cross the road there."

Disgust puckered Rob's mouth as he drew back. "Oh, ah… I don't know if I have anything that would help with that. Umm."

Jacob held up his hand and stalled the brewing offer before it could go anywhere. "That's okay. I'm going to head home and get changed, anyhow. Did you find Fozzy?"

"Oh, not yet," Rob said and glanced back over his shoulder. "I don't think we have, anyhow. If you want to finish cleaning up, I'll go check with the interns. They're still looking."

"That's okay," Jacob refused politely as he stepped toward the door. "I don't think there's anything more I can do… for my outfit. I'll come back with you. See if Fozzy is back. I do appreciate all your help, by the way. This wasn't *your* fault."

The faint emphasis he put on the penultimate word distracted Rob. He got out of Jacob's way and fell in next to him as they walked.

"Abby's a lovely person, really," he said. "She'd be devastated if anything happened to your dog, or if you'd been badly hurt. It's just that it's been so hectic here. There's the police, the lawyers, the board, and everyone just wanting to ask questions we can't answer. Usually she's much more careful."

Jacob nodded agreeably, even though that was a bigger lie than the one he'd just tried to tell. He'd pulled Abby's police sheet on the way down, and she'd been cautioned multiple times for driving carelessly, and once for driving under the influence, if not quite drunk.

The cup of tea was balanced on the arm of the couch, gently steaming honey into the air. Jacob picked it up by the rim and breathed in the heat of it.

"What'll happen to you guys?" he asked. Rob slid in behind the desk and gave him a questioning look, so Jacob expanded his point. "Now that, well, that your boss is gone."

"Don't know," Rob said. "None of us do, especially not now this whole scandal with another company has kicked off. It's a mess, but according to Abby, we just have to keep the home fires burning until someone—"

Out of the corner of his eye, Jacob saw a blur of color through the window. He swore behind his smile and lost the confiding lean of Rob's body as the door opened and Abby staggered in with an armful of dog.

Damn it. Jacob had assumed that, once he was off the leash, Fozzy would find his way home.

"Found him," Abby said as she deposited the lump of heavy dog in Jacob's arms. He winced as Fozzy rammed a bony little paw right into his ribs, and he tried to stop his tea from spilling. From the smell, Fozzy had found his way to a garbage can instead of his owner. "I don't think he's any worse for wear."

Fozzy struggled in Jacob's lap. He handed his tea to Rob and tried to get a hold of the dog, which was surprisingly muscular for something that had, twenty minutes earlier, seemed 70 percent sloth. Jacob got a faceful of hard dog skull and a lungful of sweaty dog BO. He crouched down and set Fozzy back on his paws.

"Thank God," he said and got a death grip on the dog's collar. It strained forward and he leaned back. Paper crinkled under his clothes. It sounded ridiculously loud to him, and the hard edges of the stolen notebook dug painfully into his backside. He shifted and resisted the urge to reach around and check that his shirt was covering it. "I was more worried about him than the bike."

The reminder that she wasn't the hero of the piece deflated Abby a bit. She brushed fastidiously at her shirt and tried to dislodge dog fluff and stains from the chic top.

"Look, if it needs repairs or anything, I'm happy to pay for it," she said. "I would rather just keep this between us, though. I know I should have been more careful, and I *will* be in future, but—"

"No harm done," Jacob interrupted her. He caught her look at his face and grinned. "Nothing that won't heal or get straightened out, anyhow. Fozzy was all I was really worried about. Accidents happen, and you weren't the only one not paying attention. I should have been watching where I was going as well."

She looked relieved. Jacob explored Fozzy's collar. The dog had snapped his leash on something, but there was enough left for Jacob to hang on to. He twisted it around his fingers, stood up, and gave his shirt a casual tug to make sure everything was covered.

"Thanks for finding him." He held his hand out.

She hesitated and then took it. Her soft fingers with pink polish on the nails were careful around his bruises. "You're welcome, Mr. Bell. I really am sorry. Whatever it costs to fix your bike, just send me the bill. I'm happy to pay it."

He shook her hand firmly and took the business card she offered. "I will," he said. "Like I said, though, the dog's fine, I'll heal, and the bike can be fixed. No harm done. Bye." He half turned to nod at Rob. "Bye. Thanks for the tea."

"You can stay and finish it," Abby said. She bent over to scratch Fozzy's head. "He's welcome too. We're a dog-friendly office."

Of course they were. Jacob shook his head. "Thanks, but I should go. I'll call someone to come and give me a lift."

That time she didn't try to change his mind.

CHAPTER TWELVE

YOU WOULD think that after what happened with Clayton, Jacob would have learned his lesson about meeting in coffee shops. Apparently not. He was sitting outside a Starbucks, drinking coffee and frowning at his backup phone. A scruffy blond mop lay at his feet, licking crumbs out of its beard.

Simon pulled to the side of the road, ignored the aggravated blaring from cars behind him, and leaned over the passenger seat to pop the door open.

"Since when do you have a dog?" he asked when Jacob looked up.

Jacob shrugged, drained the dregs of whatever sugar-bastardized coffee he'd been drinking, grabbed the folder, and stood up. He tugged on the dog's lead. It grunted, flattened itself resentfully against the pavement, and sighed so hard it looked like it was trying to melt.

"I borrowed him for the afternoon," Jacob said as he pinned the folder under his elbow and bent down to pick the animal up.

He shoved the dog into the footwell, climbed in, and slammed the door behind him. The dog grumbled under its breath and sniffed the carpet and the seat under Jacob's knee. As Jacob yanked on the seat belt, it propped its chin on the stained knee of his jeans and squinted suspiciously at Simon.

Simon reached down to let the dog sniff his hand. Its nose was cold and wet against his palm. "I never imagined you were a dog person," he said.

"I know," Jacob said. "I'm a cat guy. Right?"

Simon gave the dog a scratch under the chin and threw Jacob a dry look. "I was thinking more lizard."

"Too much work," Jacob said and buckled himself in. "The dog was a prop—short notice means shortcuts, and a cute dog is the oldest distraction in the book—but his owner had ended her shift when I went back. Now I'm stuck with Fozzy here until tomorrow."

Apparently Simon's fingers passed whatever test scruffy terriers were interested in, because Fozzy gave his thumb a judicious lick for approval and flopped down on the car mat. The smell of hot, tired dog already filled the car.

"Did it work, at least?" Simon asked as he watched the traffic in the mirror for a chance to pull out.

Jacob considered the question and wobbled his hand. "I got in. Whether I got anything *useful* is another matter." He tapped his fingers against the folder he'd been juggling. It was stuffed with bits of paper. "I need to sort through all of this first. Separate the useful information from the noise."

An asshole in a pickup cut off a redhead in a Subaru. The exchange of abuse slowed traffic enough for Simon to pull out from the curb.

He paused, sniffed the air, and wrinkled his nose. "Why does it smell like old milk?"

Jacob sniffed the folder and shrugged, apparently not able to smell it anymore.

"I got most of it from the trash. They really like that yogurt bar at PeaPod."

Simon snorted. "When you hacked our system, I was impressed. I'm starting to wonder if I should have just been embarrassed."

"It's industrial espionage, not James Bond," Jacob said. "For every hour I spend infiltrating corporate environments like a pilfering chameleon in a good suit, I spend five going through their coffee grounds. You'd be surprised what people throw out without shredding. Well, most places. But if it makes you feel better...." He pulled a cracked plastic oval out of his pocket and waved it in Simon's peripheral vision. "I got a few bits and pieces off the office manager's computer, but I need to buy a new computer before I can tell if it's anything interesting."

"You could use mine."

Jacob flashed a thin smile. "No offense? I prefer to keep my contacts and their anonymous Dark Net chat spaces anonymous."

"Your life is in danger." It would have been a decisive argument for most, but Jacob just shrugged. For a professed coward, he was surprisingly blasé about threats to his life more than five minutes in the future.

"So is my ability to fly without a fat customs officer sticking his sausage fingers up my ass, because your cyber team got close enough to piss my people off," Jacob said. He opened the folder and peeled bits of paper off plastic sheets. "I think I'll grab a new computer. I don't need anything custom made, an off-the-rack gaming rig should do the job."

"Do you trust anyone?" Simon asked.

Jacob glanced up from a receipt. "No," he said. "You?"

The question plucked one of the crossed wires in Simon's mind. It wasn't a hot day, but a memory of ripples of distortion rising from the sticky tarmac overlaid the reality. He knew it wasn't real, that it was the past, but part of his brain was *sure* he was still in the desert, with the heat and the itch of sweat under his uniform.

He'd known Medo, the man who flagged them down. He was an easygoing slacker with a taste for American beer and folding American money. He was supposed to have good info for them.

Then the world broke apart. Simon remembered the wave of tanned hands, the white sleeves flapping, and the weight of metal under him as he hit the brakes, and it didn't matter whether Medo had been a victim or the perpetrator. He'd still fucked them over.

Simon swallowed the dry stone in his throat and forced it back down his gullet. He could see why his mind was making the connection— friends and liars—but it wasn't the same. Nobody had gotten killed.

Except Clayton, he supposed.

"No," he admitted. "I don't. Not anymore."

A SHARP elbow nearly caught Simon in the side of the head. He growled in irritation and shoved the offending limb back onto its own side of the car and got a shirt-muffled apology from Jacob, who was halfway through getting changed into the clothes Simon had brought for him. Glancing sideways he checked out what was really putting his temper on edge—the bare line of Jacob's arm down to the fuzz-tufted hollow of his armpit, the slice of skin between hip bones and groin, exposed by the unbuttoned fly of his jeans.

He was a liar. He was a criminal. Simon glanced to where Fozzy was lying on the backseat. He was possibly a dognapper. And he was leaving. None of it mattered. Simon still wanted to drag him into his lap and kiss him until he stopped being an idiot. Although that would probably take more time than they had.

"Let me get this straight." He averted his eyes and scowled out the window at the perfectly manicured gardens and expensively uninteresting houses. Christmas decorations that side of town were apparently minimal—just twinkling lights in the garden and tasteful wreaths on the doors. The gaudiest was a neighborhood anarchist who had a wreath of red, green, and gold baubles on the door. "Your plan is to walk up, try the door, and hope no one stops us?"

Jacob pulled the polo shirt down over his head. He reached around and scratched the back of his neck as though being that close to respectability brought him out in a rash. "I'm not a cat burglar," he said. "The only house I've ever broken into was my family's when I came home late from curfew, and I'm not going to try climbing up the ivy to crawl in the bathroom window here. So we act like we're meant to be here, walk up to the door, and try to get in. If we can't, we think again. But hey, you're the Marine. If you have a better idea, let's hear it."

Cut the power, go in under cover of darkness, do a hard reset on the alarms—after they'd cased the location, either in person or by drone. He'd go in armed—with info as well as artillery. He'd also have the US government backing him, not planning to throw him into jail.

"We'll try it your way," he said.

Jacob snorted, hitched his hips up off the seat, and buttoned his fly. "Gee, thanks." He slid a business card into a lanyard, strung it around his neck, and turned it so the PeaPod logo was visible.

"And what am I supposed to be?" Simon asked.

"Cop."

Simon gave him a dirty look. "I don't look like a cop."

"You look more like a cop than anything they'd expect to see," Jacob said as he got out of the car. "You look dangerous."

A chill wriggled through Simon's chest at the casual statement and made him hesitate on his way out of the car. Most people—his doctor, his bartender, his *dad*—said dangerous, but they meant broken. Like whatever the military had done to him inside his head was worse than the ruined arm.

It wasn't anything he did, anything he said, anything he could change. It was just what he was. Apparently.

"What?" Jacob gave him a curious look over the car. "You look like I kicked our rented dog."

Simon shook his head. "Nothing."

"Now who's the liar?"

"Not wanting to talk to you about something isn't lying," Simon said. "It's just self-preservation and none of your business anymore. Let's go."

He stalked away from the car and left Jacob to catch up with him. Jacob stretched his legs enough to match strides, and when he did catch up, he'd changed the way he moved. Not a *lot*, but his shoulders were hunched like someone who spent a lot of time on the computer, and his posture was… tenser, like someone on edge. He definitely passed as a computer geek who'd been press-ganged by the local police.

Simon wanted to ask how Jacob had gotten into the business of stealing secrets for a living, but he'd just taken personal questions off the table. So it was hardly fair.

"Did you find anything about Lau?" he asked.

"I haven't had a chance to go through everything carefully," Jacob hedged. "But not yet. On the other hand, Clayton wasn't going through the company. He hired me with money from his personal account. He met me on his own. That's not how it goes when they have a board of directors on their side, you know?"

"Good use of your morning," Simon said dryly. The point wasn't lost on him, though. "So, as far as PeaPod's concerned, before Clayton turned up in the river, it was just business as usual?"

"There was one thing," Jacob said. "Clayton had called a last-minute board meeting for before Christmas. From the complaints that the office manager was getting, they weren't particularly happy about it. One of them said something about them thinking he had other things to keep him busy these days."

Simon raised an eyebrow. "Any idea what things?"

Simon got a shrug in answer to that and clenched his jaw on the need to push harder. If there was anything to find, Jacob would have found it. Or would find it when he had a chance to look through his "loot" properly. He had as much motivation as Simon. More.

They turned onto Clayton's drive and gravel crunched underfoot as they walked. His garden was just a long stretch of manicured grass, bare of detail except for a single lonely magnolia planted in the middle.

Jacob pulled a notebook out of his pocket as they reached the door. A single keypad was inset into the wall, the numbered buttons unhelpfully unworn. Flicking to the back of the book, Jacob frowned at the crib list of codes scribbled there.

While he worked his way through, Simon turned so his body was in the way of anyone who might see what they were doing. But looking up and down the street, it seemed unlikely there were going to be any curtain twitchers in the neighborhood.

When he was growing up, his family had been well-off by the standards of their neighbors. They had a nice house, a pool in the yard. They had still been part of the community, though. When he skipped school, an old lady had told his mom. When Becca snuck Dev in while their parents were at a conference, the neighbors raced each other to spill the beans on the driveway when they got back.

Simon couldn't imagine that happening here. It seemed like the sort of neighborhood that should appeal to him—he'd made a point of remaining on grunting terms with his current neighbors. But he supposed there was no point in being a loner if it wasn't a *choice*.

"Got it," Jacob said.

"How many tries?"

"Two."

"Will the security firm get an alert?"

Jacob stepped through the door and shoved the notebook into his back pocket again. "Don't know. Three is usually the doddery grandma allowance. Probably best to work quickly, though."

"The police have probably been here already." Simon stepped over the threshold and closed the door behind him. It was muggy inside, like someone had planned for a warm welcome after Christmas shopping in the cold. He was surprised no one had turned the heat off. "I'm sure they took the computers already."

"Garbage too," Jacob said. "They were looking for information about a murder, though, and one that didn't take place here, so hopefully they missed something we can use. Do you want to take upstairs or down?"

"Downstairs," Simon said. If the alarm had gone off, he would be better able to deal with the arrival of security than Jacob was. "Be quick."

Jacob loped upstairs, and the heavy wood risers creaked under his weight. "Start in the kitchen," he called down.

Simon headed down the hall to where he would have put the kitchen door if he were building a house. The architect apparently agreed, and a nudge swung the door open onto a modern, glossy teal-countered kitchen. It was also the kitchen of a depressed man.

Not dirty—Clayton probably had a cleaner. But there was still a layer of dust on the oven—more than would have accumulated in the days since his murder—and a squirrel stash of chocolate bars and bags of candy stacked in easy access on the counter. Empty wine bottles were lined up on the table like soldiers on guard.

There was a stack of mail piled up on the window over the sink— all open, none looking dealt with. The edges were smudged with butter and fingerprint powder. Simon pulled a pair of thin latex gloves out of his pocket and snapped them on. A quick sort through the pile proved that no one but banks and takeouts sent snail mail anymore. At the bottom was a letter from the University of Texas, but it was just the standard "please donate" they sent to successful alumni. Well, civilian universities, anyhow. Simon had never gotten one from boot camp.

Apparently Clayton was successful enough to warrant a personalized letter, instead of the mass-printed one. It specifically referenced his thesis and how it had influenced his development of the "PeaPod social lubrication algorithms," which sounded unpleasant.

Clayton had scribbled a note on top. *Useful for no project.* A little bit harsh, as it turned out, since someone at Syntech had found something to do with it. He snapped a scan of it with his phone. Maybe it could be useful.

He was just about to file the PDF in the cloud when his phone buzzed against his palm. Dev's name pulsed on the screen. Shit.

Simon considered just rejecting the call, but he hit the green button instead.

"—ell are you doing?" Dev snapped as Simon lifted the phone to his ear.

"Right now?" Simon deadpanned. "Going through mail."

"Don't try and be fucking clever," Dev snapped. "I told you to lie low with the hard drive until I got in touch with you. Not to chase up Nora for confidential files, and definitely not to go and bail the damn thief out."

"He wasn't booked," Simon said. "Your lawyer was going down anyhow—" Dev tried to interrupt, but Simon firmly talked over him. "And whatever is going on—since you wanted me to sit on the hard drive, I'm assuming you didn't want Jacob spilling his guts to the world that we have it."

Dev snorted. "Like that's why you did it. Don't try to kid a kidder, Simon." His temper was cooling already. He'd never been good at holding on to his anger. He'd never had to be. In the old days, him getting angry and him getting it out of his system by punching someone usually happened at the same time. "Look, I have the board climbing up my ass right now. I'm pretty sure they've got my own damn security team watching the house. I don't want to give them any ammunition until I know what the hell is going on."

"Because you're completely in the dark."

There was a tight silence, broken by the faint distinct click of Dev clenching a once-broken jaw. "Jesus, Simon, you think I'm involved?" he finally demanded.

"I don't know. If you are, you should have told me. If you *aren't*, then you should be talking to me."

Dev snorted at him. "What do you think I'm trying to do? I need to talk to you, but it can't be here. The board already thinks we were colluding. Now that you've got Jacob and all the stolen information? We can't look like we're plotting anything."

Simon left the kitchen and walked into the main room. It looked almost unused. There was a pack of cigarettes on the arm of the leather couch.

Odd. Clayton was a notorious health nut. Half of his interviews weren't about social networking or computers. They were about vegetarian lifestyles and yoga, and they ran in magazines that talked about how your body was a temple.

"My apartment," he said. "Tonight."

"I mentioned *your* security team watching me?" Dev groused.

"You've forgotten how to shake a tail?" Simon asked. "Talk to Carl. Carl Howe. He owes me enough that he'll turn a blind eye."

Dev made a guttural, irritated noise. "This whole mess is a pain in the ass."

"You think?" Simon said. "Tonight. Eight o'clock at my place."

"Fine," Dev said. "Simon, you know I'm not involved in this. I wouldn't risk it, for Callie's sake."

"If you were," Simon said. "I'd still help."

He hung up and shoved the phone into his pocket. The cigarettes bugged him. He supposed if Clayton had taken up drinking, he might have taken up smoking too. It wasn't as though Simon could judge on that front. It was just that smoking took more commitment to start with—wine went down easy—and it was harder to hide.

Back before he'd quit, he and Nora used to go through packs of gum just to avoid the pointed coughs and sniffing. It wasn't as though either of them had ever pretended they were health nuts either. The coughs would definitely have been more pointed for Clayton. Depression was a private thing. Looking at the symptoms just made it feel worse.

Simon gave himself a mental shake and shed his suspicion. Maybe the pack belonged to a neighbor or a plumber, or one of the cops who'd been through. Even if it was a clue, it wasn't one that meant anything right then.

There was another door in the corner of the room. He nudged it open and found the place where Clayton had spent most of his time. It didn't smell bad, just… in use. He noted the aroma of coffee and food, a worn leather chair with wrinkled creases from a single ass. There was a huge TV framed with gaming systems, a Blu-ray system so high-end it looked retro, and a camera on the floor in front of it. Simon crouched to pick it up, and the latch flapped open to reveal an empty memory-card slot.

"Damn," he muttered.

He set it back down and was about to stand up again when something caught his eye. Sitting on a shelf next to a stack of *Nightmare on Elm Street* DVDs was a picture of a slim dark-haired woman—girl, Simon supposed—in an old white frame. Even in a still image, her narrow blue eyes were intense and the set of her mouth stubborn.

Becca. It always amazed Simon that people who'd known them both called *him* the dangerous one.

He stood up and reached for the picture. It had been taken a while ago, probably at college and without Becca knowing, since she wasn't doing the grimace that passed for her "say cheese" face. Of course, for Clayton to be Dev's friend, he'd have been Becca's too. Back then Dev hadn't made many on his own.

Well, Becca might have thought they were friends. If Clayton had kept a picture of her in his private space, she'd probably meant more to him than that.

For a second, thoughts of an affair skittered through his head. But that was unlikely. Becca had been in love with Dev since she was fifteen, hated compromise since she was five, and ripped the head off her My Little Pony rather than share it. If she wanted Harry Clayton, she'd have gone for it and damn the consequences. Hell, she hadn't let consequences stop her from refusing further cancer treatment. If death didn't put her off doing what she wanted, then divorce certainly wouldn't have.

"Isn't that your sister?" Jacob asked.

He was lucky Simon had registered the sound of his footsteps, otherwise he would be picking his larynx out of the back of his spine.

"Yeah." He put the picture back in its place. "She's how Dev and Clayton knew each other."

There was a greasy fingerprint on the top corner of the frame, and the oils stained the age-porous wood. The direction of it made it look like the picture had been held upside down. Simon picked it back up and turned it over. The plywood back was stained with fingerprints, and the metal tags holding it in place had fresh scrapes of bright metal.

"I guess she's where he kept his secrets too," he said.

CHAPTER THIRTEEN

JACOB SHOULD have taken the downstairs. Rich people had dens, offices, libraries. That's where they kept the good secrets. All he'd found upstairs were retro soft-porn magazines, a drawer that suggested Clayton had a sleepover friend—the sexy undies could have been just for him, but the packet of sanitary napkins suggested someone fairly confident of their welcome—and a Kindle with some moderately interesting late-night reading on it.

"That guy you were asking about earlier? Did you mean *L-A-U* or *L-A-W*?" Jacob asked as he watched Simon use his key to pull the flat metal tags straight.

"*U*. Why?"

Jacob pulled the Kindle out of his pocket and thumbed it on. "Clayton had a bunch of his articles on here." He turned the device around so Simon could see the screen. "Along with… ah…. Mathilde Delacourte and…. Gregory Whittle. They're nothing to do with computers. It's all weather and rocks. No evidence that Lau was ever here, but Clayton certainly had an interest in him. He downloaded this stuff a week before he hired me."

Simon pulled the back off the frame to reveal a memory card taped to it. He picked it off, turned it over in his hand, and frowned at it as though he could intimidate the secrets out of it. Then he tucked it into the condom pocket on his jeans.

"Time to go," he said, reattached the back of the frame, and returned the picture to the shelf. "If there's anything else, we aren't going to find it."

Jacob paused for a second to glance at Simon's sister. He wondered if she'd have liked him. The answer was probably not—he didn't think his own sister would like him if she didn't share the same asshole genetics—and it was a weird question. Since when did he care what anyone thought of him?

He shoved the niggling question in with other things he didn't want to think about—was it weird to have had a crush on a Muppet as a kid, should he try to be less like the dad he hated, at some point did you have to age into loafers—and followed Simon out of the AV room. Or tried to. He bumped into Simon's back just across the threshold. The impact jarred an apology out of him.

"Sorry, I—" His attention flicked past Simon's shoulder and caught on the black gape of muzzle aimed at them. "Fuck."

"Yeah," Simon said dryly. The nudge of his elbow put Jacob more firmly behind him, and Jacob let it. He supposed it was an insult to his manliness or something, but he didn't mind. "For a dead man, Clayton gets a lot of visitors."

The arm holding the gun belonged to a tall man with broad shoulders and an oddly narrow face—as though someone had pinched it in a vise. Blood hummed in Jacob's ears, and he felt a wash of hot dizziness flood through him. It made his knees feel wonky and his stomach twist with pain. That was the guy who kicked him in the ribs, the one who tackled Clayton to the ground and cursed him when he died.

Shit. He'd always called himself a coward, but he never really thought it was true.

"I heard you were a Marine," Pinch-face said.

"I am a Marine."

Pinch-face smirked. "Yeah, whatever," he said. "It's a shame, really. Shaw told the boss we should have used you—but the boss didn't think you could be bought. Too uptight."

"Your boss is a good judge of character."

The exchange gave Jacob enough time to pull himself together and squeeze some spit back into his mouth. He licked his lips. "What do you want?"

"Same thing I wanted last time," Pinch-face said. "The data packet that you stole from Syntech."

"And I told you the going rate," Jacob said. "Why do you care what's on it anyhow?"

The man shrugged. "I don't. I'm just paid to collect it. Now give me the data, and I'll let you walk."

Simon shifted his weight to the side and moved one foot forward. The barrel of the gun twitched as Pinch-face focused on Simon. "That seems unlikely, doesn't it?"

A tight little smile pulled at the man's lips. "You might have a point there. How about this? I won't break the thief's other hand before I kill him."

"Sounds fair to me," Jacob said and took a half step backward. The gun twitched a bit farther. "I'm a fan of working fingers."

He eased in another half step, and then Pinch-face waggled the gun in his direction. "Don't try to run. You saw what happened to Clayton."

"Then you'll never get the data," Simon said as he moved forward.

The gun stayed on Jacob, but Pinch-face's attention shifted back to Simon. It was, apparently, all the distraction Simon thought he needed. He took a long, quick step and aimed a short kick at Pinch-face's knee and slapped Pinch-face's gun hand to the side at the same time. The gun went off with a muffled cough, and the bullet hammered into the floor a few inches from Jacob's feet.

Shit. Shit.

He scrambled for the oversized chair and threw himself into its shadow in a sliding fall. *Plan. Plan. Damn it.* Jacob was *good* at plans, but no one would give him the time to put together a good one. He glanced around the leather side of the chair. The gun was on the floor, lying on the probably hideously expensive black-and-white cowhide rug as Pinch-face and Simon traded blows. They moved so fast that, to Jacob, who'd mostly seen fights on TV, it looked like the blows barely connected. Pinch-face clipped the side of Simon's jaw, and he turned the stagger into a sweeping kick. Simon's fist buried in Pinch-face's gut turned into a joint lock that made Simon's face go bleak with pain as he went to his knees.

"Heard you *were* a Marine," Pinch-face panted as he drove his knuckles into Simon's armpit, "before they had to staple your arm back on."

Jacob jack-in-the-boxed to his feet, head swimming with fear and the realization that, apparently, he was going to improvise. Or piss himself. Maybe both.

"Here." He waved the Kindle in the air. "I've got the data here. Just let Simon go. This isn't anything to do with him."

Pinch-face snorted. "He should have thought of that before he interfered." He squinted as he tried to get a good look at the Kindle Jacob juggled from one hand to the other. "He's not the sort of man you leave with a grudge."

Simon twisted. His arm achieved an unnatural angle, and he hammered his fist into the side of Pinch-face's knee. It popped out from under him, and Simon threw his weight and turned Pinch-face's stagger into a fall. A scuffle of knees and elbows ended when Simon kneeled on Pinch-face and punched his head down into the rich wooden floor.

It wasn't *quite* the same noise that Clayton's head had made as it hit the ground, but it was close enough to make Jacob cringe. He didn't have time to puke, though—he doubted Pinch-Face was on his own. He scrambled over the arm of the chair and grabbed the gun. The weight of it was strange. The addition of the silencer changed the balance of the thing more than he expected. He ran to the door.

"Fucking… stay here," Simon snarled.

Jacob glanced back over his shoulder and saw Simon get to his feet, his jaw gritted so tightly that the muscles bulged under his skin and his arm swung loose and weird from his shoulder. He could probably still kick Jacob's ass, but, apparently, the unwelcome revelation that he really was a coward had left Jacob with a need to prove something. He ducked out into the hall just as a lean scruffy thug skidded down the stairs and stumbled to a stop as he saw Jacob lift the gun and aim it at him. After a second's surprise, he smirked and showed a broken tooth next to his incisor.

"Please," he said. "You're a petty thief. You go through people's garbage for a living. You've never even used a gun."

Something about him didn't read quite as dangerous as the others Jacob had met—Pinch-face and the nondescript Shaw. Simon. The sort of people who had to try to *not* look like they could kill you in a hundred different ways. This guy postured like a street tough—all attitude and snarl.

Jacob straightened his elbow and brought his free hand up to steady his grip. "I've never shot anyone," he said. The smirk dug in deeper, and the man took a step down. "I've used a gun, though, and I have the Junior ROTC ribbon at home to prove it. I'll probably puke my guts out afterward, but I'll still put a bullet through you."

He kept his hand steady and his finger curled around the trigger.

It bought him a second as the man eyed him up. "You're bluffing," he said finally, and he shifted his weight for another step.

"I'm not," Simon rasped as he stepped out through the door. Sweating and with blood clotting on his upper lip, he pointed his gun one-handed. "Move again, and I'll blow your kneecaps off."

It didn't even take a second. The thug threw his scar-knuckled hands up in the air, flashing hairy wrists and a heavy diver's watch. He folded them behind his head at a jerk of Simon's gun. Maybe their boss didn't pay enough to risk losing body parts on the job.

"On your knees," Simon said. The man folded like someone had taken a bar to the back of his legs, and his kneecaps hit the wood with a crack. Sweat beaded on his forehead as his eyes tracked Simon nervously, and he caught the tip of his tongue between his teeth.

"It was business," he said. "You've been there. Right?"

Simon snorted and then wiped bloody snot on the back of his hand. "Yeah. I've never been where you are," he said. "Anyone else here? Lie, and I'll shoot you before them."

"No. No one else. Just me and Nigel."

That would be Pinch-face, Jacob supposed. It suited him.

"Why are you here?"

The man's gaze flickered past them to the front door. Simon didn't let his attention falter, so Jacob turned around to check. A large water cooler tub that hadn't been there before sat next to the wall. It was hard to tell through the plastic, but the water looked thicker than normal and almost iridescent.

"Turn out your pockets," Simon said.

A pointed jab of Simon's gun convinced the man to do as he was told. He pulled his hands from behind his head, dug into his pockets, tossed a roll of quarters, three condoms, and a couple of birthday candles onto the floor.

"They were going to burn it," Jacob said. "There's something here that whoever hired these two really doesn't want us to find."

"Don't flatter yourself." The man put his hands back behind his head. "You weren't mentioned. It's just damage control."

"By whom?" Simon asked.

"Can't tell you."

Simon let the gun track down from the man's face to his knees, and the worn patches pulled tight over his kneecaps suddenly looked like targets. The man pulled his hands from behind his head and held them out placatingly.

"Not won't. Can't," he said. "I don't know. I've never met them. None of us have, except for Shaw. He works with a private security company, and someone called in a favor to get some work done… off the books."

"Clayton's death?"

The man shook his head. "No. That wasn't meant to happen. It *was* an accident. Things got of hand. He was meant to give us the data packet. Then we'd hold him until the boss got there. That was all."

"Why?"

The man let his hands drop to his sides. "I really don't know. The important thing was that we got the data before he could do anything with it and we kept him out of circulation for a while. Except he had to play the hero."

"Put your hands back up," Simon ordered flatly. He stepped forward. "When did your contact call you in?"

In the middle of raising his hands, the man hesitated as he thought back. "About a week before the handover with your boy."

Simon slapped the gun against his temple and coldcocked him. The man's eyes rolled back in his head and he pitched over onto his side. He dribbled spit from the corner of his mouth and blood from the knot on his forehead. Simon shoved the gun awkwardly into the waistband of his jeans and leaned down to check for a pulse.

"Is he…?"

"Fine." Simon straightened up and leaned against the wall. His mouth was a grim blood-scabbed gash. It seemed a bit on the optimistic side to Jacob, but he supposed "not quite dead" could count as fine.

"Drag him into the living room with his colleague, would you?" Simon asked.

"Does that make me the muscle?" Jacob asked. His voice sounded steadier than he thought it would. However sloppy he'd been in some regards, his lies were still on point. He copied Simon and shoved the borrowed gun into his jeans. The extra length of the silencer dug into his thigh uncomfortably as he bent down, grabbed the unconscious man's ankles, and gave his legs a tug to test the weight. The limp body slid a few slow, resistant inches. It wasn't the weight so much as the dead slog of the man.

"ROTC?" Simon asked while Jacob tried to get a good grip on the man's legs.

"What?"

"You were ROTC?"

"Junior ROTC." Jacob paused and leaned back against the anchor of his grip on the guy's old Doc Martens. It was a good lie, vague enough to be hard to disprove and specific enough to invite belief. Except it was a job lie, and it felt wro... weird... to hand it to Simon. He supposed whatever bit of him had thought taking Simon to Bali was a good idea didn't want to admit that they didn't have a personal relationship anymore. "And no, not really. I—"

Simon stuck out his hand. "Give me the gun."

It was a relief to hand the thing over. While he held it, there was always the chance that someone would expect him to do something useful with it. Jacob still felt the need to defend himself against... something.

"I have shot a gun before," he muttered as he dragged the man away from the stairs.

"Did you hit anything?" Simon sat down on the stair. He leaned his bad shoulder against the bannister.

"Yes," Jacob said indignantly.

That wasn't a lie either. He *had* hit something. Technically it wasn't what he'd meant to be aiming for, but he'd still hit it. That was... sophistry, and sophistry fell into the normal amount of lying that people do to each other. He heaved and felt the tug in his shoulders as the unconscious man shifted an inch. Then another. Once he was moving, however grudgingly, it was easier.

He dragged the man over to Pinch-face—or Nigel, he supposed, since his face had been spread by punches—and dropped his feet to the ground. The heavy rubber heels of the guy's boots bounced off the floor. When Jacob straightened up, he grabbed the tail of his shirt and pulled it up to swab his face. On the ground, Nigel groaned and pushed clots of blood from between his lips, and rolled his head to the side.

Jacob loped into the hall and wedged the door shut behind him. "I don't think they're going to be out much longer," he said. "We should go. Can you drive with your arm?"

"It'll be fine," Simon said. He sat with his dislocated arm between his thighs and his hands clasped under his knee. "Trigger the alarm on the way out. They'll probably make themselves scarce before the cops get here, but they won't have time to set the fire."

He braced his feet against the step, exhaled through his teeth, and then shoved up against his own arm. The damaged slope of his shoulder rolled under the skin. There was an audible click-pop that made Jacob cringe back into himself, and Simon exhale a hard, relieved sigh through clenched teeth.

"There. Done."

Jacob shuddered and hunched his own shoulders as though he needed confirmation they were still in place. "What the fuck are you doing?" He stepped forward but stalled when Simon growled at him. "Jesus, Si, there are doctors for that."

"By the time I get to the doctor, it'll be too swollen to jam back in," Simon said. He sounded freakishly calm for a man who shoved his fucked-up arm back into his fucked-up shoulder.

"That was not right," Jacob said.

Simon snorted, held out his good arm, and let Jacob haul him up off the stairs. The movement made him clench his jaw again and exhale hard through the pain. He got into this because of Jacob. If it had been the other way around, Jacob would have brought that up about ninety-two times by then.

He tightened his grip on Simon's hand, pulled him closer, and stretched up the inch it took to kiss him. It was quick and messy, tart with copper and wet with smeared blood between their lips. Breathing in the heat of Simon's mouth, Jacob realized he was the only one really doing the kissing. The hard lines of Simon's body hadn't relaxed into him at all.

It was the Bali question all over again. Crap. That was why one-night stands should be the rule. Simple, clear—everyone knew where they stood.

He stepped back and scrubbed the blood off his mouth on the back of his wrist. There was half an apology on the tip of his tongue, but the thought of it made him cringe. *The hell with it. Pretend nothing happened and just get on with things.* Avoidance was a proud family tradition, after all.

"Well, we didn't find anything else," he said. "So hopefully that memory card is what they were looking to destroy."

He paused, just in case, but after an unreadable second, Simon just nodded. "Clayton had to have hidden it for a reason," he said.

They went out through the backyard, just in case one of the neighbors were watching. Simon kicked the back gate open, and the lock ripped out of the wall in a tangle of broken screws and plaster dust. There was no noise, but Jacob knew that the nearest station was shoving cops into a car to make sure the rich people weren't going to be on the news.

Ignoring the twitching urge to run, they walked briskly back toward the car, looking as unsuspicious as two beat-up men carrying guns could look. When they got there, the dog was sitting up in the back, and his nose prints and slobber smeared the window. He went insane when he saw them, barked at the glass with teeth bared back to the gumline, and wagged his tail the minute they opened the doors.

"Well done," Simon ground out as he slid stiffly into the driver's seat. "You managed to find a dog that'll warn off thieves, but makes its peace if they actually get into the car."

"We like to call it pragmatic," Jacob said. He slammed the door and slouched down with his head tilted back against the headrest as he breathed out. His heart raced behind his ribs, and his balls had cringed their way back inside after the kiss, but the wisecracks made him feel a bit more like normal. Fozzy scrambled up onto his lap so he could look out the window, and his hard little paws dug into Jacob's thighs like pitons. Jacob petted him absently. The rough fur and dog heat were kind of soothing. "So he said they weren't supposed to kill Clayton. I thought they'd just… done it… before they got the information they needed, but they weren't meant to kill him at all."

Simon glanced at him. "So?"

"He wasn't the one they were worried about getting the information," Jacob said. He could already hear sirens in the distance, although maybe it wasn't for their break-in. "It was whoever he'd have taken the information to next."

"You mean the police?"

Jacob paused to consider that. "Yeah, okay, that could be some people's first port of call," he admitted. "Still, they thought they could talk him around. Why?"

CHAPTER FOURTEEN

THE CHILL from the bag of frozen peas soaked into Simon's shoulder and dug down through inflamed muscle and into bone. He didn't think it was actually doing anything to help with the pain. It was just making it cold. There were analgesics and anti-inflammatories in the bathroom cabinet, but fuck it. Since he'd fallen off the wagon, he might as well stick to what worked.

He'd grabbed the whiskey while Jacob was buying a new laptop, and he pinned the bottle against his ribs and twisted the cap off to pour himself a shot. He picked it up and paused when he felt the eyes on the back of his neck.

"What?" he asked and turned around.

Jacob hesitated and brushed the ripped cardboard and broken Styrofoam onto the floor. It was probably, Simon thought dryly, his version of being tidy. Half of it fell on the dog they'd still not managed to return to its owner and made it twitch awake at the contact.

"Since when do you drink?" he asked.

"Dulls the pain," Simon said dryly.

Jacob narrowed his blue eyes into a squint at him. "Are you quoting country music lyrics at me?"

The snort of laughter jarred Simon's shoulder and jagged pain and a trickle of ice water ran down his spine. He grimaced, tossed the whiskey back, and ignored Jacob's frown. "No," he said. "Not deliberately, anyhow. It's medicinal."

"Yeah, medicinal is a shot of brandy in your coffee when your kid comes out as gay," Jacob said. "You're an alcoholic."

The bottle was still open, and a second shot would blur the ache in his shoulder just that bit more. Just to make a point, Simon didn't pour it.

"I'm not alcoholic," he said. "I'm a problem drinker. It's different."

It sounded like bullshit, even to him. Jacob looked like he was going to call him on it, but then visibly tightened his lips to keep the words in. His chin dropped, and he went back to staring at the computer instead of Simon.

"Guess it's not my business," Jacob said.

Even through the whiskey, Simon could still taste Jacob on his tongue—the nervy quiver of a body full of too much adrenaline pressed against his own and the heady heat that jerked his cock even through the dull ache of his shoulder. He should have kissed him back. But if he did that, he might as well have said he'd go to Bali. It wouldn't change anything, just drag it out. And he couldn't afford to explain. It would let Jacob know that Simon's self-control hung by a thin thread. So he offered up the booze as a consolation prize.

"Drink is a socially acceptable coping strategy in the circles I moved in," he said, mouthing the words of the VA therapist he'd been stuck with when he first got back. "More than talking or popping pills. It's self-medication, not addiction."

Jacob *huh*'d without looking up as he pecked his way through the computer's boot-up process. "So how come you stuck to soft drinks and painkillers when you threw it out at the company softball game?"

"Less stress in my life back then." The words sounded more bitter than he'd meant them to and exposed a raw underbelly he didn't quite trust Jacob with.

"Fuck you," Jacob said flatly. He didn't look up from the computer, but his jaw was clenched so tightly that the muscle twitched under the skin. "You cracking open the bottle isn't on me. Asshole."

The hit of anger surprised Simon. "You lied to me. You *used* me."

Jacob smacked his hand on the table and looked up, his face tight with anger. It was one of the few times that Simon had seen the charm slip enough to leave Jacob looking bony and sharp. His voice was hard too. Something along the lines of a Kansas accent scraped out from under the practiced vowels.

"So I lied. Big fucking whoop. I lie to *everyone*. Even if I hadn't been working the job, I still would have lied to you about every damn thing I lied about. I'm a thief. I'm a liar. But I didn't make you any promises, Simon. It would have made my life easier, but I didn't, and I didn't pour a drink for you either. So yeah, fuck you."

"Fuck you too," Simon said.

Jacob threw up his hands in frustrated drama. "You had your chance," he said. "But someone didn't wanna go to Bali."

For a second Simon wanted to laugh again, but Jacob was still glaring at him. After a fraught second, Jacob growled in frustration and dropped his attention back to the computer. He gnawed absently on his knuckle as he tapped the memory card impatiently on the table.

Simon took a breath. A second shot would make the fight easier—lubricate all the vicious words that wanted to get out and dim the undermining flashes of humor. He could ignore the fact that—just once—Jacob had a point. Neither of them had made any promises or commitments, and even if they had, Simon's issues weren't something he could afford to hand off to someone else.

He left the whiskey, walked over to Jacob, and dropped a hand on the nape of his neck. He ran his thumb up the line of Jacob's neck to the dip under his ear before he could catch himself.

"Sorry."

"Good."

"You're meant to say 'me too, Simon.'"

"I know," Jacob said. He pulled up an empty window and typed a string of numbers into the address bar. "I ain't gonna."

Simon squeezed the tight cord of muscle at the back of Jacob's neck. The habit of touch wanted to drag Jacob's head back so he could kiss him and slant his mouth across parted lips. It was more the ache in Simon's back than any willpower that stopped him.

After a second Jacob sighed. "I should have kept my mouth shut. Like I said, not my business."

"Almost right. Not your *problem*." He slid his hand up and buried his fingers in the short scruff of hair. "Not kissing you this afternoon wasn't easy, Jake. I need to give in on something, I guess."

Jacob gave the half snort that the use of a nickname always dragged out of him and leaned back into Simon's touch, like a cat. "I'd be better for your liver."

"Not the organ I'm worried about."

He didn't wait for Jacob's response. It'd be the wrong one. It was Jacob. So he just gave his blond head a lazy shove and got up.

Simon smelled of blood and sweat, with the bitter undertone of adrenaline souring on his skin. "I'm going to shower and get changed," he said. "If Dev gets here before I'm done, he might try to punch you. Don't take it personally."

He put the whiskey in the cupboard before he went, shoved to the back behind the balsamic vinegar and the olive oil. Jacob held his tongue, and Simon wasn't sure if that was what he wanted or not.

THE WHITE scars on his shoulder looked like a net, pulled tightly and painfully over the swollen, bruised joint. Standing in front of the bathroom mirror after his shower, Simon could almost see the throb of pain keeping time with the pulse of his heart. He gingerly poked the tender skin with his other hand and clenched his jaw against the wave of sick dizziness that hit him. It was back in its joint, more or less, and—he flexed his fingers and lifted his elbow, wincing as it stalled at closer to seventy degrees than ninety—it worked, more or less.

Simon closed his eyes and tried to expel the frustration on his exhale. His shoulder was a mess. It was more likely to get worse than better, and that was the new normal he had to accept. Like it or not.

Wet hair straggled over his forehead in a dark, dripping tangle. He shoved it back with one hand as water ran down the back of his neck, and he brushed his fingers along his jaw. Stubble rasped against his fingertips, but a shave would have to wait until the next day.

Or the day afterward, depending on how his arm fared overnight. He grabbed a pack of anti-inflammatories from the cabinet and was popping pills out of the foil when his phone buzzed in the bedroom.

He hitched a towel up around his waist and dry swallowed the pills on his way to grab the phone from the bedside table. There was no number on the screen.

"Yeah," he said. He frowned when he saw the dog lying on the bed. Fozzy stared back at him with beady black eyes and then pointedly shuffled around to turn his back on Simon.

He got a staccato address briskly recited into his ear. It wasn't in San Antonio, but it was close enough. There was a pause, and then Hayes added, "You owe me twice. Someone didn't make it easy to track Lau down."

Niceties weren't as valuable as debts in their line of work—Simon's old line of work—but vanity was universal. He could hear the smugness on Hayes's end of the line, and it got him a shred more information.

"They weren't expecting anyone to look from inside. Looks like he's working for the US now."

The line went dead.

Huh. That debt was going to bankrupt him when it got called, but it was worth it. Lau had been headhunted after all—just not by another corporation. He was working for the US government. Probably the military.

He dragged on a white shirt and a pair of jeans. By the time he was done, the pills had kicked in and dropped the pain to a dull, heavy throb that he could live with. He scrubbed his hand through his damp hair and went to see what Jacob had found.

It turned out he'd found Dev. As Jacob worked on the computer, Dev stood by the window with a bottle of sparkling water and watched.

His attention shifted as Simon asked, "You get here okay?"

"I had to sneak out of my own house," Dev grumbled. "Carl can cover for me for an hour, so let's get on with it. Harry had a picture of my *wife*?"

"And my sister," Simon reminded him. "And Harry's friend. And her own person. You wouldn't have gotten away with owning Becca when she was alive. Don't try now."

Dev grunted sourly. He leaned back against the wall. From the suit he wore with reluctant style, he'd been dealing with the board or lawyers that day. That would have put him in a bad mood before he even heard Clayton's name.

"I was friends with Harry too," he said. "Did he have any pictures of me hung up on his walls?"

"To be fair, Becca was more likeable than you."

"And to be ever fairer, Clayton had a photo of your wife in his house *and* a couple of angry mercenaries who wanted to burn the house down in there too," Jacob interrupted from the couch. He shrugged under both sets of scowls. "What? I just think the latter might be relevant as well. What with them trying to kill us."

"A few weeks ago, *I* wanted to kill you," Dev pointed out. "What was Harry hiding behind Becca?"

Jacob rubbed his finger against the tip of his nose and blinked around his knuckles. "Fuck if I know, to be honest," he said. "And before anyone insults my professional skills again, I've cracked the password on it, and there's reams of what looks like pretty advanced computer code on there. It could be the codebase for a new social-media platform, databases, or a sudoku generator. I don't have the knowledge base."

"Let me see." Dev pushed himself off the window.

Jacob obediently turned the laptop toward him. Dev dropped into a crouch by the table, put his water between his feet, and frowned at screen with interest. He flicked the screen up and down in flickering jerks past patches and squares of the code.

"I thought you were a biochemist," Jacob said.

"I'm a genius," Dev said. "I pick things up. And you can't be anything in science these days without having some understanding of computers."

He hunched his shoulders and squinted at the screen as he fingertapped his way down through the file. His eyes flickered as he scanned the screen full of symbols and shortcuts.

"It looks like a predictive modeling program, only more advanced than anything we're looking at right now. Better stability, able to run comparison models side-by-side." Dev paused, and his eyes glinted as he read a string of code. "It has a support vector machine algorithm that bundles unsupervised cluster learning with—"

"Hey, genius?" Jacob said. "Can we try some shorter words for the just-smart in the room?"

Dev looked daunted by the request. He frowned, his forehead furrowed with deep lines, and scratched the back of his neck.

"I don't think there are shorter words for some of it," he said. "Basically, at the moment, we build a virtual world, release a digital version of Icarus, and see what happens. Usually it's that the computer bricks itself after a few cycles because the scenario gets too complicated for it to manage. This program could run more complicated scenarios for longer and faster than we can hope to right now. If this model of Harry's works as it should, it would be the most advanced artificial neural network in the business. He'd need some serious hardware to run it on, but it's brilliant. I mean, if this was what I was supposed to have stolen? I'd have been tempted."

Simon interrupted him. "Not really helping your case here."

"I said I would have been tempted, not that I would. Or had," Dev said. He sat back and rolled his shoulders to stretch out his back. "Steal this, and I'm stuck. It's—and I hate to say it—inspired, but it's not finished, and without Harry it might never be. Besides, *this* isn't what I'm supposed to have stolen. I don't think anyone but Harry's seen this. I would have heard the chatter about it."

Simon pulled his phone out of his pocket and drew up the list of contaminated projects. He handed it to Dev. "These were the projects using Clayton's code."

It took longer than Simon expected to get a response. Dev furrowed his brow as he studied the list of names and departments. Guilty conscience?

His arm throbbed again as gravity tugged at his bones. He gave in to it and grabbed a seat on the couch.

"This isn't right," Dev said finally. He hesitated and glared at the list like intensity could change what it said. "None of these projects should be here."

Jacob stretched over to take his computer back, pulled it up off the table, and balanced it on his folded legs. "Did you think you'd hidden them better?"

"Shut up, Jacob," Simon said, cutting off Dev's growl. "Why not?"

"They're old, mothballed projects." Dev flicked up and down through the list again and shook his head in baffled annoyance. "Most of these are over a decade old, and these last two were ghost files. The projects never made it past concept stage, and I never got around to stripping the shell-space out of the server. Things came up."

He paused, clenched his jaw, and then snapped his fingers at Jacob. "Do you still have the files you stole?"

There was a pause as Jacob pulled a confused who-me face, as though he'd never heard of any of those words.

"It's a bit late for that," Simon said. "At this point we're hardly going to turn you in."

Jacob tilted his head to look at Dev and waited until the big man rolled his eyes. "Someone was stealing from Harry, and now they're framing me. It turns out that you raiding my company was the best thing that could have happened."

"First time anyone's said that," Jacob muttered. He leaned over to grab the hard drive from the table and held it out.

Instead of taking it, Dev leaned back. He held his hands up, palms out and fingers spread. "No. When we find out who's behind this and take it to the board, I want there to be clear blue water between me and the data on that drive." He pulled a pen out of his pocket and scribbled an e-mail address on the back of a business card, digging the nib into the card when the ink didn't take the first time. "E-mail the data to this address. No one should be able to track it to me."

"What about the researchers on the project?" Simon asked. "Ryan Lau. If these projects weren't active, what was he working on?"

Dev rubbed his hand over his mouth as he thought. Then he shook his head. "I don't know," he admitted. Frustration drove him up onto his feet, and he swiped the wrinkles out of his trousers with both hands.

"After Becca got sick, and…. Well, I had more important things than business to think about. It's why the board intervened to pull Nora up out of R&D—which she still hasn't forgiven me for. It's also what gave them the foothold to push me out over this as well. I don't know what Lau was working on over that period. When I came back, he wasn't on my radar until he requested a secondment to an Alaskan research base."

It was a good opportunity to share the information that Ryan was working for the military and that he was in San Antonio. The fact that Simon held his tongue meant, he supposed, that he still wasn't entirely convinced that Dev was whiter than white in all of it. Maybe he'd just been hanging around Jacob too much, but he was getting used to not trusting people.

"I've still got some leads to follow," he said. "We'll find something."

Jacob patted his hand on the side of his laptop. "Going through the files I, um, accessed from PeaPod has given me a couple of ideas to chase up."

"Sounds very illegal. Congratulations," Dev said. He glanced down at his watch and heaved a frustrated sigh. "If I'm not going to get caught sneaking back into my own house, I have to go. If you need anything, call Nora, and she can sort it out at Syntech. I've been locked out of the servers. You probably have been too by now, Simon."

Simon shoved himself up off the couch, jaw clenched against the need to show pain, and walked him out into the hall. He closed the door behind them.

"You trust Jacob?" Dev asked.

Simon tipped his hand back and forth. "I trust him to have my back. I wouldn't trust him around your wallet."

He felt a brief pang of irrational guilt at the disloyalty, but it was the best shorthand he could come up with for his slightly… contentious… relationship with Jacob.

"The code that was stolen, the college stuff, was being used for predictive modeling," he said. "Did it do the same job as this stuff Clayton was working on?"

Dev snorted. "It's the difference between a moped and a Jaguar," he said. "To be fair Harry was always good, but this new project was a cut above. I couldn't do it."

High praise from the arrogant.

"Okay," Simon said. He tugged Dev into a rough hug, and thumped Dev's back. "Be careful. They're covering their asses right now. That's when people do stupid things."

"I'm fine." Dev gave him a careful pat on his good shoulder. "You're the one I'm worried about. Seriously. Callie'd never forgive me if something happened to her favorite uncle because of my company. It's not worth it."

"I'm not letting you go to jail for something you didn't do." Or probably even if he had done it.

"Me?" Dev asked. "Or Jake in there?"

"He hates that."

"I know. I hate being robbed." Dev grinned at him and then got onto the elevator. He glanced back down at his watch again as the doors closed, and a frown pinched his eyebrows together.

When Simon went back into the apartment, Jacob was slouched down almost horizontal on the couch. His hips were barely hanging on to the cushions, and the laptop was balanced across his crotch. He'd gotten a can of lemonade from the fridge and set it on the table next to the coaster.

Simon walked over, picked it up, and pointedly set it on the glass disc. Jacob glanced up briefly and told him, "Help yourself."

"Anything useful?"

"Maybe," Jacob said. He looked up and rubbed a fingertip over his eyelid. "Apparently I was right about the drawer. Clayton had started seeing some woman recently. He was always getting Abby to run personal errands for her—because he sucked as a boss—including, it looks like, tickets to DEF CON in Vegas next year."

"The hacker convention?"

Jacob shrugged. "If you work with computers, you care about cybersecurity. Where better to discover the various exploits out there than a roomful of people who make them for fun and profit. It doesn't mean anything other than she's interested in high-level programming. It could just be a love connection for her and Clayton, but the timing is odd."

"Do you have a name?"

"And Guest."

"Could just be a coworker."

"Not unless they're going sleep head-to-foot in that king-size bed they booked," Jacob said. "I also found evidence of some contact between Clayton and Lau. They were scheduled for an early-morning meeting, but Clayton stood Lau up. He was too busy being dead in the canal."

CHAPTER FIFTEEN

ABBY THE office manager had lived her life on the computer—schedules, to-do lists, call lists, contacts, Amazon wish lists, a password manager, and a downloaded backup of her bookmarks. The only thing missing was a daily journal. While all that unpacked on the partition he'd set up on the computer, Jacob was left with a notebook and an envelope full of Abby's expenses to go through.

"Well, Clayton's new love interest was a woman of expensive tastes." He peeled the wrapper off a Milky Way bar and took a bite. His stomach growled. They'd swung by a McDonalds on the way back to the apartment and ate quarter pounders and fries in the parking lot, but that had been hours earlier.

"You're assuming it was a woman," Simon said as he got a beer from the fridge. He leaned back against the counter and looked thoughtful as he twisted the cap off. It still wasn't anything to do with Jacob. "Maybe it was Lau."

Jacob shrugged. "Maybe. But even you don't make your love-connection appointments at the office."

Simon laughed at the joke and went back to looking through the pile of sticky coffee-stained receipts that Jacob had palmed off on him. Maybe after the job was over, Jacob mused, he should take on an intern. It was nice to have someone to hand the suckier jobs to. But he was still stuck sorting through the rest of the expenses. He finished off the Milky Way as he pulled out any receipt that didn't seem to do with PeaPod's running expenses—flowers from Tuscan Blooms, chocolates from Schakolad, and an Iron Cactus Tequila Dinner Cruise for two. Expensive tastes and a preference for staying out of the public eye.

Despite himself Jacob thought of Clayton, who would have been cuter if he'd embraced the nerd and turned out to be a lot braver—or more stupid—than you'd expect. He wondered if he'd been happy with that woman. The taste of chocolate and caramel in his mouth cloyed, suddenly sickening, and he crumpled the wrapper up to stuff between the cushions of the couch.

"Trash," Simon said.

It would put some distance between him and his thoughts. Jacob retrieved the wrapper, got up, and walked over to pointedly toss it in the trashcan. Since he wasn't the one with a drinking not-problem, he stole Simon's beer from the counter.

"Anything?" he asked as he lifted the bottle to his mouth.

Simon held up a crumpled piece of paper between two fingers. It was a to-do list for the day Clayton died. Or Jacob assumed it was from the notes about the board, the police, and sending condolences to the next of kin.

"No mention of the girlfriend," he said.

"What about the receipts? Was there anything recent?"

The beer tasted like beer, but the thought of Simon's mouth on the glass still tickled the underbelly of Jacob's lust. He tried to ignore it.

"He had chocolates delivered last week with a begging-off note," Jacob said. He made bunny ears with the hand not holding the beer and quoted. "'Sorry. Next time.' If she *was* involved in this, maybe he was buying time?"

"Maybe," Simon said, and reached for the beer. His fingers bumped against Jacob's. Jacob surrendered the beer to Simon and shoved his hands into his jeans.

"How's your shoulder?"

"It's fine," Simon said. That was obviously a lie. "How's your ribs?"

"Okay," Jacob said. He took a deep breath. It still hurt as his ribs moved around his lungs, but it was an ache instead of a stabbing pain. "I guess I'm going to live."

"Good," Simon said. Instead of taking a drink, he put the beer in the sink. "Get some sleep. You can chase our mystery woman tomorrow while I go and catch up with Mr. Lau. You can stay here overnight, if you want."

Jacob snorted. "Well, I'm sure as fuck not going back to my place," he said. "They already know where that is. Don't worry. I'll take the couch."

He'd gotten the message—no Bali, no kissing. His brain had, at least. But there was a sticky, horny part of his libido waiting with bated breath for Simon to drag him to bed. It hung on right up to the point Simon went into the bedroom and closed the door behind him.

Jacob let his breath out on a slow sigh, puffed his cheeks out, and grabbed the half-empty beer from the sink. He tilted it up to his lips and took a draft. The chill settled like an ache in his breastbone.

"Guess we both got blown off, mystery lady," he muttered. "Let's see if I can find you so we can compare notes?"

He finished the beer and went back to work.

IT WAS still dark when he woke up with that vaguely resentful feeling that meant his body clock still thought he should be asleep. He also had a crick in the back of his neck and a feeling that he was being watched. The yawn hijacked his mouth and made his eyes water and his jaw crack. He blinked his vision clear and propped himself up on his elbow. Simon sat on the coffee table, watching Jacob with his elbows resting on his knees. His face was thrown in shadow, and the lean angle of his body was all dark planes and hollows.

It was a bit weird, but Jacob knew just what to say. Vowel sounds mostly, based on the confused noise that came out of his mouth. He scrubbed his hand over his face. Waking up was never his favorite part of the day, but professional pride was on the line. He should be able to manage a few syllables.

He managed to almost get the relevant word sounds in the right order. "Wha?"

"You know why I don't drink?" Simon asked. He didn't wait for Jacob to say anything, Instead he supplied his own answer. "It's because I make bad decisions."

"Like what?"

Simon's shadowed profile was still and thoughtful, hard to read. Then he slid off the table, knelt on the floor, and leaned over Jacob's body. "Like this."

He kissed Jacob, his mouth minted and stubble scraping rough against Jacob's skin. It probably wasn't a great idea to kiss him back, but Jacob did anyhow. If he needed to, he could come up with a justification later. Even it was just "I wanted it."

It was an awkward kiss. Jacob's back was stiff, and Simon was nursing his shoulder. But it was still hot. Jacob curled his hand around the nape of Simon's neck and felt warm skin and the bristle of cropped hair against his palm. Heat crawled down his spine and into his balls and dragged at the muscles in his thighs and stomach. He propped himself up on his elbow, felt the ache as flesh moved over his ribs, and sighed a wordless protest between wet lips as Simon pulled back from him.

"Come to bed," Simon said.

The invitation caught Jacob off guard. He had expected, and would admit he probably deserved, another rejection. His libido jeered, "I told you so," in the direction of the rest of his brain. He tried to tug Simon back down and nipped at the curve of Simon's lower lip.

"We could stay here," he said. "It wouldn't be the first time."

That time the wet and sloppy kiss pushed Jacob back down into the cushions. Simon's mouth crushed down on Jacob's, scraped teeth and stole his breath on a gasp…. He ran his hand up Jacob's thigh and squeezed the hard bulge of his cock through his jeans. The rough caress made Jacob groan and dragged his hips up off the couch in an aching, physical demand for *more*.

"Fuck," Jacob groaned into Simon's mouth and dragged the word out over his tongue with the last of the air in his lungs. The next hot and heady breath he took was stolen straight from Simon's mouth. "The bedroom's a long way away."

"Two minutes."

"We'd need to take trail mix."

Simon's mouth arched against Jacob's with a sly curve of humor, and he flexed his fingers in a lazy caress. "It's where the lube is."

"Fine," Jacob drawled with mock resentment. "You've talked me into it."

Simon rocked back on his heels and stood up in a single fluid motion. His muscles clenched and stretched with elegant efficiency. For a second, Jacob just sprawled back on the couch and admired the moonlit view of six foot and a bit of lean, practical muscle. Simon looked like the sort of arty gray-scale nude you could hang on the wall and not scandalize your vaguely homophobic aunt.

Well, the heavy erection tenting the front of Simon's white silk boxers might give Auntie Julie a bit of a turn. Fuck her, though. She was cheap as well as a bigot, so it wasn't even worth keeping her sweet for presents.

"You coming or not?" Simon asked.

Jacob gave him a sloping lazy grin. "Just admiring the view."

Simon crossed his arms over his chest. "Take your time."

"Naw. Done now."

Jacob scrambled to his feet. He was a lot less graceful than Simon had been and not helped by the ache in his balls as his jeans creased over his groin, but he still got there. He dragged his shirt off and tossed it behind him. For once, Simon didn't complain that the floor wasn't where clothes lived. He just hooked his fingers in the waistband of Jacob's jeans and tugged him closer.

That was definitely where Jacob wanted to be, but....

"Bad decision, or... chew your arm off in the morning bad decision?" he asked.

Simon shrugged his shoulder—the off-kilter slope that ran from his good shoulder down to his scarred one. "My decision."

That was good enough. Jacob let Simon reel him in, chewed a kiss into his unscarred shoulder, and licked salt from skin pulled tight over a hard slab of muscle. He reached around, slid his hands down the back of Simon's boxers, and grabbed his ass.

"I like your ass," he said.

Simon caught Jacob's face in his hands and tilted it back as his thumbs grazed over the bony line of Jacob's cheekbones. He stared at him for a second and then scraped an impatient kiss over Jacob's mouth, hard enough to bruise his lips. Jacob pulled him closer and dug his fingers into the curve of Simon's firm muscle and flesh until he could feel the hard jut of Simon's cock pressed against his stomach.

"I like you," Simon said. His mouth twitched with wicked amusement. "Although that could be the drink talking."

They stumbled into the bedroom between kisses and gropes and nearly tripped over the dog as it made itself scarce. The open curtains let in enough light to illuminate the large bare room. Other than the bed—king-size, memory-foam, and 600-count Egyptian-cotton sheets of luxury—the hotel room the other night had more character.

Simon twisted around long enough to close the door after them, and Jacob took advantage of the moment to lean into Simon's back. He wrapped his arms around Simon's lean stomach, pressed a kiss to his scarred shoulder, and the heat of his skin and the rough texture of the scars like threads against his lips. It was a tentative touch at first—sometimes Simon liked it, sometimes it made him tense—but the sharp hiss of reaction encouraged Jacob to let his mouth wander.

"Not into dogging, then?" he teased, and the words slid between his lips and wet skin.

He felt the groan drag itself up from Simon's diaphragm. "That's bad."

Jacob snorted. "You were in the Marines," he said as he hooked his thumbs into the waistband of Simon's boxers. The cool silk bunched under his fingers and then slid down over Simon's hips and freed his cock. "You've heard worse."

"No. Marines only make jokes when they're funny." His voice cracked on the last word, and his breath caught in his throat as Jacob wrapped his fingers around Simon's cock. "Fuck, Jake."

Jacob dragged his hand back and felt the stretch and slide of delicate skin under his fingers. "That's the idea."

Simon's long weight settled against Jacob—not quite leaning, but relaxed. Simon reached around and gripped Jacob's thigh with one hand for support as he swore between clenched teeth. After a few teasing strokes, Jacob let go of Simon's cock and cupped his balls instead. He fondled them and squeezed carefully to feel the tightening twitch of the sac up toward Simon's body.

Jacob's cock was so hard it hurt under his jeans. He pressed against Simon's hip, and the pressure made pleasure throb through his gut. Anticipation clenched his ass and up his spine to the back of his skull.

After a second, Simon took his hand, shifted it to his cock, and wrapped both their fingers around the hard shaft. He set the pace and pumped Jacob's hand along his cock in quick, hard jolts. Jacob rested his chin on Simon's good shoulder, caught between the sweaty eroticism of watching—the head of Simon's cock was wet and eager in the moonlight— and the need to just fuck.

When lust won the toss, Jacob turned his head to wet open-mouthed kisses and bruises against the stubbled skin under his jaw. He felt the reaction in the sudden tightness under his mouth as Simon gritted his teeth and his tendons tightened all down his throat.

Jacob smirked, and his lips slid over his spit-wet skin. Every time. Simon was a slut for hickeys. If his boxers hadn't already been down around his thighs, Jacob could have gotten them there with a bite. He scraped his teeth along the clenched ridge of Simon's jaw and dragged a growl out of him. It was enough. Simon twisted around, grabbed Jacob's wrists in his hands, and shoved him backward to the bed. Onto the bed in a smirking sprawl.

The sheets were just as nice as he remembered. He stretched out on the cold, crisp cotton and hung his legs over the edge of the mattress as his bare feet touched the floor while Simon kicked his boxers off.

"You pick them up, and I get to go on top," Jacob said.

Simon snorted but left them where they lay. He grabbed the waistband of Jacob's jeans, his knuckles pressed against his stomach, and pulled until Jacob's ass hung off the bed and Simon stood between his knees.

"You go where I put you," he said as he popped the button on Jacob's jeans. He yanked them down roughly, and the scrape of denim over his erection made Jacob gasp and sweat at the sharp jolt of pleasure and pain. Simon paused for a second and looked down at him with an oddly bitter tilt of his mouth. "For tonight, anyhow."

Simon grabbed a handful of denim and flipped Jacob over onto his stomach. Jacob sucked in a startled breath at the sudden movement—the sheets smelled of green jasmine and laundry—and the vulnerable swing of his balls between his thighs. He twisted his hands in the sheets and gave in to the petty impulse to wrinkle the cotton.

"Control freak."

"Liar."

Fair enough. Before he could come up with a retort, he felt Simon's hands grip his ass firmly and pull the cheeks apart. His wet tongue against Jacob's hole made him curse, the *fuck* strangled in his throat and muffled as he pressed his head into the mattress.

Simon's tongue circled the pucker of his hole and then pushed against the raised thread of his taint. Pleasure jerked Jacob's hip forward, and his cock rubbed against the mattress, but Simon just followed him.

Slick wetness and the pressure of flexible muscle. The sloppy kiss to the base of his balls. Jacob gasped, twisted his head to the side, pressed his face into the crook of his arm, and swore raggedly against his skin. Okay. So everyone had their thing they were a slut for. Point made.

It was weird having someone pick up his kinks, though. Reading people was usually his thing. He supposed that was what happened when you hooked up with someone for longer than a couple of weeks in New York. The mystery in the relationship just up and died.

He rocked his hips, his aching cock slid over the expensive sheets, and his legs felt like weighted spaghetti. By the time Simon was done with him, he was sodden with sweat and frustration. He couldn't have moved even if he wanted to when Simon braced his arm on the bed, the mattress pitched under his weight, and he stretched his long body up the bed to grab the lube from the bedside table.

Jacob straightened his legs and lifted his ass into the air. The long muscles in his thighs trembled down to his knees and nearly buckled when Simon slid a gel-slippery finger into his ass. He pushed back, wanting *more*, and groaned when Simon obliged with three fingers. It didn't hurt, but he could feel the stretch of it in his ass and the promise of more. Then they were gone and he whined in protest.

"Say you want me to fuck you," Simon told him.

"Isn't it obvious?"

"Just say it."

Simple enough, but Jacob still hesitated. He wasn't even sure why. The words caught in his throat like they were shy. He rolled over onto his back and kicked his jeans the rest of the way down to his ankles. Simon rolled a condom onto his cock while he waited for an answer. Jacob was pretty sure he was going to get fucked whether he said it or not. He just didn't know why he didn't want to say it.

"I want you," Jacob finally got out. He was pretty sure the "fuck me" had been there when the thought started in his head, but somehow it didn't make it all the way to his tongue. It felt awkward for a second. Then he let it go and grabbed Simon's hand to pull him down onto the bed. The long, warm heat of Simon's body sprawled on top of Jacob, heavily enough to pin him in place. Jacob reached up, buried his fingers in Simon's hair, and used the handhold to pull him down for a kiss. He mouthed the challenge against Simon's lips. "So get on with it already."

"And I'm the control freak?" Simon asked as he ran his hand down Jacob's back and over his ass. His fingers gripped the lean muscles of Jacob's thigh.

"Mmmm-hmmm," Jacob agreed.

Simon rolled them both over so he was splayed out on the sheets and Jacob straddled his hips. His hands on Jacob's thighs, sliding up to his ass, got him into position over Simon's cock. Jacob bit the inside of his lip as he reached back to grab it and felt the pulse against his fingers as he lowered himself down onto it.

He exhaled raggedly as he felt the cock fill him up. The pressure of it was just close enough to pain to make the pleasure sweeter. Sweat trickled down his stomach and itched in his abs as Simon tightened his grip on his hips to hold Jacob in place.

That was how it worked. Jacob might be on top, but Simon was still in. He set the pace. He directed the action. Of course he did that even when it was Jacob fucking him. Control freak.

Jacob arched his back and braced his weight on Simon's thighs instead of risking the chill-red shoulder, with its scatter of scars, as Simon pushed up into him with slow, steady thrusts. The head of his cock bumped Jacob's prostate with every other push and jolted slaps of pleasure up Jacob's spine.

Jacob kept one hand braced on Simon's thigh for balance, and the muscles flexed against his fingers as he grabbed his cock with the other. He dragged his hand in an impatient rhythm, squeezed at the base, and swept his thumb over the slick head on the upstroke.

His balls felt hot and heavy between his thighs and tight with the need to come.

"Si," he gasped, his voice ragged and pleading. "I can't...."

"Yeah, you can."

Jacob clenched his jaw, tilted his head back, and swore quietly at the ceiling as pleasure built ruthlessly. He *needed* to come. Simon's thrusts picked up pace as he buried his cock deeper inside Jacob and his fingers dug into Jacob's hips hard enough to bruise. The muscles in his thigh clenched, and Simon came with a last jolting thrust and a twisting pulse inside Jacob.

He flopped back onto the bed, licked the sweat off his lips between ragged breaths, and watched Jacob with hooded eyes. Jacob leaned forward, and the pressure against his cock cramped pleasure back to his ass. He kissed the salt off Simon's lips.

"Suck me off," he said.

Simon snorted a laugh into his mouth and shoved him off onto the bed. He licked his way down Jacob's body and chewed marks generously over the ripples of muscle. When he reached Jacob's hip bone, he lingered to suck a stinging bruise into the tight stretch of skin. Once the red stain was made to his satisfaction, he finally wrapped his lips around Jacob's cock. His mouth was hot, and his tongue was slick and pushed up firmly against the underside of the shaft as he bobbed his head.

Everything clenched, from his toes to his jaw, and Jacob arched up off the bed as he came, and a ragged groan dragged out of him.

Simon let Jacob's cock slide out of his mouth and pressed a sticky kiss onto the flat of Jacob's stomach. Then he rolled off the bed, stood up, and stripped the used condom off his cock. He padded across the dark room, into the bathroom. A trashcan rattled and then the sound of water running.

When he came back and crawled into bed, he was clean and cool, while Jacob was still sweaty and sticky. Not that Jacob moved. He just lay there and waited to see whether he'd fall asleep before guilt outweighed his resentment.

Nope.

"I should go wash," he said. Not that he moved.

Simon tucked a damp hand behind his neck and stroked his thumb along the sensitive hollow under his ear. "It doesn't bother me."

In that case Jacob wasn't going to bother. He closed his eyes, stretched until the knots in his muscles released with satisfying pops of pleasure, and then grabbed a pillow to fold under his head. After a minute of half dozing, he snorted.

"What?" Simon asked.

"Bad decisions," he said around a yawn. "This job has been one bad decision after another."

"Including me."

"Oh yeah. Caring is the worst decision. Makes you…." He stopped to yawn again and managed to mumble out the final "stupid" before he got dragged down into sleep.

CHAPTER SIXTEEN

SIMON LAY in bed and tried to ignore the pulse in his shoulder out of existence. He listened to Jacob move through the apartment. It was stupid. He could just get up and confirm that Jacob wasn't getting up to anything he shouldn't—it wasn't as though Jacob could pretend it was unfounded—but that felt like a step he couldn't take back.

It felt like he couldn't step either way—to or from—in case he couldn't take it back.

So instead he lay in a bed that smelled of sex that shouldn't have happened and traced Jacob by the disturbances he made to the familiar soundscape of the apartment. The rattle of the pan drawer under the sink—he knew it was that drawer from the catch and jolt caused by a kinked runner he hadn't gotten around to fixing—and the clink of the glass bottles as the door to the fridge was pulled open. The scrape and clatter of drawers being banged as Jacob looked for something in particular, and the hiss-pop-splutter of the burner catching on the oven. All to a backing track of snatches of Nickelback and Charli XCX lyrics.

There was the sound of something breaking, a wet cracking, and a muttered curse. "Fuck."

Water gushed and slopped about.

Simon closed his eyes to the view of the ceiling and sighed. It would have been easier if Jacob *had* tried to pull something. It turned out he was good at that. Cooking? Not so much. And Simon was probably going to have to eat it.

It wasn't the biggest concern of the day. That was somewhere between Jacob being convicted of a murder he didn't commit and Simon letting Jacob make a fool of him again—but maybe that was why he dwelled on it.

The door nudged open, which made Simon open his eyes, and Jacob leaned in around the jamb. He was shirtless and scruffy. The borrowed jeans were low around lean hips. Was it just a coincidence that the lack of shirt showed off lean muscle *and* the dapple of bruises over his side?

"Don't bother pretending to be asleep."

Simon propped himself up on his elbow. The sheet slid down around his waist and folded over his hip.

"I wasn't going to."

Jacob snorted at him and flashed a grin. "I made breakfast."

If he'd been trying to ingratiate himself, to somehow bargain bad food into an advantage, Simon would have shot him down. Instead he looked cocky, as though he were about to make a point. Smug looked good on him.

"Is it, or has it ever been, on fire?" Simon asked as he sat up. He pulled his knees up, and the cotton sagged in the middle as he rested his elbows on the shelf they made.

"Nope," Jacob said.

"Would you be happy feeding it to a small child?"

Jacob narrowed his eyes in thought. "How small?" he asked. "I mean, it's not breakfast's fault that babies can't digest chilies."

"Tell me that you didn't feed a baby chilies," Simon said as he threw the sheets back and got out of bed. He grabbed a pair of jeans from the back of a chair, gave them a desert-habit shake, and pulled them up over his legs.

Jacob leaned against the door and watched with unabashed appreciation.

"Hey, I'm the one who knew not to feed babies chilies," he said. "I bet you'd put tabasco in formula."

"I have a niece."

"So do I," Jacob said, and pushed himself off the door. "And *my* sister didn't marry a millionaire, so I have to spend time with them."

Simon buttoned his jeans and scowled. "I spend time with Callie."

"Fun time," Jacob said. "Not trying to force the little monsters to eat their breakfast instead of sticking it up their own butts."

No, just helping a teenager cope with the death of her mom when she refused to admit she was anything but "old for her years" time. Although she had admittedly never tried to put her granola anywhere inappropriate that he knew about. Simon followed Jacob out of the bedroom. Breakfast smelled like eggs and vinegar.

Resigned to having to eat at least some of Jacob's food, Simon hooked a stool out from under the breakfast bar and hopped up on it. "Do you get along with any of your family?"

Jacob snorted, his back to Simon as he did something at the oven. "No. They're horrible, and I'm a liar and a thief."

An apology tickled the back of Simon's throat and wanted to protest that he hadn't meant it. Except he had, and Jacob didn't respond as though the words had any sting. It was just a fact.

"Do any of them know what you do?"

The long muscles in Jacob's back stretched and played under lightly tanned skin as he reached up to get a plate from the cupboard.

"Hell no," Jacob said. He turned around and slid a plate of scrambled eggs in front of Simon. It looked edible—crispier than normal—but edible. Jacob handed Simon a fork. "I mentioned I'm a liar, right?"

Simon poked gently at the eggs and turned them over to uncover wilted peppers and black, half-moon shards that, after an exploratory prod, he guessed were mushrooms. It could have been worse. He finally bit the bullet, lifted a forkful to his mouth, and chewed it cautiously. Crunchy and wet in the wrong proportions, but the flavors were… there. He swallowed and ran his tongue around the back of his teeth to feel the grittiness.

"Must be lonely."

"No. Not really." Jacob dished himself up a plate of eggs and scraped the bottom of the pan to season the dish with charred egg bits. He added salt and enough tabasco to drown the taste and held the plate as he ate. "I don't need saving from myself, Si."

Simon took another bite of eggs. It still tasted of… taste. "So, that leaves me saving you from street fights and kidnappings, just not from yourself?"

"Point taken," Jacob said. He turned, opened the fridge, and grabbed a carton of milk. He left the door open as the cold leached out to goose pimple his skin. Then he splashed milk into a glass and, realizing he only had one out, a coffee cup from the night before. He put it back and closed the fridge precisely five seconds before Simon was going to have to say something. Simon got the glass and left Jacob to wash his hot sauce and burned eggs down with dingy beige coffee-flavored milk. Even Jacob made a face, although it didn't stop him taking another drink.

He swallowed and wiped his mouth on the back of his hand. "How are you going to approach Lau?"

"I'll see how he reacts to my turning up. Then decide," Simon said. He pushed a lump of runny egg—how had he managed to have some runny and some burned black—around the plate. The wedge of self-doubt in his chest made him feel like a teenager again, scared to ask anything in case someone guessed what he really meant. "So, about last night?"

Jacob scraped the last of the eggs and pepper out of a puddle of sauce and licked them off his fork. He hunched a bare shoulder. "It was last night. I get it. I mean, really, I get it. Maybe I didn't mean to lie to you—that much—but I did. If I were you, I'd have left me in jail or to the guns. So it's fine. Bad decisions and Bali—neither are for you. I mean, fuck you a bit, but I understand."

Simon grimaced, and the corners of his mouth twisted down. "I didn't mean that."

Jacob dumped his plate and fork in the sink, and the white stoneware seemed to sink under the greasy water. He wiped his hands on his hips. "Yeah, you did."

Maybe a bit, Simon supposed. Not as much as Jacob thought.

"I'm not like you, Jacob," he said. "I have a life. I have a family. I have a dad who's already lost one child. I can't go to Bali, and I can't have you in my life—"

His throat closed up around what he was going to say, trapping the "not if you're going to leave again" somewhere between his diaphragm and his Adam's apple. It was too raw, too close to that irrevocable step. He swallowed, worked his throat around the knot, and found something a little bit less honest to sub in.

"Not even if I wanted to."

And he did. It just didn't change anything. Not for him and not for Jacob, to judge by the resigned shrug Simon got before Jacob headed off to get dressed. Left alone Simon stared down at his plate as though the answer might be somewhere in the congealing eggs. The tick of toenails on wooden floors jarred him from his introspection, and he looked down into Fozzy's hopeful teddy-bear face. With a sigh he leaned over and set the plate down in front of the dog.

"At least you're easily pleased," he said. The dog, face-first in the eggy leftovers, twitched an ear at him in acknowledgment.

Simon gave his bony head a scratch and then he pushed himself up. Enough. Wallowing wouldn't change anything, and while he wanted Jacob to stay, he didn't want it to be in a jail cell.

MARION, TEXAS wasn't exactly the sort of place you'd expect a hotshot climate researcher to put down roots. It was sun-bleached and dusty, and the Old-West-fronted brick buildings rattled on their foundations as a train dragged a mile of freight cars past the town.

Simon guided his car through the empty streets of the business district—abandoned at eight thirty, except for a few shop owners dragging stock out onto the pavement and a tired-looking man who pushed a broom from one end of the block to the other. His phone, tossed onto the seat next to him, gave him directions in a stilted voice that took him off smooth asphalt and onto cracked, rutted concrete.

When the phone finally congratulated him on reaching his destination, Simon rolled past low white houses on patches of scrubby green lawn. Some of them were neat, with painted fences and matching trim, while others had rust-stained roofs and had let the desert take dusty bites out of their gardens.

Lau's house had a battered kettle barbecue on his lawn. Rust ran down its legs to stain the grass, and the fence had been pulled over to make room for a wilted, electric-blue Plymouth to sit on its rims. The drive was full of a hard-used pickup, the bed of it full of tarps, and the sides caked with streaks of dried mud.

Simon pulled up on the dusty verge behind the pickup, blocking it in, and got out. The air was still chilly, but the watery sunlight had started to warm it up. He paused for a second to check out the car's sleek blue lines under the coating of dust. Plymouths weren't his car, but it was a pretty bit of muscle to leave rotting on a lawn. He flicked the thought out of his head. Even when he had more time on his hands, his Firebird was still lodging expensively at the mechanic waiting for him to source a drive belt and a manifold. That was enough of a hobby.

The steps up to Lau's door creaked under his weight. It made Simon tense with pointless reaction, and he realized his mouth tasted of dust and pennies again. On edge. After yesterday it made sense. He swallowed the taste away and glanced around to gauge whether it was his brain misfiring or his instincts picking up on something wrong.

In the lot opposite, a swing rattled on its chains in front of a boarded-up house. Down the street a middle-aged woman in a T-shirt dress was hanging up her washing on the line. It was the cotton flapping in the wind that made his mouth sour.

Not real. Or at least not immediate.

He turned and hammered on the door. His irritation added a bit of extra force to the blows, and the side of his hand stung. The door was sturdier than it looked. Simon thumped it one last time and turned to check the street again. That time he wasn't looking for a threat. He was looking for surveillance. Nothing installed that he could identify, but that meant nothing. He'd been out for a couple of years, enough time for the tech to bypass him.

The door wrenched open, and Lau glared out at him and squinted as he pulled his glasses down from his forehead and set them on his nose. When he recognized Simon, surprise supplanted the scowl for a second and then gave way to fear.

"I didn't tell Clayton anything," he said as he backed up from the door. "I don't know what Syntech thinks happened, but it was nothing to do with me. Okay?"

Simon's stomach knotted, a hollow ball of dread squeezed up against his spine, and he took a second to be glad that Jacob wasn't with him. He stepped forward to block the door with his body when Lau tried to shove it shut.

"How about we talk about that inside?"

Lau looked like he'd rather do anything else, but it wasn't as though Simon were giving him a choice. He stepped back reluctantly and gave Simon enough room to get into the house.

THE COFFEE was black and bitter, stewed to the point of being Turkish, and hot enough it was nearly bubbling. Simon let it sit and cool on the table in front of him. Lau drank it like water. He had to have an asbestos mouth. Either that or his nerves were so bad he didn't care about scorching off his taste buds.

It was obvious his nerves were bad enough that he'd lost weight. Lau'd been stocky before. Not fat, but solid and calfy—the sort of man who did geolocation treasure-hunt hikes into the mountains and posted selfies on rock faces. Now he looked skinny, and his jock-amiable face was pared down into sharp lines and angles.

"Do you know what happened to Clayton?"

Lau twisted his hands around his Star Wars mug—he had climber's knuckles, all scars and lumps—and took a slurping drink of coffee. "He's dead."

"Do you know why?"

"Do you?"

"Pretend I don't know anything." It was still too close to the truth. But he didn't want to let Lau in on that fact, not when Lau seemed to think he was still working for Syntech.

Lau slurped his coffee and twisted his hands. "I'm not supposed to talk about this. I signed a nondisclosure agreement. Hell, I signed it twice."

"So did I."

Not lately, not about this. It still seemed to work on Lau, who nodded and took a deep breath. "Okay."

It looked like Jacob wasn't the only one who knew how to manipulate people. The only difference was that Jacob had natural talent, and Simon had studied interrogation techniques. He wasn't sure who came out ahead there, morally speaking.

"I think he… I can't shake the idea he died because I called him," Lau said. He added a scoffing little laugh at the end, a nervous cue for Simon to disagree with him. "Like, stupid, right?"

He looked hopefully at Simon, eyes in search of some reassurance that he hadn't fucked up. All he got was a noncommittal grunt, while Simon scrambled at the pieces of information behind his carefully expressionless face.

"When?" he asked. "When did you first make contact?"

Doubt flickered over Lau's face—surely Simon should have known that—but guilt and fear battered it back. "Eight months ago, when the causal-reasoning…" He took a look at Simon's face and tried again. "When the program kept having irretrievable crashes, I recognized Clayton's input on the code we were using. I beta'd on the PeaPod's location-sharing app before they sold it off. So I assumed he was in the loop on the project. I contacted him to ask for some advice."

Dates flipped by in Simon's head as he constructed the timeline and stacked the days, one on top of the other. Eight months put Lau in Alaska—

officially put Lau in Alaska—and a couple of weeks before he "resigned" from Syntech to make his own way home. It also possibly highlighted one of Simon's people as a turncoat, but that could be handled later.

"He didn't believe you?"

Lau shook his head and freed a hand from his cup to shove his glasses back up on his nose.

"Didn't have a clue," he said. "Look, I fessed up to the mistake at the time, and I haven't had any contact with him since."

Simon raised his eyebrow. "Really?"

Whatever confidence Lau had pulled out of the conversation and the coffee drained out of his face. "I don't know what you mean."

"He thought he was meeting you for coffee on the day he died."

Lau put his coffee down on the table with a too-hard clack. "I didn't contact him," he said. Simon waited, and Lau broke miserably in the silence. "Fuck. Fine. You know what? Yeah, I was supposed to meet him that day. I didn't contact him, though. Clayton tracked me down and asked to meet."

"And you said yes."

"Yeah. I should have said no, but I didn't," Lau said it cockily, all "so what" attitude and jutting chin. But his hands shook, and he kept licking his lips. "So? I didn't talk to him. You can't throw me in jail for planning to have a coffee with someone. Maybe I had a thing for him?"

"You could still be fired. We don't have to give reason—"

"Good," Lau spat back. Then he promptly winced back from the word as though it had surprised him. He didn't retract it, though. "Ramsey, if I wanted to work for the government, I'd have gone to Russia to dissolve clouds. I just want to go back to work in the lab, on my actual field of study. When I was recruited, Porter told me we were going to reverse climate change."

"Dev talks a good game."

"He talks a big game," Lau corrected him. "That's what I liked— the ambition to actually change the world with science. *Literally* change the world. Instead I'm working on targeting algorithms to use with Icarus. I'm not *stupid*, you don't need to target clouds." He paused to rub the heel of his hand against his forehead. "I'm stuck out here in the train station of Texas with no one to talk to. Look. I appreciate that being put in charge of this project was a great opportunity for me, but I just want to get back into the labs and get back into my own field again. You're related to Porter. You can talk to him. Get me reassigned."

"What did he say when you asked him?"

Lau sagged back into the couch. It was new enough to creak under him, maybe only eight months or so old.

"That I'd committed to his project and had to see it through." He spit the words out like they tasted bad. "That things would be changing soon and to have patience."

The way he said the words sounded like a direct quote, the sort of disappointing e-mail you memorized and grumbled about to your friends. Except they didn't sound like Dev. Not even a Dev who had forgotten how much he hated authority and was running black-site labs behind Simon's back. Dev didn't value patience. It wasn't a trait he'd ever name-check to anyone. Dev would have told Lau to grit through it or complete the project if he wanted out of it that badly.

"When did you last speak to Dev, to Mr. Porter?"

"Yesterday? Yesterday morning," Lau said. Then he shifted. Clearly the habit of precision made him uncomfortable. "I mean, not personally. I talked to the project lead, like always."

"And they told you to be patient?"

"Yeah. But it's been three years since they put me on this project. It was only ever meant to be a brief secondment and—"

Copper pennies on his tongue and dust in Simon's nose—the sudden hit of adrenaline dragged down the relief he'd felt a second before. Stupid fucking brain. He clenched his jaw and tried to hold on to what he'd just learned—that Lau had never spoken to Dev directly and that the project started three years earlier—when Dev was busy not accepting that Becca was dying.

It was what he'd wanted—needed—to hear, and apparently that was enough to kick off a fight or flight reaction.

"Are you all right?" Lau looked at him with concern.

"Too much coffee," Simon lied thinly. He ignored the itch at the nape of his neck and leaned forward. "Who is your project lead again?"

Confusion made Lau screw dark eyebrows together over his nose. "What? Hold on. I thought she sent you?"

He had started to push himself up off the couch, hands up and frustrated, when the bullet punched through the glass window. The shatter of glass gave Simon a second to react, but his muscles were clenched with the expectation of violence, and he was in motion before he even consciously knew he needed to be.

He lunged over the coffee table, sending the mugs flying, and tackled Lau back onto the couch. It wasn't enough, but it jolted the center of his mass out of the sniper's sights. The bullet caught his shoulder and punched through the flesh and bone without drama.

It was rarely as cinematic as you expected. Not in the moment.

They landed on the cushions with a thud. Lau started to hyperventilate as the situation hit him, and Simon rolled them both onto the floor. Under the tranqing blanket of the painkiller he'd taken earlier, Simon's shoulder started to scream again. He ignored it and folded his arms over both their heads.

Blood spread over the floor and soaked into the carpet along with the spilled stewed coffee. Either the shooter had seen that he'd missed or he just liked to make sure. Either way he kept firing and perforated the wooden walls of the house. Bullets ripped into the cushions, punctured the leather and sent the stuffing flying. The noise was deafening, and then it stopped.

"What the hell! What the hell?" Lau spluttered. He reached up, touched his head, took away bloody fingers, and stared at them in shock as they started to shake. "What the *fuck*?"

Simon rolled off him and to his feet. He grabbed Lau and dragged the shaken, shocky man up and stuck his shoulder under his arm when he staggered. Blood dripped on his jacket and onto the back of his hand.

"Move," he said. "We need to move, Lau. Now. Come on."

They stagger-ran into the kitchen and out through the back door. Behind them Simon heard a boot kick the front door in.

CHAPTER SEVENTEEN

THERE WERE—BARRING the exceptions that proved the rule—only ever two options when it came to on-hold music. It was either 80s pop—Jacob had spent more hours listening to "Walking in Memphis" than was humane—or classical music if it was performed by an orchestra with no soul.

Tuscan Blooms had picked the former.

Jacob pinned the phone between his shoulder and his ear as he reached back to dry his ass on one of Simon's towels. He absently hummed along to the Smiths as he passed the towel between his legs and gave his balls a quick dry. He tossed the towel at the laundry basket, turned toward the bedroom, and paused when he found Fozzy staring at him from the bed.

"Don't judge," he told the dog. "I saw what you were doing last night. You're gonna lick that thing to a nub."

Fozzy blinked his beady little eyes, heaved a sigh, and lay down. Still staring.

Jacob shrugged, grabbed his jeans, and held them up to assess the stains. He imagined them on someone else and how he'd judge them, then sighed and tossed them after the towel. Too scruffy for what he wanted to pull off. He went to Simon's wardrobe and flicked through the perfectly pressed and hung dress pants.

Hot as hell on Simon. Not quite right.

A quick hunt through the drawers turned up a pair of black chinos and a fitted gray T-shirt. The fit wasn't exactly tailored, but he didn't want to look too good either. He was just shoving his feet into his sneakers when the harried florist in Tuscan Blooms picked up the phone.

"Hello," she said. "I'm *so* sorry for the wait. It's just really busy here today. How can I help you?"

Jacob switched ears. He could imagine how busy it was. He'd donated a couple of grand and recruited some online contacts to spam the florist with telephone orders. Considering the sense of humor of most of the people on that board, there would be some pretty inappropriate bouquets sent the next day.

"I wanted to order a wreath?"

"Of course. Friend or family?"

"Business associate," Jacob said. He sat down on the bed and scruffed Fozzy's ears as he talked. "Ah, sort of. My employer passed away, and we're sending flowers from the office. We have an account with you."

He said it confidently.

"Oh, I'm sorry to hear that," the florist said. In the background a phone rang. He could hear her moving around in an attempt to dim the noise. "Could I just get where you're calling from?"

"PeaPod," Jacob said. He rhymed off the address while he pulled his foot up onto the bed to tie his laces.

"Oh," the woman said. "Your employer was Harry Clayton, the man found in the river."

"Yes," Jacob said. He hesitated with his fingers hooked through the loops in the laces as he scrabbled through phrases for the most useful social interaction. "It's awful. We don't really know what happened, though, and we can't talk about it."

The faintly terse note—the implication of official censure on discussion—worked well enough. The florist muttered an abashed apology and took Jacob's order.

"And where do you want the flowers sent?"

Jacob gave her Clayton's address, told her to bill the office, and hung up while she was distracted by the phones going behind her. He clicked the screen off, looked down at Fozzy, and gave him a poke in the side to make him grunt and open his eyes.

"Not that you seem worried," he said. "But let's get you walked and back to your owner before I go to grab myself some brunch."

THE CHEAP canvas lead stretched taut from Jacob's fist to the catch on the dog's collar—not *quite* long enough for Fozzy to reach the scattered pastry crumbs.

"She said she doesn't want him back," the barista said apologetically as she flicked the drooping crest of her mohawk back from her face. "He wasn't even her dog, but when she broke up with her boyfriend and *he* wanted the dog...." She let her shrug convey every single bad decision ever made during a breakup.

Jacob gave up on trying to reel Fozzy back in and let go of the lead. The dog disappeared under the table and licked noisily at the ground.

"Well, she can't palm him off on me," Jacob said. "Just give him back to her when she comes in."

"She quit," the barista said. She held up her hands before Jacob could say anything. He could see letters tattooed on the crease of her palms. "I've got a parrot. He hates dogs."

"So do I," Jacob said. "Look, just give him to whoever wants a free dog."

"I can't keep him here," she protested. Over her head the menu—artistically chalked on an old-school chalkboard—advertised chai, vitamin water, and Chinese lily tea alongside the lattes and Earl Grey. Gluten-free scones and triple white-chocolate macaroons were the sole confectionary on offer. "Dogs aren't allowed. I'll have to get someone to take him to the pound."

Jacob shrugged. "At least he'll get four hots and a cot," he said. "I don't want a dog."

He ignored the barista's distressed look, left the coffee shop, and let the door slam behind him to make the bells jingle. He got halfway down the street before the hook in his atrophied conscience found something to sink into.

How was he going to explain it to Simon? He'd probably had a dog when he was a kid, and Jacob could imagine the expression of chilly disappointment on his face when Jacob explained Fozzy's fate. He'd probably go and find the damn thing and adopt it out from under the needle.

Jacob stalked back to the coffee shop. The bells jangled their warning of return and made the barista look up from behind the counter. Relief hit her face, and she quickly made a brusque excuse to whomever she was talking to and hung up.

"Oh, God. Thank you," she said. "I was going to try to get someone to take him, but dogs need space, you know? You *have* changed your mind?"

It was a dog. It was Christmas. Either his nephew or Simon's niece could get a puppy from Santa this year.

"Yeah," he said. "I'll have a chocolate orange latte to go... and the dog."

She spooled in Fozzy from behind the counter and wrapped the leash around her hands until he waddled out, dripping water from his beard.

"Coffee's on the house." She grinned at him as she held out the lead. "Thanks. I'd have felt like shit if anything happened to him. He's a nice dog."

He took the dog *and* the coffee to go.

THE WAITER at the Iron Cactus was tall, young, and either gay, bi, or vain enough that he'd take flirting where he could find it. It helped that he was agog at the opportunity to be involved, however peripherally, in a murder investigation.

Dark hair flopped in Andy's face as he leaned over to look at the image Jacob flashed on his phone. Harry Clayton stared seriously out of the screen through the heavy black-framed glasses he'd worn before he went for contacts. It was from a Google search, but it looked enough like an official ID to pass.

"That's him," the waiter said as he tapped the screen with a finger. Chipped black nail polish retreated toward his cuticles. He glanced up and gave Jacob a sliding, conspiratorial grin. "I'm a computer sci major, so when I recognized his name, I made sure I was working that night. Thought we might get talking."

"Did you?" Jacob asked. He angled the phone so it looked like he was recording the conversation. Andy believed he was being interviewed by a reporter from the San Antonio *Express-News* about the recent tragedy. Jacob had considered cop, but that needed a bit more prep time. People were more forthcoming with police—even when they were lying—but too many police shows meant they wanted badge flashes and business cards. And saying you were a cop was an actual crime.

Andy pouted and shrugged. "He was *not* interested in small talk," he said as he straightened up. He waggled his eyebrows suggestively. "Not with me anyhow."

"Hard to imagine," Jacob said, eyes flicking appreciatively to Andy's arms. It was a fairly safe area. Even if Andy wasn't gay, most guys didn't mind if you checked out their muscles. It was when you slid lower that the homophobia started to creep in. They were nice arms too, although not as nice as some. Back to the topic at hand. "He'd booked a cruise, hadn't he? Was it for a work party or…?"

"No. I mean, she was in the business. They were talking location-tracking algorithms when they came in. But it was a date, y'know? She was wearing a 'look at my boobs' dress. Clayton was flashing his Silk card around like we might have missed it."

"First date?"

"Naw," Andy said immediately. "She was in flats. With that dress? She knew he was short, and twitchy about it. That's at least a couple of dates in, and I actually had the feeling it was a special occasion or something? An anniversary maybe?"

"Did you get her name?"

"No. Like I said, Clayton made the booking. I might have a picture, though? We usually snap a couple on the cruises for the website." Andy hesitated for the first time and glanced over his shoulder. "I'm not sure I should be showing them to you. I mean, she didn't sign a waiver or anything."

It was the sort of moral qualm that just begged to be overruled.

"Look, I'm not going to use it," Jacob said. "I just want to find her. Besides, who's going to know? Come on. You can trust me."

Just in case his charm wasn't enough to seal the deal, Jacob pulled his wallet out. After a quick bit of mental arithmetic weighed how much he wanted the picture and how much a reporter would want the picture, he pulled out a hundred and tucked it into Andy's palm. He thought the bit of subterfuge sold it more than the bill itself.

"Hold on," Andy said. "I'll need to go check the computer. Be right back."

He loped off inside. Jacob leaned against a rail and looked down to check that Fozzy was where he'd left him. He was, and he seemed happy enough. The dog had splashed a full dish of water into a puddle on the ground and was watching other dogs stick their nose in the empty dish.

So, the dog was a dick. Jacob liked him a bit more for that.

His phone buzzed in his hand, and his sister's name appeared on the screen when he looked down. Crap. He'd forgotten to call her, hadn't he? Jacob hesitated and then banished the call with an auto-texted promise to call back in five minutes. She gave him five seconds and called back again. Jacob rejected the call and set it to "Do not disturb" as Andy came back from the restaurant. He was carrying his phone and gestured apologetically over his shoulder at the girl behind the bar.

"Sorry," he said. "I have to hurry. The manager will be in soon. Can I get your number?"

Jacob raised his eyebrows at him. Andy just widened his eyes and looked innocent. "To text you the image."

"That all?"

A slow hot smile spread across Andy's face. He caught his lower lip between his teeth and took a quick look down Jacob's lean dark-clad body. "Not necessarily."

Andy was no Simon, but it was nice to be appreciated. It was also nice to get his own way without feeling guilty about his manipulation. Jacob delivered his number in packages of three digits at a time while Andy tapped it into his phone. After a second he hit Send. Jacob checked his messages, and there was the unfamiliar number and a picture thumbnail.

"Thank you," he said and handed over another hundred.

Andy took the cash and tucked it into the pocket of his tight jeans. "Call me sometime," he said. "If you need anything else."

He turned, jogged back into the restaurant, and dodged the wet cloth the bartender chucked at him. Jacob tilted his head to the side and watched him go. Andy had long legs and a tight ass in black jeans that fit a lot better than Jacob's did. In Jacob's imagination he had ink in the small of his back to match his arms and scrollwork over lean hips.

Nice view and no urge to chase after it at all. He hoped that whatever it was with Simon—and no, he wasn't giving it a damn name—it was going to wear off eventually. Otherwise he and his hand were going to have to get married.

He shook his head and started through the maze of tables—all carefully arranged to look unarranged—and down the stairs to the Riverwalk. He flipped through his phone as he walked and pulled up the picture that Andy had sent him.

The mystery woman was tall and toned, elegant in black lace and with a ribbon woven through her dark hair. The breadth of her shoulders and the defined muscle suggested martial arts, and the fact she showed them off in a strapless dress betrayed confidence.

When his sister played soccer semicompetitively in school, she spent most of her time trying to hide her muscles, as though someone would revoke her girl card if they saw them. Clayton's mystery woman clearly didn't care who saw them. So the flats were an off note. A woman with those shoulders, in that dress, would expect her partner to deal with her height. Maybe she just preferred flats, of course, but a manipulator recognized a manipulator.

And he was pretty sure he'd recognize that particular manipulator if he saw her again. The photo caught her profile. It was partially obscured by the artful sweep of wavy dark brown hair, but it was distinctive. She had warm-looking tawny skin, a Roman nose with a dinted bridge, a faintly weak chin, and the hint of a very good fake smile. It was a fairly striking face.

He saved the photo, got to the bottom of the stairs, and collected Fozzy from the tree he'd been tied to. The dog looked unenthusiastic at having to walk again, but grunted and grumbled along at Jacob's heels as they headed away. Tourists sat at tables outside the restaurants and took selfies with the sun and Christmas decorations in the background. A bride and groom posed on one of the bridges and held each other while they tried not to squint as their pictures were taken.

Jacob wrapped the leash around his wrist and sidestepped a jogger. The sweating girl gasping out a thanks as her ponytail flapped past. He opened his contacts. The missed call from his sister sat there accusingly. Jacob skipped it and found Tuscan Bloom's number.

It was lunchtime, and the money he'd put up for nuisance orders had just run out. The florist he spoke to that morning had to have been ready for a break. He paused between the jostle of tourists and the wedding guests and tapped the number with his phone.

A man answered it. Jacob felt his shoulders relax. He'd thought his setup would work, but the best laid plans of mice and fools… and all that.

"Yes," he said. This time the voice belonged to his tutor at his university, a burned-out adjunct who stalked through life like a White Rabbit in a panic about being late. It wasn't an impression—Mr. Norman had been German and sang baritone—but the irritated timbre, the confidence that what he was saying was too important for pleasantries was borrowed. "This is Ryan. Called from PeaPod. Our account number is 20043. My assistant was on with your company earlier this morning regarding an arrangement we wanted sent out?"

He paused abruptly and sighed heavily when the florist didn't immediately take up the thread of the conversation.

"Well?" he snapped.

"Sorry," the man said. Jacob could hear the click of a keyboard. "It's been a hectic morning. We've had a lot of orders come in. Just give me a second."

Jacob snorted. It was loud enough to make one of the wedding guests turn. A man in a morning suit with a calla lily on the lapel scowled at him. He covered the phone with his hand and mouthed "Sucker for a wedding."

Jacob *tch*ed down the line at the man who was still hunting for the order.

"Look. We're happy to go forward with the order," he said. "I just want to check it's going to the right address. Unlike everything else Engels ordered this morning."

"Okay," the man said. "I've got your order here. It's going to—"

"It should be going to the same address as the last arrangement we sent." Jacob interrupted. "Not to Mr. Clayton's home address. Just check that. I don't have time to clear up this mess today."

There was a pause that was full of irritated key clicks, and the man came back with, "Okay. I can change that for you now," he said. "So the arrangement is now being sent to 17902 La Cantera Parkway. Is that right?"

Probably. Flowers didn't seem like the sort of thing PeaPod usually sent out, but maybe there was a hippy working there.

"That's right," Jacob said. He heaved his best put-upon sigh, got another glare from the irritable weddinggoer, and headed away from the noise. "And did he tell you no lavender? None."

"Ah, no," the man said. "Nothing about that. But we weren't going to include…."

"Just put a note," Jacob said sharply. "Last thing we need is someone else dying. You know, fixing other people's mistakes is not what I need to be doing right now."

He hung up abruptly and left the florist to—hopefully—mutter more about what a dick Jacob was than wonder if he should have given out the address. A quick property search should turn up the mystery woman's address. He glanced down at Fozzy, who listened to him with his head cocked to one side and his bat-tuft ears folded over.

"Yeah. I know," he said. "I have to call my sister. You're lucky, Fozzy. None of your littermates have mastered the keypad."

The call to his sister went about as well as a call could to someone waiting to pick you up from a flight you weren't on. He had forgotten about that.

CHAPTER EIGHTEEN

EMERGENCY RESPONSE times in San Antonio hovered at the seven-minute mark. The shooters would know that too. That gave them six minutes to carry out the kill order on Ryan. Simon dragged the swearing scientist across the scrubby backyard.

"What the hell is going on?" Ryan asked as he swiped blood out of his eye with his sleeve. "Who are they? Why are they after you?"

"They're not after me." Simon kicked the post of the fence down and shoved Ryan across the listing chain-link. He pulled his keys out of his pocket and shoved them into Ryan's hands. "I'll lead them off. You head back around to the front and take my car."

"But—"

Glass smashed in the kitchen window and someone took a shot over the kitchen sink. Simon yanked Ryan out of the way and made him stagger as the bullet kicked up a rut in the dirt. It was enough to convince Ryan that it wasn't the time to argue. He stuck to Simon's side as they took off at a run through the maze of lots and randomly angled houses. Behind them two men burst out of the house and gave chase. There'd be a third in a car, waiting to cut them off on the road.

"Who was she? Who was your contact?" Simon demanded. He grabbed Ryan's sleeve and swung him around a tight corner. A kid stared out the window at them, sticky looking and huge-eyed under a plastic tiara. Simon grimaced and gestured for the boy to get down and put enough force into the gesture that it read like a shout. The kid hesitated and then dropped out of sight.

"I... I don't know if I should tell you," Ryan said. Blood dropped off his chin, and his scalp wound bled with wet enthusiasm until it soaked into the collar of his ragged T-shirt. He licked it off his lips, grimaced at the taste of it, and glanced back over his shoulder. A shot rang out, and he flinched and staggered as the surprise broke his stride. "This only happened *after* I talked to you."

Maybe. They might have planned to snatch him the same as they had Clayton, and the objective had only changed when they saw that

Simon was there. Unlikely it would have made a lot of difference in the long run. It hadn't for Clayton.

The shooters lagged. Simon's *arm* might be a mess, but there was nothing wrong with his legs. And Ryan free-climbed for a hobby. It might not make him any faster, but he had stamina. Simon gritted his teeth and dragged a faster pace out of his muscles—just enough to turn the lead into room to maneuver. With a grunt of effort, Ryan kept pace.

There was a rotting carcass of a pickup on blocks in a dusty garden, nudged up against a peeling metal playset.

"Hide there. Break for the car," Simon gritted out. "I'll catch up with you in town. Then you tell me who the hell is behind this. They aren't on your side."

Ryan started to argue, but there wasn't time for that. Simon shouldered him behind the truck and kicked his feet out from under him. Ryan hit the ground with a shocked huff as the air left his lungs, and Simon kept going. He hit the swings on the way past and made the chains rattle and sway.

Once the blood was up during a chase, it was easier to keep hunting ghosts than stop and look for the real target.

A quick check over his shoulder showed that Ryan had rolled under the car. Simon dodged around the side of a building and then another. There was a shed in one of the gardens—sturdy plastic, with a halfhearted lock on the door.

He ducked in behind it and rethought leaning on it when he felt it rock under his weight. His gun was a tempting presence against his ribs, but the thought of the kid's face at the window kept his hand away from it. There were numerous gunnies in his past who'd rip him a new one for it, but he'd rather get shot than know he'd killed a little kid.

It was bad enough knowing that he already might have—some time, some campaign.

He tipped his head to the side as he listened. He could hear sirens in the distance. They might not be coming there, but someone in the neighborhood yelled that she'd called the police.

A voice barked an order to split left. Simon wiped his hand over his mouth, tasted salt, and—for some reason—thought about Jacob. Then he lunged out from his shelter and tackled the lean beaky-faced man closest to him.

He tried to favor his shoulder and used the opposite one to dig into the man's gut, but the impact jolted pain through him anyhow. He ignored it and headbutted the man, who ended up on top of him, and drove the crown of his head into the man's chin. The impact snapped the man's jaw shut, and he spluttered blood over Simon's face.

Simon twisted his hips and threw the spluttering, swearing man off him. Leaving his opponent to cough as blood ran down his throat, Simon scrambled to his feet and stamped on the man's wrist. Bones cracked, and the gun fell out of suddenly nerveless fingers.

"Fucking rent-a-cop," the man garbled out over his ragged tongue. He pulled his knees up to his chest and drove them into Simon's stomach in a kick that lifted his hips off the ground. His heels made contact and sent Simon flying backward into the plastic shed. It pitched over, the panels cracked under his weight, and he went with it. The gun went flying as he lost his hold on it.

He grabbed blindly for something, and closed his fingers around the shaft of a—he glanced over quickly—rake. That would have to do. He got back on his feet, swung the rake up and around, and then froze. There was a man with dead eyes and a nondescript face pointing a gun at his head. Not good.

Simon let the tool drop and held up his hands. None of the options that flicked through his head ended well under those circumstances. So he needed to buy time until he could change the circumstances.

"Shaw. Long time, no see. How's Denis?"

Amusement pinched Shaw's mouth into an unremarkable smile. His gaze dropped briefly to Simon's side where his jacket was hanging open. It took a microsecond to register the gun and then his attention was back on Simon.

"You should have gone for your gun. I've read your file. I'm sure you're a better shot than Milo here."

"Lot of people around here who aren't involved in this," Simon said.

"I didn't take you for a bleeding heart."

"Kids," Simon said as he glanced around. "Thin walls and shoot-outs don't mix."

Shaw looked around. His lip curled with the sort of contempt that looked personal. "Place like this? They don't have much to look forward to anyhow." He flicked his attention back before Simon could take advantage of the momentary distraction. "You know, my information says that Syntech's cut you loose. If you're looking for work, I could always use a man with your skillset."

Milo had gotten back to his feet. He spit out blood and mopped at his face with his sleeve. "Screw that," he got out, slurring his words over his tongue. "Rent-a-cop made me bite off my *tongue*. He put my friends in the hospital. I'm going to make him pay—"

He stopped abruptly as Shaw pulled his backup gun and pointed it in his direction. Shaw's eyes didn't shift from Simon's face, but the muzzle of the gun still ended up pointed at the merc's center of mass.

"You don't get a vote, Milo," Shaw told him mildly. "If you and your friends were as skilled as Mr. Ramsey here, this situation would never have gotten so... messy. Now, pick up your tongue and go find our target."

Milo glared at his boss with murder in his eyes.

That time Shaw glanced away from Simon. It was just a quick flick of his eyes and a minor adjustment of his aim—two inches down, one across—but the threat was clear. Milo blanched and crouched. He fumbled in the dirt for the wet bit of muscle he'd just spat out. He scraped it up out of the dirt and was shoving it into his pocket when the chokey growl of a car's ignition coughed to life behind them.

Shaw's mouth tightened with annoyance as he put the pieces together. "Playing the martyr, Ramsey? That's going to get you killed one of these days." He lifted the gun slightly and aimed it at Simon's head. "Sooner rather than later. And for what? You think we won't find Lau? He's a scientist in a borrowed car, how far is he going to get? To the police station in what the locals like to call a town?"

"I think he'll head to Syntech and tell Dev what's going on," Simon said. He gave a tight smile in response to Shaw's skeptical look. "Well, I'll be dead before I find out how it plays out. I might as well be optimistic."

Shaw snorted a brief huff of laughter and curled his finger around the trigger. Simon's brain went into overdrive. He scrambled through the bits and pieces that he knew and tried to shove them into the gaps of the things he didn't. Something had changed between a screwup that killed Clayton and the decision to send a team to murder Lau.

"The job's burned, isn't it?" he said.

Shaw tilted his head to the side to consider Simon and decided to answer. "Not exactly," he said. "Think of it more as undergoing restructuring. When one door doesn't take you where you want to go, then you find another, don't you? When my employer made it clear she didn't have the balls to deliver the results, I went over her head. Men like you and me, Ramsey, we do what needs to be done. We don't let sentiment get in the way."

"Speak for yourself."

Shaw chuckled. "Fair point. You are the sentimental type, but I bet you'd still sell that pretty boyfriend of yours out if you had to. Although I guess we'll never find out, since I don't think you'll be seeing him again." He paused for a second and then allowed himself another sentence. "I'm telling you, if the bitch had let me run things my way from the start, it would never have gotten this messy."

The wail of sirens cut through the air like screaming cats, and Shaw's attention snapped away from Simon. It was a narrow window of opportunity, but it was the only one Simon was going to get. He lunged forward, tackled Shaw, and rammed his shoulder into his lean stomach.

There was nothing graceful about the fight. It was quick and nasty—dirty tricks and rabbit punches. Simon brute-forced Shaw around and used Shaw's body as a shield against Milo's gun. The wail of the sirens got closer, and Simon could see the calculation flicker in Milo's eyes. If he were arrested, it would cause repercussions that could impact his career. Not only that. He'd already admitted the job was a mess. The last thing he wanted was for whoever was pulling his strings to decide that door didn't work either and just burn it all.

Right then Shaw needed an exit plan more than he needed Simon dead. His foot slipped in the mud. Maybe it was on purpose. Maybe Simon had just gotten lucky. He didn't really care. He got behind Shaw, hooked his arm around Shaw's neck, dug his fist in under his jaw, and dragged him backward.

"Get out of here," he snapped at Milo. "I see you again, I snap his neck."

Milo didn't hesitate. He did as he was told. His gun went in the holster, and he backed away, hands held up in a halfhearted gesture of surrender. Blood had scabbed on his chin and his throat and was drying on his shirt.

"Who's the woman?" Simon asked.

Simon felt the muscles under Shaw's jaw flex as he swallowed. "You know I won't tell you that. And I know you don't want to deal with the police any more than I do. Considering your boyfriend is the prime suspect, and your boss is implicated, they'll be real interested to find you here, won't they?"

True, unfortunately. Simon licked his lips and weighed the likelihood that he'd be able to convince the police of his version of events. It wasn't good, and the sirens were too close to give him time to plan.

"You can't fix this, Ramsey," Shaw said. "It's too late for that. All you can do is try and let it be as painless as possible. It's just business."

"It's my family, the people I love," Simon said. "It's my life, Shaw. It's not happening. I don't care who it hurts."

He shoved Shaw and released his chokehold as Shaw lurched forward. Before Shaw could regain his balance, Simon turned and ran. He wasn't fast enough. A gun barked once, and he felt the punch of it hit his leg. He staggered, caught himself, and dodged down the narrow alley between two buildings. His leg felt shocked and numb under him—wet and warm—but it didn't hurt. Yet.

The sirens screamed, and Simon could hear the police yelling orders and instructions out on the road. He pressed the heel of his hand to his thigh and tried to hold the blood in. It was hot as it bubbled through his fingers.

"Sooner or later, Ramsey," Shaw yelled after him. "Unless you back off, I will get another chance to kill you. So tell you what. Crawl back into your bottle and stay out of my way."

His leg started to hurt. Simon took his jacket off and ripped the lining out of it to pack into the wound. The bullet had punched a wormhole of flesh from the meat of his outer thigh, missing bone, muscle, and arteries. It was bleeding wet and red, soaking through the silk of the lining with disheartening speed, and throbbed with pain in time to his heartbeat.

It could have been worse.

He put the jacket back on, buttoned it to hide the gun and the torn lining, and pushed himself off the side of the house. Three deep breaths and then he made himself walk out into the street. He ignored the hot-burn pain of traumatized flesh that wanted to hobble him.

People stumbled out of houses—parents with children hugging their legs, teenagers with their cameras held up to catch the action, shuffling, squinting night-shift workers shocked out of what was their midnight. Simon slid into the flow of bodies and let it carry him behind the barrier of police cars and bodies.

Shaw had told him who "the bitch" was, after all. He had too much information. Back when he'd been in the Marines, Simon hadn't had any hobbies and his vices had been tame. He hadn't been a drinker. He certainly hadn't been a drunk. His vices weren't a secret, but nobody who'd just read his military record would think he'd ever crawl into a bottle, never mind that he'd already crawled back out of it. Only someone who knew him later—someone who had access to Syntech.

Jacob knew he drank, and he was an untrustworthy sham of a human being, but Simon trusted him anyhow. It might not be his first instinct, but he did.

Dev had access and knew Simon, but Lau had been recruited when Becca was dying. Maybe Simon could wrap his head around Dev committing corporate espionage and killing Clayton in a grand fuckup. The idea that he would have left Becca and Callie to do it? No.

Neither of them were women. That only left one option.

His train of thought faltered, derailed, and he staggered into a yawning man in sleep shorts and badly done tattoos. The man glared at him through bloodshot eyes, shoved him away, and grumbled under his breath as he stomped across the rough asphalt on bare feet.

Simon stood where he was, frozen in the middle of the street as his brain finally found the matching piece for the hole in what they knew.

He knew who'd stolen Clayton's project. He had no idea why, but he knew who.

"Hey, move," a woman with a squawking toddler on her hip snapped impatiently. She shoved at Simon until he stepped out of her way, and then she dragged her kids past him. Jarred out of his thoughts, Simon quickly started to walk again. The brief respite had given his leg time to decide that it did really hurt, and it cramped with pain as he pushed his way through the small crowd of residents.

Dev needed to know.

Simon pulled his phone out of his pocket and grimaced at the spider-web-smashed screen. That wasn't going to work. He dropped it back into his pocket and turned around to scan the crowd. The man he'd bumped into earlier was leaning against a battered Ford pickup, drinking something out of a Starbucks cup and scowling at the cops.

"Hey," Simon said as he walked over. "Could you give me a ride into a town? I have a meeting to get to."

Tattoos drained the Starbucks cup with a grimace and wiped his mouth on his sleeve. "You don't have your own car?"

Simon didn't lie as reflexively as Jacob, but that didn't mean he couldn't. He jerked his thumb toward the cars. "It's in there." He just didn't see why he needed to. There were easier ways to get people to do what you want. He pulled out his wallet and tugged a wad of cash out of it. "I can pay."

Tattoos rubbed his chin and weighed the money against the possibility that Simon was shady. The money won. He boosted himself up into the car, crumpled the Starbucks mug up, and tossed it over his shoulder.

"Get in," Tattoos said as he flicked the driver's side visor down. A spare set of keys fell into his waiting hand. "Where do you want to go?"

"Town," Simon said. The anesthetic effect of shock had worn off. It felt like someone was poking hot pliers into his leg. He'd had worse, but the combination of pain and adrenaline made his brain twitch. The back of his tongue felt gritty with sand, and he could feel the blood itch in his ear. A quick rub of his hand confirmed there wasn't any there. He licked dry lips, reminded himself he was crazy, and smiled thinly at Tattoos. "I'll tell you where when we get there."

CHAPTER NINETEEN

IT TURNED out someone had thought of the property search already. The house on La Cantera was owned by *About Time LLC*. Jacob supposed it was a comfort, in a way. He wouldn't want to be outsmarted and framed by someone who didn't think ahead.

He stood at the counter in the mall vet with Fozzy's lead double-wrapped around his wrist, and tapped the details out for Simon—assuming he ever checked his phone. Posters on the wall told him to fix his pet and check for ticks. In what he guessed was some sort of visual aid, there was a jar of the fat things crawling over each other on the counter. Jacob stood a good distance from them. He hit Send just as the young receptionist bopped out of the back, full of apologies for the delay.

"One of the cats got out," she said as she blotted the bloody backs of her hands on her scrubs. "He's a monster. I'm sorry. You wanted to get your puppy checked out?"

Jacob knelt down, picked Fozzy up, and grunted at the weight of the little barrel body in his arms. He set the dog down on the counter and hung on to his collar as his paws scrabbled in an attempt to run.

"Well, he's sort of mine," he said. "I was dating this guy for, like, a week? Now he's blown town and left me with this scruffbag."

The girl's eyes went huge with dismay. "Oh no." She took Fozzy's head in her hands and scritched his ears, which made the dog go cross-eyed. "You poor sweetie. Did your daddy go off without you? That's just horrible, but,"—her attention flicked up to Jacob—"we can't take him. It's policy. Otherwise—"

"No, that's fine," Jacob reassured her. "It's just… obviously this guy isn't the most reliable. So I just want to get scruffy here checked over. Make sure he's healthy before I find someone to take him on."

It was actually the truth. That was weird, but if it did the job….

"Oh, no problem, then," the girl said. She dropped down on her stool and pushed over to the computer with her sneaker toes. She tapped the keys with businesslike speed. "I can fit you in—"

"Today?" Jacob suggested. He tried his best smile when she looked up and her face squinched into dismay again. "I have a meeting to get to," he said apologetically. "I can't leave him in my apartment all day. I'll pay for kenneling him for the day? Please?"

He wasn't sure if it was his puppy eyes or Fozzy's that did the trick, but the girl gave in. "Okay," she said. "I can fit him in... late, late this afternoon. Is that okay?"

"More than okay," Jacob said. He gave her his details, his phone number, and the dog. If anything happened to him, at least the dog would be with someone who would take care of it.

He rolled mental eyes at himself as he walked out of the shop. The breakup couldn't come soon enough, as far as he was concerned, before he started strip-mining his bank accounts to fund orphanages instead of keeping Bali cabana boys in suntan oil.

There he was, back on familiar ground—lying.

OVERSIZED WREATHS of blue and silver Christmas baubles hung on the main gates, and a tasteful twenty-foot tree, strung with elegant glass snowflakes, stood outside the luxury apartment block. Most of the windows were bare, except for the occasional tasteful spray of orchids, but someone on the second floor had filled their balcony with a family of light-up snowmen.

Jacob perched on the low wall outside and idly swung his foot as he sipped his toffee latte and waited for someone to pick up the phone. He'd just started to wonder if they'd given the staff leave for Christmas when the call was answered.

"Hello," a smooth male voice said. "The Residences."

"Is that Kim?" Jacob asked. He'd had a roommate from Nantucket once, and he let his voice settle into the remembered cadences. "My assistant was speaking to you last week?"

He waited expectantly, ready to throw his fictional hard-done-by assistant under the bus if Kim was on duty. Instead the voice on the phone corrected him pleasantly.

"Actually this is Chris. I'm the location manager. How can I help you?"

"I just wanted to apologize ahead of time," Jacob said. "I'm going to be late for my viewing. Fox Bellamy."

There was a pause on the other end of the line. Jacob sipped his coffee and waited for Chris to finish his panicked schedule check. He wiped the pad of his thumb over his lower lip and caught a stray dollop of cream. Right on cue Chris cleared his throat apologetically.

"I'm afraid I can't find your appointment in our system, Mr. Bellamy. Are you sure it was for today?"

"I'm only in town for today," Jacob said. He pulled the phone away from his ear for a second, checked the time and added ten minutes. "I was supposed to be there for one twenty? The booking might have been under my assistant's name? Dan Adler."

There was another pause while Chris fruitlessly checked through the files. "I'm sorry. We don't have you booked in for a viewing. I can only apologize. Kim must have gotten the dates wrong, or misfiled your call...."

He sounded like his teeth were gritted. Based on the reviews online, this wasn't Kim's first screwup. She was name-checked more than once over bad service and bad recordkeeping. It was convenient to have a scapegoat to blame the mislaid appointment on.

"That's a shame," Jacob said. "I thought your apartments looked nice, but I have other buildings to see."

"I could fit you in... New Year?" Chris offered.

"Sorry," Jacob said. "I'm being seconded to the local office, and I don't have time to waste getting settled in. If I can't see the apartment this afternoon, I can't see it."

He paused to give Chris the opportunity to do the work for him. Bless him, he stepped up to the plate.

"When could you make it?" Chris asked, and the tenor of the phone altered as he tucked it under his ear. Papers shuffled around.

"If I don't hit any traffic, one thirty should be fine. After that I have other viewings all afternoon."

"That's...." There was a short huff of breath, and Chris edited whatever he'd been going to say. "That's fine, Mr. Bellamy. Just ask for me when you arrive, and I'll show you around?"

"Perfect," Jacob said. "I'll see you soon."

He hung up and nursed the last few mouthfuls of coffee as he scrolled through Amazon for "sorry about the whole airport thing" Christmas presents. For a small surcharge, Amazon even wrapped it for him. With a new coffeemaker heading to his sister—it would probably get there before he did—he made one last call.

A carefully measured five minutes late, Jacob hopped off the wall, tossed his empty cup in the bin, and headed past the oversized glittering Christmas tree on his way to the lobby.

"—AS YOU can see," Chris said as he opened the doors to the main bathroom. If he was irritated at the ad hoc walk-through, he didn't show it, and kept a smile on his face as he pointed out the best features of the elegant rooms. "Everything is finished to the highest specifications."

It was all white tile and claw-foot bath, the stark monochrome broken up by a splash of gold and red in the towels and shower curtain. Jacob's brain derailed and skipped "on the job" to head straight for a brief potent fantasy of fucking Simon in that bath. Wet, scarred flesh, callused fingers, and the smell of come and lavender on Jacob's skin. The tight, lean stretch of Simon's body under the milky water, the spread of his thighs, and the jut of his cock out of the bubbles.

He licked his lips as he imagined the taste of soap and wet flesh, and pulled his attention back to the job.

"It's nice," Jacob said. "But I'd prefer to be on the first floor. Are there any apartments available there?"

He didn't offer a justification, just waited expectantly. Chris's smoothly pleasant facade slipped for a second, and a muscle tightened under a slightly scarred cheek. Then he pulled it back.

"We do," he said. "But only one of the three-room family units. They're more expensive."

Jacob just waited. After a beat Chris gestured for Jacob to leave the room ahead of him. He kept up a running patter as they walked down the corridor to the elevator and then rode between floors in the brushed-steel box.

"This unit was actually just renovated and redecorated," Chris said when they stopped outside 14891. He opened the doors, stepped inside, and did a quick check around the space. Jacob stepped through behind and tripped into Chris hard enough to make the other man stagger. They stumbled backward into the room, a waltz of klutzes as they stepped around each other's feet. Chris grabbed Jacob's arm to support his weight and dropped his phone and keys.

"Sorry," Jacob said as he caught his balance and straightened up. "Long flight. Are you all right? I'm so sorry."

It was hard not to accept an apology. While Chris accepted his, Jacob ducked down and grabbed the phone and keys. He hung onto them and spun his apologies seamlessly into praise for the apartment.

"Oh, this I like. Would this be the unit I would have?" He walked away from Chris and into the bedroom. "Does it come furnished?"

He kept the small talk going as he walked quickly through the rooms. Does that rate include everything? When could he move in? What happened to the last resident? Do you allow dogs? By the time a frustrated Chris managed to ask, Can I have my—, he was so relieved to have them pressed back into his hands that he didn't count his keys.

Just in time too, as five minutes early, Chris's phone rang.

"Don't worry," Jacob told him generously. "You take that. I'll just have a look around."

Chris gave him a tight smile, turned his back, and headed for the bathroom as he had a terse, irritated argument about a delivery of a truckload of washing powder and bleach with whomever was on the other end. Jacob left him to it and headed into the other room. He made a brief circuit of the narrow, curved kitchen and then went to stick his head into the bedroom.

"—telling you, I didn't order—"

"Chris? I have to go to another meeting," Jacob interrupted and glanced down at his bare wrist in a mime of timekeeping. "I can let myself out, if that would be easier."

Chris tucked the phone against his shoulder. "Ah, that's not necessary—"

"No, no problem," Jacob said pleasantly. "I know the way. I will call tomorrow about the lease."

He waved his hand carelessly and left. Sometimes the easiest way to get people to let you do something was to just not give them a chance to argue. He left the apartment, walked briskly down the hall, and stopped at the elevator to send the car down to the ground floor. Just in case anyone asked.

A quick jog took him to the mystery woman's door, and the master key he'd filched from Chris's keyring got him inside. He pulled a pair of balled-up latex gloves out of his pocket, pulled them on, and snapped the fingers into place as he looked around.

The layout was a mirror image of the other apartment, and the decor was a slightly more shopworn version of the same grays and greige. No personal touches. No clutter—except for a stack of paperwork on the coffee table, weighted down by a coffee cup. Jacob sat down on the shiny edge of the cushion and moved the cup. He lifted it to his nose to take a sniff as he caught a hint of something acrid on the air.

It had been a while since whoever lived there had made coffee. A lip-stained cigarette butt floated in the dregs of what had probably once been quite good bourbon.

He flicked through the stack. Red pen was slashed and scribbled over the pages and notes and corrections elbowed for space between the printed lines, but it was nothing that Jacob could parse. A few sections looked similar to the code they looked at the night before, or the code he'd seen on screen during a *CSI: Cyber* rerun last week.

Jacob pulled his phone out to scan a couple of the pages. He had three images uploading to the cloud when he heard a key in the lock.

"Shit," he mouthed. "Fuck."

He shoved the papers back together, set the boozy cup back on top, and scrambled off the couch. His hands shook with the sudden jolt of adrenaline... and fear. Mostly fear. The bruise on the back of his hand was still livid enough he could see it through the latex glove.

A quick list of escape options ran through his brain as he glanced around the room. The balcony caught his attention for a second, and then he snorted. That was it. No more action movies. They gave him ridiculous ideas.

Jacob scrambled over the arm of the couch, dashed into the crescent-moon kitchen, and went down on his knees behind the counter. His kneecaps cracked against the hard tiles and made him bite back a curse, but at least it gave him more than one exit if he needed it.

At eye level there was a stack of pill boxes—allergy medication, thyroid, a bottle of B12, and syringes. Jacob stared at them but didn't really see them as he listened to the door open and someone come into the room. It was the voice that caught his attention at first, an accent far from home and with a vaguely familiar smoky contralto. Then the name on the medications came into focus.

Nora Reyes. In the months Jacob had spent infiltrating Syntech, he'd never had any reason to focus on her. He'd done his research, though. She'd been the deceased Becca Porter's roommate at college and Devon's lab partner. Porter had hired her right after Syntech was founded and rescued her from the life of an associate lecturer.

The image of the paper Simon had found at Clayton's house flashed through Jacob's head. *Useful for no project.* "No" wasn't a negative. It was a nickname.

"Simon, where the hell are you? I need to talk to you," Nora said. She sounded sharp and clipped the words off between her teeth as though she were angry or nervous…. A lighter flicked, and she sucked in air. Collecting herself…? "It's all gotten out of hand. This wasn't what it was meant to be like. I just wanted… needed…. I need to talk to you. Call me back when you get this. It's important. Please."

Jacob shifted forward and tried to peer around the edge of the counter. He needed to get out of there and call Simon—let him know what was going on. A small disruptive part of his brain tried to ahem its way into the discourse—or we *could* blackmail her—but that was not the part of his brain he wanted to listen to today.

Tomorrow…. Well, tomorrow's bad ideas deserved their chance to make their case.

He couldn't see Nora. In his head he mapped out the apartment and moved a static mental cutout of the dark-haired woman from one spot to another. She could have walked over to the windows. It was a good view to brood over. If she was, and if she was alone, Jacob could maybe get to the door and out without her catching him. She'd know someone had been in the flat, but not who.

A sharp metallic click interrupted his thoughts. It was an indictment of the last few weeks that Jacob immediately knew it was a gun. His balls tried to squeeze back up into his groin and fought his dropped stomach for space as he froze.

"We haven't met," Nora said, a bitter half laugh trembling in her words, "but you, Mr. Archer, have been a royal pain in my ass."

Jacob closed his eyes for a second. He wished he'd taken the time for a piss after he finished his coffee. It wasn't exactly dignified, dying with wet pants. He opened his eyes, sat back on his haunches, and turned around.

The dark elegant woman, whose photo was currently taking up space in his phone's memory, was standing in front of him. She'd lost five inches in height because she left her shoes behind in favor of sneaking up on him with silk-muffled feet, and there was a small classy-looking gun in her hand. It was aimed at Jacob's head, and her hand was rock steady all the way to her shoulder.

He didn't think she was bluffing about knowing how to use it.

"You haven't exactly made my life easier," he said. "You framed me for murder."

Her mouth twisted, and the generous red curve turned into a thin, sour line. "You deserved it. Harry wouldn't be dead if it weren't for you. None of this would be happening if it weren't for you." Her voice cracked when she said Clayton's name, but her eyes were dry as she jerked the gun. "Get up. You put yourself in the middle of this. Now you get a front row to how it ends."

Chapter Twenty

MARION, TEXAS had one thing going for it. No one gave a man in a bloody suit carrying a bag from the convenience store a second look as he limped into the bathroom. The lock was broken. Simon wedged the door shut and kicked the scarred chunk of wood under it with the heel of his shoe. The exertion of doing that broke a sour sweat on him, and a wave of dizzying nausea washed over him.

He leaned on the sink, flexed his fingers against the cracked china, and waited for the sickness to ebb. Once it did he turned the cold tap on full, cupped his hands under the stream, and splashed it over his face. Icy rivulets ran down his chest and funneled along the line of muscle to his stomach. It cleared his head, slapped the dopey distance of shock out of him, and made him realize he was thirsty. He licked the water off his lips to cut the dust on his tongue.

His reflection in the fly-spotted mirror looked combat ready, with dust caked on his skin and blood sprayed over his cheek and temples. It set his nerves on edge—made them hot and itchy under his skin and made his muscles ache with trigger-ready eagerness. His therapist would call it paranoia, but with Shaw in the wind, Simon called it good sense. But then he supposed that's what he'd say if he were paranoid.

There'd been no sign of Lau on the circuit of the town that Simon had bribed his yawning chauffeur to take. He was either on his way to Syntech to blow the whistle or he was on the run. Simon couldn't blame him either way.

There was also the off chance that Shaw had Lau. Simon hoped not, but there wasn't anything he could do about it anymore.

He stripped his trousers off. Blood had glued the fabric to his leg, and it tore away the thin scab over the wound as it peeled off. Simon grimaced and drew his lips back from his teeth at the needle of pain that wriggled through the meat of his thigh. Fresh blood oozed sluggishly from the broken-open wound.

He grabbed the rough first-aid supplies he'd grabbed from the shelves—gauze pads, oversized Band-Aids, and antibiotic cream. He covered the worm-track wound with a blob of white cream from one end to the other, and it went pink around the edges as the blood mixed with it. Simon slapped a pad over it, pressed it down with his palm to spread the cream, and secured it with Band-Aids.

Blood and stained water ran down his leg. Simon used a handful of paper towels from the dispenser to roughly wipe his leg off. Then he shook out the jeans he'd grabbed on his way through the store and pulled them on. The cheap denim clung to his wet skin, and stains showed dark against the prefaded fabric.

It would do.

The bin at the door was knee height and smelled like vomit and baby shit. Simon lifted out a handful of trash, dumped his bloody bits and pieces in, and covered them over. He washed his hands quickly in the sink, dried them on his hips, and wrestled the door open again.

No one bothered to give him a second look on the way out. He stopped at the cash machine.

There was a teenager loitering outside on the hood of an ancient Chevy that was as much primer as paint. He was nursing along a cigarette like a drunk with his last beer as he fiddled with a cracked-screen iPhone.

"Loan me your car," Simon said as he walked over.

The kid looked up and screwed his face up in contemptuous dismissal. Then he saw the handful of fifties that Simon held out. His eyes went wide, and he squinted.

"This legit?" he asked suspiciously.

"What do you care?"

After he thought about that for a second, the kid realized it was a good deal and slid off the car. He fished the keys out of his pocket and held them out, but he hung on to the fob with a tight grip until the cash was in his hand.

"Phone too," Simon said. "One call."

The kid had already counted the number of bills he held, thumbed his way through the stack with a licked thumb. Simon could have asked for a kidney and probably gotten some serious consideration. He handed the phone over without question.

Once the sweaty plastic and glass was in his hand, Simon hesitated. He *needed* to know that Jacob was okay. The doubt was an anxious weight in his chest, but... if there was anyone that he could count on to take care of himself first, it was Jacob. He called Devon instead as loyalty overrode guilt at the choice.

It rang drearily in his ear until it clicked over to voice mail. An anonymous voice mildly told Simon that there was no room to leave a message before it hung up on him. Shit. He pulled up the texts—winced out of the boob-heavy message thread—and typed out a brusque order to *Answer the damn phone. Simon.* It wouldn't help if Dev was busy or in the lab, but it might just be that he didn't recognize the number and was screening.

"You said one call," the kid said.

"I lied," Simon said as he waited for the message to send. Once it did he tried again. That time Dev answered it immediately.

"Why the hell aren't you using your phone?" he grumbled at Simon. There was pop music in the background, something upbeat and relentless, and the sound of Callie telling her dad to say hi from her.

"It's broken," Simon said. "Where are you?"

"In the car," Dev said. "Callie got in a fight at school. They're trying to suspend her for punching some boy who was harassing her. It's ridiculous—"

"Good," Simon said. "Look, has Nora been to the house in the last few days?"

"Nora?" Dev repeated. He sounded baffled. "I don't know. I guess she might have…. Callie says she came over a couple of days ago to drop off some stuff from work. I thought it was just couriered over."

"Call the security team in," Simon said. "Have them sweep the building."

There was a pause, and then Devon said, "Hold on a second."

After a breath the engine and music cut off and Simon heard the heavy clunk of the door closing. When Devon spoke again, his voice sounded like he was in the open air.

"You think Nora's involved?" He sounded skeptical. Simon didn't blame him. Time served, Nora had been more a part of the family than Simon had been. When she was getting chemo, Becca had sent Simon selfies of her and Nora grinning and confident—before the doctors said it wasn't working.

"I'm pretty sure," Simon said. "It all fits. According to my source, this all started four years ago. When you took your sabbatical and Nora stepped in."

It took a second, but not as long as Simon had expected. Maybe Dev had had his suspicions already and just needed a lens to focus them.

"Shit. I'll have to let the board know," Dev said.

"I can't prove it," Simon said. "Not yet."

"They couldn't prove I was involved. Didn't stop them ousting me. I expect they'll do the same with Nora. Where are you?"

"On my way back," Simon said. "I'll let you know when I get there."

"Is there any way we can keep this in-house?" Dev asked. Self-consciously he added, "Becca loved her."

"She was responsible for killing Clayton, Dev."

"Not directly," Dev said. "You said yourself, he wasn't meant to die. And a jail term for Nora won't bring him back."

He didn't look it, but Dev had always been too forgiving. The people he loved could treat him like a dog, and he'd make excuses for them—his mom, his brother, even Becca when they'd been younger. Simon wasn't like that. The only person he'd ever forgiven was Jacob.

"I'll try," he said.

He didn't say how hard. Dev seemed to accept it anyhow.

"Call me when you get in," he said.

The phone went dead. Hopefully he'd just hung up. Simon grimaced, but he would just have to have faith. He wiped the number from the phone's memory. Done, he tossed it back to the kid with a grunt of thanks and climbed into the car.

Despite the battered appearance, the engine rattled to life without too much trouble. Simon shifted into drive, hit the gas, peeled away from the curb, and screeched out of town.

Simon had taken forty minutes to get to Marion. He wanted to see how fast he could get back to San Antonio.

IT TOOK thirty. The Chevy's exhaust rattled like a dying smoker's cough, and the cab was filled with the burned-toast smell of smoldering wires. Simon ditched it at his apartment building and dragged himself out. His injured leg had stiffened as he drove, and a dull ache throbbed up into his groin as he put weight on it. Blood had seeped through his make-do bandage and dried into a stiff red-brown patch on his jeans.

He had to look like shit. One of his neighbors was walking her dog, doing a circuit of the green space in a designer dress and old sneakers.

She started to yell a protest about him leaving an oil-pissing wreck in the forecourt, but changed her mind when she got a good look at him.

Simon limped inside, gritted his teeth against the weakness in his leg, and took the elevator up. As he leaned back against the car, he felt the slime of sweat run down his spine to the small of his back. He let himself into his apartment and impatiently stripped off his sour-smelling, sweat-damp shirt.

The kitchen was clean, the surfaces so scrubbed down that Simon could still smell the bleach. There was also a pan handle sticking out of the garbage can, which twitched a resigned smile out of Simon. No sign of Jacob or his borrowed dog, though.

Half-naked, unbuttoned jeans hanging loose around his hips, Simon hobbled into the bedroom and grabbed his old emergency phone from the drawer. He popped it open and swapped the sim card from his smashed phone. His fingers fumbled at the delicate task.

It had buzzed twice on the drive there, but the ringtone shrieked out before it got strangled in the cracked speakers. He'd tried to answer—on the off chance it might connect—but jolts of sound was all the battered piece of tech could manage.

The plan was to make himself presentable, get to Dev, and confront Nora. That plan changed when the phone booted up and he saw two voice mails from Nora waiting for him.

He hesitated as dread settled in his gut with cold certainty, and then he tapped the icon. The first message was from someone who knew their cover was blown. The second was from someone who'd found an ace in the hole.

"I have Mr. Archer," she said. Her voice was cool and professional, detached, as though she were scheduling a meeting instead of a hostage exchange. "We need to meet. Call me, and I'll tell you where."

There were a lot of things that Simon knew he should do—contact Dev, call the police, be smart, and be tactical. What he did was call Nora back.

"What do you want?"

IT WASN'T where he'd have chosen to meet, but it was somewhere out of the way. The red struts of the bridge stood out dramatically against the pale sky and punched through the heavy foliage that led to the Incarnate

Word campus. It was strung with reams of Christmas lights that waited to be turned on at dusk.

Nora stood by the metal rail in the shadow of the trees with her arm hooked around Jacob's.

For a second, as he stood in front of them, Simon wondered if it had all been one very elaborate double-cross. The suspicion should have dug its hooks in. Jacob was hardly above betraying him. But it couldn't find any traction. It just skated over the surface of his brain and was gone.

"You okay?" He searched Jacob's pale, tight face. The aging bruises stood out like paint on his skin.

Jacob looked at him like he was an idiot.

"No," he said. "Not so much."

He shifted his weight. In the second before Nora yanked him back into her side, Simon got a glimpse of something black and deadly looking jammed into Jacob's ribs. He stepped forward as anger propelled him like a hand in the small of his back.

"Don't," Nora warned him and ground the muzzle deeper into Jacob's ribs until he winced. "Not if you want to keep him."

Simon stopped like someone had nailed his feet to the bridge.

"Nora," he said. "What the fuck are you doing?"

She gave him a tight red smile that didn't reach over her cheekbones.

"I know you aren't the genius in the family," she said. "But haven't you put it together yet?"

Jacob cleared his throat. "She's Clayton's mystery woman," he said. "If that helps clear anything up."

Simon worked his jaw from one side to the other and pretended the pop of the damaged hinge released some of the wire-tight tension in his spine.

"I misspoke," he said, his voice clipped and curt with anger. "I've got the what. You stole Harry's code so you could run some sort of stealth research product behind Dev's back. You killed Harry. You framed Jacob for it. Sound about right?"

Nora's eyes flickered, and emotion tightened her lips. "I didn't kill Harry," she said.

"He's dead."

"That wasn't what I wanted."

"No," Simon admitted. "I know that. You wanted to talk to him."

"Yes."

"Since he was dead, though," Simon continued, without acknowledging he'd heard her, "you went ahead and sent all the information on what *you'd* done to PeaPod and blamed Dev for it. Next step—and I can't take credit for working this out, since you actually told me—would have been regretfully stepping up to take over after Dev got forced out of the company."

"Sounds like he's got your number," Jacob said.

Nora tightened her fingers on his arm and dug them in through his shirt. "If I were you," she hissed. "I'd shut up. None of this would have happened if it weren't for you. Nobody would have been hurt."

"If you hadn't *started* this, nobody would have gotten hurt," Simon growled. "Fuck, Nora, we were friends. You and Dev have known each other—"

"*Becca* was my friend," Nora spat. Emotion flushed her face as her voice rose. "I knew *Becca* since we were in school. Dev was along for the ride—the plus-one to Becca's company. Now she's *gone*, and what do I have?"

"What did you *want?*" Simon asked. Below them, people in the park paused and looked up. He could imagine their curious expressions. "Dev would have given it to you. You just had to ask."

"Why should I have to ask?" Nora spat back at him. "Why should I ask for him to give me something, when I'd earned it? I broke my back when Becca was sick, taking over the company and being there for the three of them. I went to the hospital, I had sleepovers for Callie when *I* hadn't slept in a week because I was trying to deal with the board. I cooked fucking casseroles. I had to look it up on the Internet to learn how. Then she died, and Dev came back to Syntech and pissed on all my hard work. Every contract I'd sweated blood negotiating, every project that he hadn't thought up, just shoved into storage. It wasn't fair."

Targeting algorithms and a new identity with inky government fingerprints all over it for Lau.

"The DoD deal," he said. "Nora, you knew Dev wouldn't agree to that. First time it came up, you knew he'd blackball the deal when he got back."

She twisted her mouth to the side and hitched one shoulder in a wry shrug. "I thought he might respect me enough to hear me out," she said. "When he didn't, I realized that he never would. But I didn't want to take his company. I wanted to set up my own. With the projects *I'd* been working on, the contracts that *I'd* set up."

"Using Syntech research and intellectual property." Jacob shook his head. The long shadows from the bridge flickered across his face like bars. "Trust me—this is my wheelhouse—they never would have let you get away with it."

It was Simon who corrected him. "She would have," he said. He watched Nora's face as he talked—the uneasy mixture of pride, confidence, and shame that set around her mouth. "The DoD isn't fond of their contractors giving out the details of their covert projects. If her plan had worked, she'd have disappeared, and her projects would have gone with her. Except it didn't work, did it, Nora?"

"You think I don't know that?" Nora said. The bitterness in her voice seemed to catch her by surprise. She hesitated and then let go of Jacob's arm and held her hands up. He stumbled away from her and then stopped as though he wasn't sure what he should do. The gun rested against the cup of Nora's palm—small, dark, and nearly hidden. "It wasn't meant to be like this, Simon. No one was meant to get hurt. I just wanted something for myself. Now I don't know what to do. No one's listening to me anymore, and I don't know how to fix any of this. I need your help."

It should have been pathetic. Somehow, though, Nora managed to hang on to a certain spare dignity. The bare bones of her honesty kept her back straight. Whatever she'd done that she was ashamed of, she wasn't ashamed to ask for help.

The dull thump was low enough that Simon barely noticed it. Then something flicked his ear, and Nora jolted backward. Her eyes went wide, as if she'd seen something that surprised her, and she reached up to grab her shoulder. That was when Simon saw the blood, oozing out of the cloth she was squeezing between her fingers.

CHAPTER TWENTY-ONE

IT TOOK Jacob longer than it should to realize what happened. There was nothing cinematic about it—no ear-rattling bang, no dramatic spray of gore—just a jolt and a gasp. Then he saw the blood dripping onto the bridge and put the pieces together.

Nora's gasp turned into a sigh and a long, slow hum of defeat, and she slid down the side of the bridge. There was something almost graceful about it, in the designer silk drape of her suit and the neat tuck of shiny leather heels under her folded legs.

"Fuck," Jacob said. His eyes were glued to Nora's hand as the blood welled between her fingers and trickled down between her knuckles.

"Jake, get down." Simon grabbed his arm and tugged him down into a crouch. He held his gun in the other hand, tucked discreetly down at his thigh. "We need to get out of here."

"What about her?" Jacob asked.

"That's her problem," Simon said grimly. There was a smear of blood on his cheek and his mouth as more shots pinged off the bridge. They chipped the red paint and scraped raw lines in the metal. "You're mine. Follow me."

Dark head ducked under the level of the railings, he headed toward the stairs down to the park. Jacob glanced after him, and some irreverent part of his brain wondered how Simon made crab-walking appear elegant and dangerous. Then he looked back down at Nora.

Simon was right. After everything Nora had done to Jacob, it was hardly his problem that her chickens had come home to roost. Except she looked shaken and small, and he'd been there. Mostly because of her, but still.

"I never even thought to make a rule against this." He pulled her arm over his shoulder and helped her up into a crouch. Her weight settled on his shoulder, and she muttered something grateful between clenched teeth. Jacob snorted and got her moving. He ducked as they stumbled after Simon. "Yeah? You want to pay me back? Anyone asks, you offered me money."

Jacob's mouth was so dry his tongue tasted like felt, and he could smell the blood and sweat coming off Nora. Her fingers dug into his shoulder, and she gasped raggedly. It made him want to apologize for hurting her, but there was no way for him not to.

He took his gaze off Simon's broad back for a second and glanced down through a gap in the bridge. There were two men walking across the grass at as close to a run as they could get without drawing attention. They carried their jackets draped over their arms. It looked awkward, but good for hiding things.

"Did it never occur to you, when you were hiring these guys, that you'd gone too far?" Jacob asked.

Nora snorted. "I didn't hire them," she said. "Laramie, my contact at the DoD, put me in touch with Shaw when I found out you'd robbed us. I hired Shaw, and he found the others. Like I said, without you none of this would have happened."

"If you hadn't conned Clayton, none of this would have happened," Jacob shot back.

They reached the steps down where Simon was waiting for them. He gave Jacob an annoyed look, and he answered with a shrug. It wasn't like Jacob had any good reason for what he was doing. Simon shook his head, gave a barely there twitch of his chin, and dropped the issue.

He sent Jacob and Nora down the steps ahead of him. Jacob had to half drag Nora, and her weight nearly toppled them both as she tripped over her feet.

"We need to get out of here," Simon said as they reached the bottom.

"We need to call the cops," Jacob protested. "This is the one time they'd actually be useful."

Simon handed him his phone. "Feel free, as soon as we're out of range of their cell jammer," he said. His mouth twitched with annoyance as he looked at Nora. "When your rent-a-thugs started trying to kill people, didn't it occur to you *then* that things were getting out of hand?"

She huffed a laugh between clenched teeth. "Like I said, they aren't listening to me anymore," she said. "Shaw went behind my back to Laramie, and now he's been put in charge. I answer to him."

"So none of this was your fault?" Jacob asked skeptically.

"No," Nora said quietly. "It was my fault, but it's not what I had planned. I told Shaw I didn't want anyone hurt, that we didn't need to hurt anyone. If I'd just had a chance to talk to Harry, none of this would have happened."

Simon shook his head and shoved them into motion. He was limping, Jacob noted. Worry tweaked at him, but their current situation seemed more pressing. As they reached the edge of the trees, he saw one of the two men stop on the grass. The man dropped his jacket and lifted a weirdly long gun.

It coughed. From where Jacob stood it sounded like a polite "ahem" when you blocked the aisle in a mall. Nora dragged him down to his knees as she swore and clutched her shoulder and fresh blood welled from the injury. The bullet hit a tree instead of him and spit out splinters.

Simon turned and raised his gun in one smooth movement. He went still, and his shoulders dropped as though he'd just found an opportunity to relax. Then he fired back. The crack of the gunshot was a lot more like what Jacob expected from watching TV.

The shooter staggered and fell over. He clutched at his leg with one hand, and blood soaked into the grass in a rapidly spreading puddle that suggested something important had been hit. Someone screamed. Maybe, Jacob thought woozily, the same people he'd seen earlier. The shooter's friend was frozen in place and hesitated as he tried to work out what to do.

"Move." Simon spat the order at them. He twisted at the waist and kept the gun pointed at the man still on his feet.

Stones dug into Jacob's hands as he pushed himself to his feet. Although it increasingly looked like a bad idea, he helped Nora back up as well. She put her weight on him for a second and then pushed him away.

"I'm okay," she said. "I don't need help."

It was a lie. Her voice shook and her skin had gone a washed-out taupe color—gray under the soft topaz brown of her skin tone. Jacob thought he might challenge her, but decided he'd done enough. He stepped to Simon.

"Si...."

"Go," Simon said, but didn't shift his attention. With the hand that wasn't holding the gun, he gestured toward the path. "Walk fast. Don't run. I'll be behind you."

Five steps later it occurred to Jacob that he should have waited or made some sort of protest. The whole "no, not without you" moment.

Except that wasn't in Jacob's nature, not even for Simon. Besides, he wasn't the badass.

He walked quickly along the path and occasionally broke into two steps worth of a jog before he managed to slow down. It didn't make him stand out. A few people headed toward the sound of gunfire, but most had the good sense not to. Nora had paused to kick off her heels and stumbled along doggedly behind him with her shoes in her hand.

Jacob glanced over his shoulder. The tight knot in his chest relaxed a couple of notches when he saw Simon loping along after him, although he still favored one leg.

"What happened?" Jacob asked when they paused in the middle of the path. "Why did they give up?"

"Public attention," Simon said flatly. He put a hand in the small of Jacob's back to get him moving again. A quick look at Nora took in the grim set of her mouth and the way she stumbled again. He tucked his arm around her waist, ignored her twitch of reaction at the contact, and held her hand up as they walked. "Right now that's the last thing Shaw wants."

"He *just* tried to kill us in a public park," Jacob pointed out.

"No, he tried to kill Nora," Simon corrected. "Killing her before she could talk to us was worth the risk, if they could do it quickly and cleanly. A public slaughter? Bit too much heat for his purposes. Not when he still has other options."

They briskly cut across the grass. Jacob continued to try Simon's phone and waited for a connection to click back on. As they got closer to the gates, there were more people to move through. Two women carried infants in their arms. Other children hung on to their skirts with grass-stained hands. Still more loitered near a bench, craning their necks.

"I think someone got shot," one said and bent down to scoot a little boy out of Jacob's way. "Probably gangs or something."

She gave Nora a curious look and her eyes twitched with suspicion. Except Nora, in her designer—if slightly soggy—suit didn't look right for the unfolding story. Jacob thought of a couple of lies that would have cemented that doubt. He didn't see the point of telling them.

That was new. He must be sick.

A couple of kids with smartphones raised them and, with cameras streaming, headed into the park. One of them walked backward and talked into the camera as they went. Before they got too far, the park officials who'd finally turned up shooed them back to safety.

Jacob turned around and walked sideways. One of the park people had a walkie instead of a phone and talked intently into it as she gestured and wiped her face on her sleeve. There was a stain on her tan shirt that could have been blood or mud.

"The cops will be here soon," he said. "It kinda goes against the grain, but should we wait for them?"

Simon glanced around to clock the same woman that Jacob had. He thought about it for a second and then shook his head.

"I'd rather be in control of that particular conversation," he said. "Nora's in no condition to make a statement right now, and if we get separated.... Shaw's a professional. It wouldn't be too hard for him to get to someone in a hospital. Or a jail. You're still a person of interest, remember?"

Jacob shoved his hand through his hair. His fingers caught in the sweated-in mats, and he flashed a smirk over at Simon. It might have been a bit shaky around the edges, but he thought it was a pretty good effort under the circumstances.

"Yeah. Well, I'm used to that," he said. "People are always interested in me."

"That's because you lie," Simon pointed out. They squeezed through the log jam at the gates and stepped out onto the pavement. "How much of what you told me about yourself was even true?"

Jacob hesitated. "I don't know," he said. "A... reasonable percentage? Over half at least."

Simon snorted. "Keep walking."

THE PARKING garage was dimly lit and full of the heavy smell of old oil and exhaust fumes. It was hot too, and the air was sticky under the low concrete canopies. Jacob fidgeted nervously in place as Simon propped Nora against the hood of a silver Porsche.

The elevator wasn't working—yellow tape and an apology had been strung over the doors. A one-ramp walk wiped Nora out. Simon too. He'd keep on until his leg fell off, but he'd gone tight over the temples, and his limp had gotten worse.

Nora braced her hands against the sleek slope of metal and tried to push herself up. Her hand left bloody prints on the paintwork, and they smeared like gory finger paints when she slipped.

"That's going to give somebody nightmares," Jacob muttered. He wiped his hands on his thighs, scrubbed the sweat off his palms into the denim, and held one out. "Give me the keys. I'll get the car."

Simon looked at him. "You can't drive."

"I lied." Jacob shrugged. He wriggled his fingers. "I can drive. Give me the keys."

Disappointment settled in the lines of Simon's face. He snorted, twisted his mouth, and said, "Of course you did." He pulled the fob—no keys required, of course—out of his pocket and tossed them to Jacob. "Black Lexus. Syntech plates. Fourth level."

Jacob caught it. The plastic felt like a lump of ice in his hand. He could drive. It didn't mean he wanted to. The last time he'd been behind the wheel of a car, he'd been sixteen and taking his test under the influence of half of one of his sister's Valium. Still, he closed his fingers around the fob. It wasn't as though the basic process of moving the car would have to change. He didn't even have to take it on the road, just roll it down a couple flights.

There was no reason to sweat like a pig at a barbecue.

"Won't be long," he said.

He jogged up the ramp. The soles of his sneakers scraped on the rough concrete, and he grabbed the wall to swing around the corner at the top. Next floor the lights fluttered on as the motion sensor caught his movement and bathed the dim structure in weak yellow light. There were around twenty cars scattered through the space, most of them suburban-nice and a few dusty and battered.

He walked halfway down the lane and then hit the fob. Headlights flashed a few spaces down, and the car clicked as the locks disengaged. The Lexus was parked between two Jeeps, both close enough that it was going to be tight to get into the door.

"Open spaces everywhere—" His voice sounded small in the rubbery silence. "—and he has to park between the two biggest cars here."

At least he'd reversed in.

Jacob took a breath, exhaled, and puffed his cheeks out. It was the sort of moment where you remembered some nugget of folksy childhood wisdom from your dad. Except the only good advice his dad ever gave Jacob was "don't work hard, work smart."

"Yeah. Well, close enough, I guess," Jacob muttered. He took a deep breath, peeled one foot up off the floor, and headed for the car. It was drive or admit he'd lied, and he had never willingly done the latter in his life.

There was just enough room to squeeze between the Lexus and the Jeep. Simon hadn't been so careful, Jacob noticed. There were scratches all over the door of the Jeep, dug into the paintwork at about hip-height on a tall man. He supposed he was kind of pleased that Simon had been worried enough about him to be careless with a car. He reached for the door.

CHAPTER TWENTY-TWO

"I'M GOING to die," Nora said as Simon sliced up the seam of her trousers.

Her voice was scratchy and shaken. It was the voice of a younger Nora Reyes, the one Becca had known at school. The voice of the girl she'd shared a room and classes with, who'd ducked through the background of Skype calls when Simon talked to his sister and once tracked him down to get a taped birthday message for Becca.

Despite what she'd done, Simon couldn't help but feel sympathy for that girl. He ripped the expensive strip of fabric off.

"You aren't going to die."

The words came out on autopilot—prestrung and loaded in his brain for just this sort of occasion. But this time it was probably true. There might be damage to the joint, but she wasn't bleeding heavily enough to have damaged an artery. That meant she'd survive long enough to get treatment. He'd seen people take a lot more damage and walk, or at least limp, away from it.

He pressed the wad of fabric to the hole in her shoulder and blood squelched around his fingers. He glanced around and waited to hear the growl of the engine. Jacob should have gotten to the car by then.

"Not from being shot." Nora nagged his attention again. She gave him a thin smile with lips that had blanched down to a pale, almost-chalky pink, and she flicked the fingers of her good hand out in a gesture that encompassed more than the garage. "From this. Either to stop me exposing them, or to make an example of me for exposing them."

"This isn't the sort of thing the US government murders people over," he told her. He took his hand away, and she reached up to hold the makeshift bandage in place. "Trust me. You're small potatoes."

"People do kill each other over this, though," she said. Her mouth tightened, and she added bitterly, "I did, didn't I? Poor Harry. He died thinking he'd been a fool."

"Wasn't he?"

Nora shook her head. "No. Me and your thief have that in common. We started off by stealing something, but then we fell in love."

"Jacob would be surprised to hear that," Simon muttered and ignored the pinch in his heart at the idea. Nora ignored him.

"I should have told Harry what I'd done," she said. "Except, it didn't seem to matter anymore. I loved him, and he was helping me *anyhow*. I didn't have to lie to him. He wanted to help me. So why rock the boat? Then I saw the files that the thief had accessed, and I knew it was about to fall apart. I just didn't realize how... conclusively."

"I'm not a priest," Simon said. "And I don't want to forgive you."

She blinked at him and then lifted one shoulder in a resigned shrug. Her mouth pleated into a perversely amused smile. "Who else have I got to tell? All my friends are dead."

"Nora—"

A punch of concussive force from above cut Simon off and made him stagger as the structure shifted under his feet. The shriek of disturbed alarms filled the air, along with the smell of burning oil and smoke. After a still moment, the building's sprinkler system kicked in and pissed lukewarm water on him that did nothing to dispel the *heat and dust on his tongue and the itch of his own blood ringing in his ears*. Memory was stronger than the distant sensation of water misting on his skin.

He *wanted* to yell for Jacob, but his brain was like a funnel. It squeezed in around the edges and left less and less room for anything that wasn't a shopworn replay of old actions. He took a deep breath, held it, and struggled to hold on to control.

"What the hell," Nora said, her voice scratchy and distorted through the static rustle in his ears. She was back on her feet but leaned heavily on the car. "What happened?"

His voice had to squeeze out of his throat. "Explosion. We have to go."

"What about...?"

"He's dead," Simon said. It didn't hurt. He just felt empty, and flat competency stood in for reaction. Maybe he'd feel something later, but whiskey could help with that. "We're not. Move."

He dragged her off the car, held her up by his grip on her bicep, and marched her toward the stairs. Under the cacophony of dueling alarms— horns and klaxons and wails—he caught the scuff of feet on stairs.

It could have been aid, but that was... convenient and fast.

"Fuck."

"They want me," Nora said. Her body turned into dead weight as she stopped helping him. "Just go."

He yanked her along with him. "You aren't getting out of this. You're going to testify against your 'friend' Laramie and clear Dev's name. You owe Becca that much. You owe Callie that much. She's lost her mom, she's losing you—you can't take her dad away too."

Invoking the kid worked. Nora's shoulders slumped as the defiance drained out of her. She dredged some energy up from somewhere and staggered along with him toward the ramp. Two steps down the oily concrete slope, and a familiar black Jeep rolled up to block their path. Behind the tinted glass, Simon could see Shaw's smug smile. The car settled back on its tires as the brakes were pressed and the door cracked open.

Simon drew his gun in one easy movement and fired. Bullets pocked the reinforced glass and pinned Shaw behind the door. The sound echoed back off the walls and made his already-compromised ears ache.

"Back up." Simon pushed Nora with his shoulder.

They retreated just as the puffy-mouthed Milo and two other men burst out of the stairwell. Simon snapped off two shots, scattered them, and hit one in the arm. The injured man staggered, tripped his companions, and fired back blindly. Simon dodged into the cover of an old blue Toyota, glanced around, and tried to focus through the smog of old actions as they jostled for primacy in his brain. Fire above, enemies here, and below....

"You got a plan, Ramsey?" Shaw asked as he appeared at the top of the ramp. He was wearing a bulletproof vest buckled tight under his jacket and carrying a semiautomatic. Simon cursed and pushed Nora farther into the cover of the car. "Because I can't see how this is going to end well for you."

The odds hadn't been good. They had just gotten worse.

"You blew up my car."

"Yes," Shaw agreed cheerfully. "With your history and that VA file, no one would have questioned it. Taking Nora along with you is a bit odder, but once it came to light that you were working together to destroy Dev Porter.... Well, then it's just tidy, isn't it? This, though, ah... this is more of a mess. Come out."

Simon blinked dust out of his eyes—*sandy boots and loose trousers approached the Jeep, framed by the starburst of shattered glass.* He snorted.

"Get fucked."

"I don't have time for this," Shaw said flatly. "You've already made this messy. I can make it very messy. That'll be painful."

Simon fired around the bumper of the car. He missed and gouged a chunk out of the ground. Shaw jumped back. He spat out a curse and stitched gunfire across the front of the. The tires popped in ribbons of rubber. The chassis shuddered under the impact and jarred Simon's bones.

"Can you run?" he asked Nora.

She shook her head. "I don't think so."

"Try."

He crawled to the back of the car. Shaw said something, but it didn't seem worth it to pay attention. Simon crouched at the bumper, tried to ignore the tearing ache in his thigh, and then lunged out. He fired off three shots in quick succession, scattered the goons, and caught Shaw square in the chest. The vest stopped it from being fatal, but it still knocked him back on his heels.

Impact with the ground ripped something loose in Simon's shoulder. It felt like hot wire pulled the joint apart, and the arm went loose and awkward. He switched the gun to his other hand and took another shot as he rolled onto his knees. Milo went down with a shattered shin and dropped his gun like an amateur.

Shaw hadn't.

The impact caught Simon in the chest and knocked him off balance. He grunted out a ragged noise that gave on being a curse halfway through, and he tried to lift the gun. Neither arm would cooperate. Shaw stepped forward and roughly twisted the weapon out of his hand.

"You're a loyal bastard," Shaw said mildly. "I'll give you that. It's not going to do you any good, though."

"You think Dev will let this go?" Simon asked raggedly and clenched his jaw against the pain. "Trust me. That's not one of his strengths."

Shaw pressed the gun against Simon's temple, hard enough to bruise. "Then I guess I'll have to kill him too."

Simon closed his eyes. A shot rang out. Since blackness didn't follow—just the bloody throb he already had—he opened his eyes again.

"Put your hands up," a woman yelled. "Hands in the air. San Antonio PD. Get those hands where I can see them."

Black-clad figures in SWAT gear burst out of the stairwell and up the ramp, guns up and ready. Milo made a move for his gun, and his fingers closed around the butt. When a barked command to drop it didn't work, one of the officers shot him in the head. The rest glanced from the messily dead man to Shaw, put their arms up, and tossed their guns compliantly.

Simon looked up the barrel of the gun to Shaw and bared his teeth in a miserable grin. He could taste blood on his tongue. "Go for it."

After a second Shaw smiled thinly and stepped back. He obeyed the yelled commands to drop the gun, went down onto his knees, and folded his arms behind his head. One of the SWAT officers grabbed him and wrenched his arms back to cuff him. The rest of the men were cuffed and pushed flat onto the ground, and two officers helped Nora up from where she'd been hiding.

It was over. Simon thought about it for a second and decided to lie down.

"Hey. You. You okay?" he heard someone ask from a distance. A face appeared in his vision, blurred and intent. "Shit. He's hurt. Call in the paramedics. Hey, Ramsey. You're Ramsey, right? You're going to be okay. All right? You hear me?"

The SWAT guy was not, Simon thought with the mild calm of shock, nearly as good a liar as Jacob.

He faded out before the paramedics got there.

WAKING UP in hospitals was becoming a habit.

Simon lay without opening his eyes and listened to the beep of monitoring machines and the sigh-huff of a respirator. He had a tube in his nose—he could feel the dry itch of it—and the cool cloud of enough painkillers that he probably had an IV in too.

It hurt—he could tell that even through the opioids—but not enough that he could access how much damage he'd done.

"Mr. Ramsey?"

He grimaced around the dirty wool taste in his mouth, peeled his gummy lips apart, and opened his eyes. Big blue eyes and a severe crop of gray hair swam in his vision and came into focus as he blinked. The nurse was tall and stern-looking, with one of those easy, mobile faces that could flip into warm with a twitch.

She raised her eyebrows at him. "We weren't expecting to see you just yet," she said.

He shrugged, or tried to. It wasn't entirely clear that his shoulders cooperated. The memory of that loose broken jiggle as he hit the concrete came back to him, and the nettle ache of dulled pain was still in his shoulder. If he'd done enough damage....

What was worse? The thought of losing the use of his arm or that he gave a damn about that when Jacob was dead? He closed his eyes again and pressed his head back into the pillow. The nurse mistook it for pain and gently patted his arm.

"Don't worry," she said. "We'll top up the pain relief in a minute."

A minute in hospital time was usually more like an hour or two. It had to wait until the summoned doctor had checked him over. That was familiar too—clinical, gloved hands and questions that felt more like a status report than actual concern with your health. When they started treating you like a malfunctioning machine, it usually meant you'd done some real damage.

"The police want to talk to you," the stern nurse said when the doctors had finally left. "Do you feel up to it?"

"Not yet," he begged off tiredly.

She nodded understandingly and patted his hand again. "Your brother's lawyers have put them off," she said. "They won't bother you until you're ready. He wanted me to call him when you woke up, so he could bring your niece over."

The in-law part of Dev's relation to Simon didn't seem all that important right then. He let the "brother" go uncorrected and nodded his permission for the contact. The nurse started out into the hall—apparently Syntech health insurance covered a private room, or that might have been the police influence—and stopped.

"And here's someone else who's been waiting for you to wake up," she said and stepped out of the way. The quirk to her smile was reluctantly charmed, won over despite herself. "Don't tire him out."

Simon rolled his head to the side and expected to see Nora. He had the image of her in his head—with one arm done up in a sling and excuses on her lips now that she could see a way out.

It wasn't her.

Jacob shuffled in wearing oversized blue hospital pajamas and with a burn shiny on his cheek from ear to chin. He looked.... He looked like shit, but he wasn't dead. Simon stared at him and blinked to make sure his drug-addled brain hadn't caused hallucinations.

"Hey." The word slipped over his tongue half formed.

"Hey," Jacob said back. He started to grin, but then thought better of it as the blistered skin on his jaw puckered. His expression settled into something close to vulnerable. "You got shot. I thought you were trained for this sort of thing."

"I thought you were dead," Simon countered.

"Oh. No. I'm okay," Jacob said earnestly.

It wasn't funny. Except it was. Simon snorted out a laugh that hurt and managed to convince one arm to cooperate enough to reach for Jacob. He grabbed hold of his hand, squeezed the fingers roughly, and dragged him down into a hug. Relief filled his chest like warm air and bubbles and pushed the pain out to the corners.

Burn ointment was slick against his cheek, and Jacob still smelled sharply of smoke and explosives. He held himself stiffly against Simon and neither pulled back from the hug nor leaned into it. It took a second for Simon to work out it wasn't rejection. Jacob just didn't want to hurt him. Jacob's body hovered awkwardly over the bed, bent at the waist and propped up on his elbow.

"The car blew up," Simon said.

"Yeah," Jacob agreed. His breath tickled Simon's jaw and was warm in the soft patch just under the point of the hinge. "The bomb went off when the Lexus's doors relocked."

That was automatic on cars from the Syntech carpool. The doors locked when the engine went on. A safety feature Dev had put in after some idiot drove with a company laptop in the backseat and the doors unlocked. One red light and an enterprising theft had nearly cost the company millions.

"You should be a smear on the roof of that garage," Simon said. He let go of Jacob, not because he wanted to, but because the effort needed to hold his arm up burned through the pain meds. "Why aren't you?"

Jacob sat down carefully on the side of the bed, and the mattress dipped under his weight. Discomfort crawled to the surface of his thick liar's hide.

"I can't drive," he said. "I mean, I probably *can* do it, but I don't. So I decided to call the police instead. But the car locked itself anyhow, when I got far enough away."

"You saved the day."

Jacob wrinkled his nose. "I broke into a flop sweat and called Detective Really-Bad-Mother-Figure to bail me out," he said. "Not quite the same. She was already on the way. A guy got shot in a park and then a parking garage blew up. But I filled her in on what the SWAT team could expect."

"You did good."

"Yeah. Well, you scared the crap out of me," Jacob said. He sounded aggrieved. He took Simon's hand, laced their fingers together, and frowned at the result as though he expected something else. Simon squeezed his hand and felt the give of elegant bones under tanned skin. "Anyhow, Nora admitted everything to the cops while you were in surgery. Don't know what's going to happen next, but I guess I'm not a suspect in Clayton's death anymore."

That meant he didn't have any reason to stay in San Antonio, didn't it? All the giddy, relieved heat in Simon's chest turned to clammy mist. It wasn't that he wanted to trap Jacob, but even though Jacob was alive, he was still going to lose him. It was… draining.

"That's a relief," Simon said.

"Yeah." Jacob huffed out a sigh. "No kidding. I'm considering a change in career after this."

"Really?"

"Naw. Probably not," Jacob said. He turned Simon's hand over and idly tidied the wrinkled edges of tape around the drip plugged in between his knuckles. "Oh, have you sorted out presents for your niece for Christmas? I've got a dog begging…."

Simon raised his eyebrows and let Jacob explain his tale of indigent Fozzy. It didn't take as long as he might have hoped.

"Thanks, but I'd kind of like to still have a job when I leave here," he said.

"Ah well." Jacob shrugged off the disappointment. "My sister is already pissed at me for missing my flight. I might as well *really* irritate her."

He stood up, and his hand slid out of Simon's too easily.

"You're leaving," Simon said.

"Yeah," Jacob said. He tugged at his baggy sweatshirt. "I need to get some clothes, clean up properly."

"I meant, in general. You're leaving."

Jacob shuffled his feet and looked awkward in a way that Simon couldn't recall seeing on him before. Scared, angry, unhappy—he'd been all of those. Never unsure.

"Yeah. Well, it's what I do," he said, and the corner of his mouth twisted up. "I leave. Left home, left school, left a normal life behind. I mean, why not, right?"

Simon couldn't answer that. It was, he thought bitterly, probably the right decision. Shaw wasn't dead, and even if Nora testified, the mess wouldn't be easy to clean up. There was still her contact with the DoD to indict, Lau to find, and a whole corporate mess to clear up at Syntech. Jacob was better off out of it.

"I'd give you a lift to the airport," he said wryly as he glanced down at himself. "But... do you want me to call you a taxi?"

Jacob waved his phone. "I can Uber."

"Okay." Simon swallowed, and regret tasted like pill dust and dry mouth. "I guess this is it, then. Bali, here you come?"

"Portland, actually. Turns out dead people don't pay their bills, and I'm not good with money. So I get to spend more time with my sister and her kids." Jacob shoved his hands into his pockets and hunched his shoulders under his borrowed clothes. It made him look younger than he was—all angles and awkwardness. He folded his lower lip between his teeth. "You know, I'm usually really good at this."

"What?"

"Manipulating conversations," Jacob said. "You know, you think whatever you're saying is your idea. However, I've actually structured what we were talking about so you only really have a couple of responses that make sense—the one I want and a really unattractive option. You, though, you're just missing the cues. I mean, at any point you could ask me to stay."

"I don't know if I should," Simon said.

Jacob's eyes widened for a second. Then he folded his emotion away under a laugh and a mugged expression of comic dismay. It was the first time Simon had been *sure* that Jacob was lying to him about something.

"Okay. Well, that wraps that up," Jacob said. He waved one hand in casual farewell and turned to go. "Have a good—"

Simon propped himself up on his elbow. His stomach ached as he creased the wound, but he caught Jacob's arm. "Look at me, Jake. I'm an invalid… and a drunk….” It was a bitter admission to make, and the back of his brain had already tagged face-saving modifiers on to it. It was true, though. The only thing he wanted as much as Jacob right then was a glass of whiskey. “This whole mess? It isn’t over, not even halfway. You, though, you’re free and clear. So maybe you’re better off going to your sister.”

“You’ve never met my sister,” Jacob joked nervously, and a smile twitched over his mouth. When Simon didn’t smile back, he schooled his face back to seriousness. “Look, I don’t know how to do this. My dad never cared about anyone, my mom cared too much about him to care for anyone else, and the only person I’m close to is my sister—and we hate each other.”

Simon gave in to the throbbing pain in his stomach and slouched back into the pillows. He was sweating like he’d run the obstacle course. “I love you. I just do. You don’t have to say it back. I just don’t know if I’m good for you.”

“Well, we know I’m not good for you,” Jacob said. He leaned back down over the bed and carefully positioned his arms and shoulders. “Maybe it’ll cancel each other out?”

The kiss was careful and slow—dry lips and the taste of blood. Simon could feel his better judgment weaken. It was hard to do the right thing when it wasn’t what you wanted to do. When *who* you wanted to do had a hand twisted in your hair and his tongue in your mouth.

“You’re good for me.” The words were raw and honest in Simon’s throat. Jacob was bad for him as well, but that was life, wasn’t it? “Will you stay?”

Jacob’s mouth against his slid into a smirk, and Jacob lifted his head. Humor slicing through his eyes like a knife. “I’ll think about it.”

Simon laughed. It hurt, but he did it anyhow. “Asshole,” he said. That was the least of it, of course. Asshole, liar, thief, neurotically unreliable—but he was Simon’s unreliable, dishonest asshole, wasn’t he?

TA MOORE genuinely believed that she was a Cabbage Patch Kid when she was a small child. This was the start of a lifelong attachment to the weird and fantastic. These days she lives in a market town on the Northern Irish coast and her friends have a rule that she can only send them three weird and disturbing links a month (although she still holds that a DIY penis bifurcation guide is interesting, not disturbing). She believes that adding 'in space!' to anything makes it at least 40% cooler, will try to pet pretty much any animal she meets (this includes snakes, excludes bugs), and once lied to her friend that she had climbed all the way up to Tintagel Castle in Cornwall, when actually she'd only gotten to the beach, realized it was really high, and chickened out.

She aspires to being a cynical misanthrope, but is unfortunately held back by a sunny disposition and an inability to be mean to strangers. If TA Moore is mean to you, that means you're friends now.

Website: www.nevertobetold.co.uk
Facebook: www.facebook.com/TA.Moores
Twitter: @tammy_moore

TA MOORE

DOG DAYS

The world ends not with a bang, but with a downpour. Tornadoes spin through the heart of London, New York cooks in a heat wave that melts tarmac, and Russia freezes under an ever-thickening layer of permafrost. People rally at first—organizing aid drops and evacuating populations—but the weather is only getting worse.

In Durham, mild-mannered academic Danny Fennick has battened down to sit out the storm. He grew up in the Scottish Highlands, so he's seen harsh winters before. Besides, he has an advantage. He's a werewolf. Or, to be precise, a weredog. Less impressive, but still useful.

Except the other werewolves don't believe this is any ordinary winter, and they're coming down over the Wall to mark their new territory. Including Danny's ex, Jack—the Crown Prince Pup of the Numitor's pack—and the prince's brother, who wants to kill him.

A wolf winter isn't white. It's red as blood.

www.dreamspinnerpress.com

A DAY
MAKES

Mary Calmes

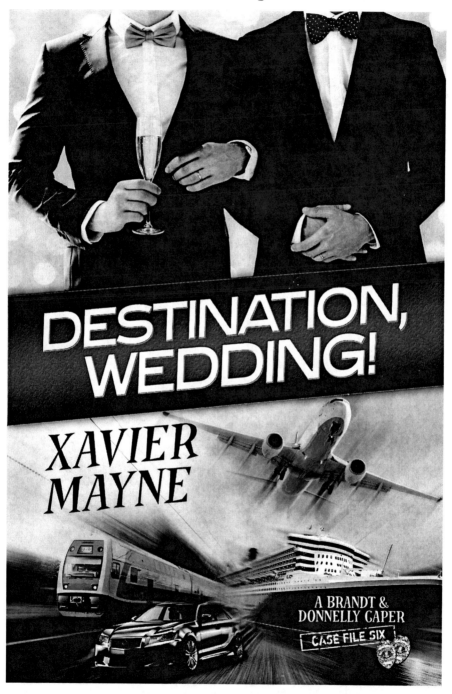

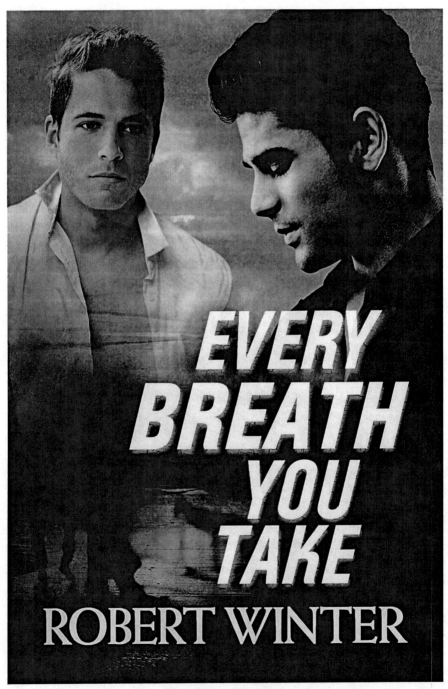

CPSIA information can be obtained
at www.ICGtesting.com
Printed in the USA
FFOW02n2310300617
37386FF